FATAL HAPPINESS

Rachel Bukey

NORTH
WEST
CORNER
BOOKS

Kenmore, WA

Northwest Corner Books published by Epicenter Press

Epicenter Press
6524 NE 181st St. Suite 2
Kenmore, WA 98028.
www.Epicenterpress.com
www.Coffeetownpress.com
www.Camelpress.com

For more information go to: www.Epicenterpress.com
Author Website: www.rachelbukey.com

Fatal Happiness
Copyright © 20221 by Rachel Bukey

ISBN: 9781603816984 (trade paper)
ISBN: 9781603816991 (ebook)

Printed in the United States of America

This book is dedicated to the memory of Waverly Fitzgerald.

Acknowledgments

I am especially indebted to each of the authors quoted in my chapter headings. Their books inspired me with unique insights and passionate theories on happiness. Thanks to Tal Ben-Shahar, Rachel Hollis, Kavita Khajuria, Mark Manson, Zelana Montminy, Gretchen Rubin, Sharon Salzberg, Emily Esfahani Smith and Ruth Whippman.

Like all novels, Fatal Happiness evolved through the input and guidance of many writing friends. I am most grateful to Waverly Fitzgerald who read the first, second and third drafts. My writing life began because of Waverly's encouragement and her wisdom and insight continues to sustain me now. She was the best teacher.

Thanks to Phil Garrett and Jennifer McCord at Epicenter Press for your guidance and patience throughout the publishing process. Thanks to designer, Rudy Ramos, for taking an idea and transforming it into a great cover.

Many thanks to the brilliant authors in my writing group: Linda Anderson, Curt Colbert, Martha Crites and Janis Wildy. The camaraderie we've developed over the years, even over Zoom, keep me going and keep me writing. Your knowledge, skills and perceptive suggestions always improve my work. Special thanks to Martha and Janis for reading the complete manuscript of Fatal Happiness. Your superb recommendations and generous support helped me take it to the finish line. Janis, I am so grateful for our fabulous Fridays. Thank you for your time, for our spirited discussions and for getting me through.

Thanks to my daughters, Elizabeth and Julianne, for your loving care and creative support. My own pursuit of happiness begins and ends with you. Last and most important, thanks to Dave for always being my first reader and my biggest fan. Your love and encouragement mean everything.

CHAPTER ONE

"We all have something to give, large or small. It may be a smile, or an attentive conversation. . . .. Any act of generosity – whether material or of the spirit – is a meaningful expression of kindness." Sharon Salzberg, *Real Happiness*.

I was on my way to Happiness Class – wishing I were headed just about anywhere else – when I got a call from my friend Alex. I pulled into the parking lot and picked up.

"Hey. What's up? Don't tell me you're skipping class tonight. I can't face a lecture on *The Four Pillars of Happiness* without you."

"Forget the class. I don't need it anymore. Meet me at Oliver's Twist instead. You won't believe what happened." Her voice sounded odd – squeaky with excitement, or possibly terror.

"What happened?"

"I need to tell you in person. Just drive right on past the Phinney Neighborhood Center and meet me at the bar. It's just a few blocks up on Greenwood." I thought about it.

"Come on, Ann," she said. "If you did your happiness homework, you'd know how important it is to connect with your friends."

Alex and I had been roommates at Macalester College. We'd lost touch when she left for Harvard Law School, and I stayed in Minneapolis to teach English. A few years later, I had a journalism degree from Northwestern and a job offer at *The Seattle Times*. Meanwhile, Alex had clerked for a First Circuit Judge and worked as a federal prosecutor in Boston before taking a position in one of the top law firms here in Seattle. Just last year she'd noticed my byline in the paper and looked me up.

I remembered Alex as fun and outrageous in college, and I needed a friend. Especially now that I'm single again and not

1

speaking to my sister Nancy. Those things are connected, but I don't want to think about that. Sure, Alex had changed a little. Outrageous had turned to brash and sometimes abrasive. Still, she was fun, always up for something new. Who else could I have convinced to take this class with me? I had no choice, but she did. With Alex along for the ride, I thought we might even have a good time. I had no idea.

"Okay. I'm on my way."

I drove to the bar thinking about how my editor, Jeff Skinner, had roped me into taking a happiness class, of all things.

Jeff wanted a series of articles about how people deal with stress, and he picked me to write them. I think he worries about me after the trauma of the last year. Maybe he hoped I'd find a better way to handle my own stress, or maybe he was just thinking of the newspaper. We had to be flexible to cut costs these days, get along with fewer reporters covering more stories – no more staying safe in our previous niches. Sure, I wanted to step away from the education stories I'd been hired to cover years ago, I wanted an opportunity to really show my investigative chops. Instead, I'd written about executives in high-stress jobs, the stress of homelessness and of people caring for their elderly parents. Then Jeff suggested I write about this happiness craze. I thought he was joking. Nope. Not only did Jeff believe there was something to it, he had a friend who taught happiness classes and he wanted me to meet her.

Mary Summers and I first met several weeks ago at the Green Lake Library, a beautiful old historic Carnegie structure, all high box-beam ceilings, wood details and huge windows. I stood at a display of new arrivals near the front door when Mary sailed in with a smile and a warm greeting.

"You're Ann Dexter!" She'd said, her voice soft and melodious. "I recognize you from your photo on *The Seattle Times* website," When she extended a well-manicured hand in greeting, I dropped the book on Swedish Death Cleaning like a hot potato and followed in her wake to the small meeting room she'd reserved for us. Mary moved through the space gracefully, with her head high and her gray curly hair brushing her squared shoulders. She was tall and lean and carried herself like a dancer. We sat facing each other, and I found myself smiling back at her, reflecting the warm enthusiasm she exuded. She even smelled like fresh air and sunshine, and I wondered how she'd managed that. I guessed she was in her early sixties, but it was hard to tell. Only the gray hair and laugh lines suggested her age. Her eyes were clear blue and her complexion flawless.

We'd spent nearly an hour talking about my articles on stress and specifically how her happiness class helps individuals cope.

"There's no magical way to go from stress to happiness, Ann," she'd said. "Which is why I present several happiness theories over the course of my eight-week class. We'll look at scientific studies outlining ways to re-wire our brains for happiness, mathematical models, psychological guides, personal tendencies, happiness projects and happiness lists."

"If you'll just give me the syllabus, I'll go from there," I'd said.

She raised an eyebrow. "I've saved a place for you in the class starting next week Wednesday at four. You'll get the syllabus then."

"I don't think so," I'd replied. "I mean, I can't take the class."

Mary smiled at me. "Of course, you can. You have to experience it to write about it."

In my moment of hesitation, she added, "I told Jeff I'd waive the fee for you."

She'd talked to Jeff about this. Now I had to say yes. "Okay."

"I'm sure you'll enjoy it," she said. "You may even make some lasting connections in the class. Happiness flows from meaningful relationships with others."

Maybe that's why I asked Alex to take the class with me. I needed the company. Or maybe I secretly hoped to find something worthwhile in it. If I were honest, I hadn't been happy in a very long time. Not only do my personal relationships need an upgrade, but my job is also precarious. I live in fear of being fired. So many of my colleagues have been let go over the past year, and others have been encouraged to take early retirement. Print journalism is hanging on for dear life. I can't lose my job. What would I do? I sure wouldn't go back to teaching. No. I need this job. I'll just have to find a way to write a killer article on happiness and move on.

I pulled into a parking place just down the street from Oliver's Twist, zipped up my raincoat and headed to the bar with a quick check of my watch: 4:05 and so gray it felt like dusk on this dreary first day of November. When the clocks fall back an hour next week, The Big Dark will begin in earnest around here. Ugh. The twinkly white lights surrounding the large street-facing window made me smile – a welcome beacon in the dark. As I pushed open the door into the lively and crowded space, the bartender looked up and smiled. Boy, he was easy to look at – all dark curly hair and sexy eyes. I smiled back, noticing how his muscles strained the short sleeves of his black t-shirt as he shook the cocktail. Reminding myself why I was here, I turned my attention from the bartender to the rest of the room and spotted Alex in the very back perusing the cocktail menu. She looked every bit the high-powered lawyer she is: dark gray suit, emerald silk blouse and her signature black heels. Her nearly black hair was messy around her face and brushed her shoulders. She looked up at me with shiny dark eyes.

"Hey. Thanks for coming," she said. "Check out these drinks – very clever."

I looked at the cocktail menu she'd handed to me. Most drinks had Dickensian character names or were related in some way to the author's work. One could order a *Pickwick Papers* and an *Old Sally*, among others.

"I think I'll try a Miss Nancy," Alex told the waitress, then looked at me. "Oh, sorry." She knows I'm not speaking to my sister, Nancy. I nodded and looked at the ingredients for the drink: gin, rhubarb syrup, lemon, orange bitters and bubbly. Served *up*. Perfect description of my sister as well as the Dickens' character: strong, not too sweet, bubbly, usually up.

"I'll stick with a glass of Pinot Grigio," I said, turning to Alex as the waitress went off with our order.

"Okay, tell me what happened. You look like you might burst."

"So, here's the news. Matt Downey," she said, making a noise in her throat – somewhere between a choke and a laugh. Then she took a deep breath and continued. "He's dead! His cleaning lady found him drowned in his hot tub this morning."

"What? That lawyer at work who makes your life miserable. He's dead?"

"The very same. Un-fucking believable, right?"

"Wow. That's intense." The waitress arrived with our drinks and Alex took a large gulp of hers while I watched her face, trying to gauge how she was feeling right now. Certainly not happy.

"May he rot in hell!" She raised her glass in my direction before taking another swig.

"Alex! The man is dead." I reminded her. "You can't be happy about that. Not really." I looked around the room and lowered my voice, hoping no one was eavesdropping.

"Oh, yes I can. It's kind of Dickensian. Remember that scene in *A Christmas Carol* when the Ghost of Christmas Yet to Come shows Scrooge some ragged old folks picking through Scrooge's belongings, including the very night shirt he died in, hoping to sell them before his body is even cold?"

I blinked, remembering the scene well. "I'm glad he's dead." I said in a low voice. "That's what the character says. Happy to profit from Scrooge's death."

"Right?" said Alex. "It's no secret that Matt Downey was a first-class asshole. Many a time I've wished him dead. Maybe not out loud. I wished he'd just disappear."

"He's a human being, Alex. You wanted him out of your life, your working life, but not dead." I felt goose bumps on my neck and looked up to see if someone had opened the door. No. I turned back to my friend.

"Don't be naive, Ann. Now there is one fewer egotistical, womanizing jerk in this world. One less man to add to the #MeToo list. Not a bad thing."

Alex shifted her long legs, crossing and re-crossing them before kicking off her three-inch heels. She leaned over the table and looked directly into my eyes.

"Okay. Here's the bad news." she said. "The cops think I killed him."

"Did you?" The question was out of my mouth before I could take it back.

"Very funny. Of course not! You know I could never. I mean, that's absurd. I'm sure it was an accident." Alex leaned back, took a breath, and rolled her neck before continuing. "He had a blood alcohol level of point two. He probably fell asleep and slipped under water, drowned and never woke up."

"Why are you a suspect then?" I asked.

"The police think I might have been the last person to see Matt alive." She took a big gulp of her drink before continuing. "We worked late last night on a proposal for some new clients and then, when Matt didn't show up this morning, I made the presentation by myself." Alex burst into a huge smile. "I nailed that, by the way."

"When did you find out he was dead?" I asked, wondering a little about my friend's stability.

"When Dennis called me into his office this morning and introduced me to two homicide detectives. He told me they had brought some bad news – that Matt Downey had died."

"How did you react?" I asked.

I said the first thing that popped into my head: *I wondered why he didn't show up for the Jefferson-Stone meeting this morning.* It seemed so unreal. Then they asked me how late we'd worked together last night, what time I left the office and what I did afterwards. I told them I went for a run to de-stress then went home to get a good night's sleep before this morning's meeting. They actually asked me if I'd run alone or if anyone could vouch for my whereabouts."

"They were asking if you had an alibi." I said.

"Can you believe it? Then they asked me if I knew Matt's plans for the evening. It was Halloween. Did he have a party to go to? How would I know? He was totally condescending to me when I'd told him my plans."

"What did he say?"

"*What a good girl you are Alex. Early to bed, early to rise.* One of the cops smirked. He knew exactly how Matt intended that jab. Assholes of the male species always recognize their own kind." She took a sip of her drink. "Then he asked me straight out how I would describe my relationship with Matthew Downey."

"Oh no. What did you say?"

"I told him our relationship was professional, that we'd worked together for over two years now."

"Good."

"Yeah. But then the other cop, the good cop, asked me if I would describe Matt as a friend, as well as a colleague."

"And?" I asked, worried she'd said something she'd regret.

"Well, I started sweating because I didn't want to lie, but I didn't want them to know how I really felt about Matt either, so I just said, *No. I would not describe Matt Downey as my friend.* Then Dennis interrupted. Said something like, *Surely Alex, you, and Matt work so well together, not friends*? The old partners are so naïve." She shook her head.

"Go on."

"Right. I told them I have respect for Matt as a lawyer – he's an aggressive advocate – but that my feelings stop there. I also stopped talking. I folded my hands in my lap, gritted my teeth, and vowed to shut up – just what I would advise a client to do under the same circumstances."

"Good," I said. "Did they stop asking questions then?"

"No. They asked me point blank how I felt about Matt Downey's death. Then Dennis got all protective and told the cop that his question was uncalled for, saying something like, *here, here gentlemen, Alexandra is as shocked as I am about Matt's death. I resent your suggestion that she could feel any other way.* Then he pretty much kicked them out of his office. It was great."

"Wow." I said, trying to figure out how to process what Alex had told me. "What happens now?"

"No idea," Alex said, all the color drained from her face. "All I know is Matt's dead. And I'm a suspect."

CHAPTER TWO

"Happiness is a critical factor for work, and work is a critical factor for happiness." Gretchen Rubin, *The Happiness Project*.

I drove home thinking about Alex, how convenient it was that the man who'd made her life miserable was now dead. Her reaction to it made me queasy though. Was she happy about it? Or just relieved? I couldn't imagine Alex killing anyone. Not even a guy who made her work life miserable. Maybe it had been an accident. The guy had too much to drink, passed out, slipped under the water, and drowned. Wouldn't you wake up when you started inhaling water? Unless someone held you under. Never mind. Not my business. I had a bad track record for getting involved in things I shouldn't. Matt Downey is dead. Alex is a suspect. Under all that bravado, she must be terrified. I could be a friend and stand by her through this, but I'd best let the police do their investigation. I had enough weighing me down these days.

When I got home, I got the usual enthusiastic greeting from my Golden Retriever, Pooch, wagging her entire backside, picking up a tennis ball and running to the back door to be let out. I let her sniff around the yard while I checked my phone messages. There were two: one from Betty Pedersen, my real estate agent, wanting to confirm my move-out date; and one from Winkie, a woman from Happiness class, wanting to know if I was okay and why Alex and I hadn't shown up for class. I decided to call Betty first, even though I was less prepared for that one. I had barely started packing and she wanted to schedule the stagers for next week. I called her back and said, yes, I'd be ready. It's time to sell this house and move on. The house is filled with memories of my husband Ben, our short marriage, and his premature death to non-Hodgkin's lymphoma. We'd hoped to raise children here. When we couldn't conceive, we both got tested for infertility. That led to his diagnosis. The rest is a cruel and sad story.

Since Ben, I'd dated other men, most recently someone I met during my investigation into a suspicious suicide of a young widow a couple of years ago. That relationship is history now that he's dating my sister. Oh, I think I always knew that Victor would be a better match for my slightly woo-woo sister than for me. Still, the reality of their relationship is too new, too raw for me to forgive them. The image of them on my sofa, in this very house, still rankles every time I enter that room. Re-arranging the furniture did not help. It's time for a new chapter.

The reality of packing up and finding a place to stay while the house is on the market has been overwhelming. Lucky for me, the profile I created of me and my dog Pooch on Housecarers.com paid off. In just a few days I'm scheduled to meet with a couple who need a house and dog sitter for six months starting soon. It's also fortunate that these people are willing to exchange dog and house care for rent. I sure can't afford to pay rent and my mortgage. Fingers crossed that they like us.

I took a deep breath and called Winkie back. Yes, a grown woman whose name rhymes with one of those spongy yellow cakes infused with faux whipped cream. No wonder she needs a happiness class. Maybe she should just change her name and see if that helps.

"Hi Ann! I'm so glad you called back. We missed you and Alex at class tonight. Everything okay?"

I debated whether to tell her about Matt Downey but figured it would be in the news anyway.

"Actually, someone that Alex works with died unexpectedly and Alex was pretty upset about it."

"Oh no! I'm so sorry to hear that! Was she close to him?"

"It's Matt Downey."

"Is that the lawyer she's had such a hard time with?"

"It is."

"Oh my." Winkie was quiet for a long moment.

"How was class?" I asked, to fill the void.

"Oh, you know. *The Four Pillars of Happiness*. Did you read it? We talked a lot about the first pillar: Belonging. Mary kept trying to suggest that connections to our families bring love, but most people had a lot of bad things to say about their families. You know, Emily's father has dementia and makes her life miserable. Then that young guy talked about how his father wouldn't pay for his college tuition when he switched majors. Like that. Which reminded me of you. Families. How's your sister? She still dating your ex?"

Sorry now that I had mentioned Nancy and Victor, I wasn't sure how to respond.

"Uh, I'm not sure actually, but I'm fine with it."

"Really? You sounded furious when you talked about it at happy hour a few weeks ago." When I didn't say anything else, she continued talking about the happiness class.

"We also talked a lot about the transcendence pillar. You know – being connected to a higher reality."

"Religion?" I asked, ready to get on my soapbox about that one.

"Not necessarily," Winkie said. "More like that feeling of flow, being in the zone when you're deep into something you love doing. Mary gave the example of writing – you might relate to that. To me doing something you love sounds more like you're creating your own reality. Which I think is important. You can't just pretend to be happy when your life is terrible. You do something about it, right? It's called being pro-active."

I was struck by Winkie's intelligent comments. I'm afraid I'd dismissed her as one of the one percent club who played golf and bridge, probably served on the opera board. Her problems always seemed so insignificant to me: she'd been passed over to play in a tennis tournament even though her skills were great. She also complained about her ex-husband a lot. I'd heard enough about the class.

"Thanks for filling me in, Winkie, but I'd better go. I'm busy getting ready to move and I'm nowhere near ready."

"I forgot you were putting your house on the market. Hope it sells quick. Have you found a new place?" Before I could answer, she said, "Let me know if you want the contact information for my decorator once you have. Marianne did a fabulous job with my houseboat!"

"Thanks, Winkie." I said, thinking, decorator? You've got to be kidding. I could never afford a decorator.

* * *

I arrived at *The Seattle Times* the next morning trying to conjure a positive attitude despite the current atmosphere of doom and gloom around here. There are more, pink slips every month. When I walked into the newsroom, a place usually buzzing with conversation and the clicking of computer keys, I noticed it was deadly quiet. I saw Jack Brenner, one of the *Times's* founding family members, in the fishbowl with my editor, Jeff Skinner, gesticulating wildly. I could not make out the words but could feel the vibrations of anger seeping through the glass. So could everyone else in the room, hence the quiet. I tiptoed over to the technology pod where Poppy – my favorite technology guru – was working away at her computer, apparently oblivious to the goings-on around her. I tapped her on the shoulder, and she jumped, took off her headphones and shook her head at me.

"Don't do that! You always scare the hell out of me when you do that."

"Sorry, sorry. What the heck is going on around here?" I gestured to the fishbowl where Jeff stood listening, the pent-up fury obvious in his face, while Brenner talked at him.

She shrugged. "Brenner just announced that they have to cut more full-time staff. He sent an email about it while you were out. No names yet, but everyone's shaking in their boots."

I felt the knot tighten in my gut. I can't afford to lose my job. It's the only thing I've got left.

"Well, we know you'll keep your job." I said to Poppy. "Technology is where it's at."

"You too, Ann. Just keep on rolling out that blog and you're set, as long as the funding keeps coming in for that."

Poppy was referring to the grant we'd received to write an education blog. The *Times* had already cut a couple of education reporters, leaving only two of us to handle higher education and one to write about pre-K through elementary. Then, riding in on a white horse, a foundation interested in something called "solution journalism" offered us money in exchange for experimenting with a different kind of education writing – a positive take on education where we focus on identifying and assessing *promising* educational programs and innovations, rather than complaining about what's going wrong. I get it and I like it. Once the education blog was born, Jeff hired a couple of interns to give us a younger voice and asked me to supervise them. Did I mention that interns work cheap, and the *Times* needs to save money wherever it can? Maybe Jeff means to back me out of the education niche altogether, which would be great if he also gave me the more serious assignments I've been asking for. Instead, it's stress and happiness class. Yes, I'm worried. I'm worried that the next step for me is out the door.

"You ready for the camera this afternoon?" Poppy asked.

I gave her a blank look, searching my brain for what she was talking about.

"The video about the blog," she reminded me.

"Right, right! That's today." I'd totally forgotten. "Who else are you filming?" I asked, wishing I'd put some thought into what I was wearing today, maybe put on a little makeup.

"Just you and Lindy." She said.

"Really, just me and Lindy? Okay, that's great." Lindy was the most attractive member of the team – all shoulder-length blonde hair and sparkling blue eyes, beautiful smile, just out of WSU. Who cares? They asked me because they want content, right? Maybe they can show Lindy's face and just use my voice. Okay, never mind. I gritted my teeth and chided myself for the negative self-talk, trying to remember some happiness tricks.

Poppy noticed the cloud cross my face. "Don't worry," she said. "You look great. Maybe add a scarf for some color. Here, try this."

Poppy unwrapped the brightly colored scarf from around her neck and offered it to me. The infinity scarf felt light in my hands and still warm. Just putting it on made me feel younger and daring with its dabs of fiery orange-red poppies on a black background.

"Thanks Poppy." I smiled and arranged the scarf over my ratty off-white V-neck sweater to hide the small food spot—probably my morning oatmeal—dotting my chest.

Back in my cubicle, I tried to focus on what I'd say about the blog. Where to begin? I woke up my computer and clicked on the document I'd started the other day, when Jeff first suggested the video, hoping I had enough in there to sound intelligent. I scanned the notes from our initial meeting and the other piece I'm working on about a new education program in California called the *support and improve* model. It's a highly progressive plan allocating a ton of money for teacher professional development, schools, and infrastructure. This is positive stuff, perfect for an upbeat video. Of course, I'll have to suppress the negative comparison with Washington – how we rank forty-seventh out of the fifty states in class size and how, despite passing an initiative mandating smaller class size, there's no money to do it.

For the video, I'll just talk about how exciting the California model is, as an example of a positive solution, and leave off the part about how Washington has no money to replicate it. Excellent.

"What are you smiling about?" I looked up to see my editor looming over my cubicle's half-wall.

"Hey, Jeff. Just putting the final touches on what I'm going to say in our video. Three o'clock this afternoon, right?"

"Right." He removed the stacks of papers from the only other chair in here, placed them next to the other piles of stuff on my desk and sat down.

"Nice scarf. I'm glad someone around here is still smiling."

"Thanks. It's Poppy's. And yeah, I heard. I saw you in with Brenner. Jesus, Jeff, do I even want to know whose head is on the chopping block?"

"You're safe. For now," he said. "The Pacific Magazine staff will be cut, and the book and arts reviewers."

"Just like in the schools —the arts are the first to go." I launched into my pet diatribe. Then I thought about our Arts reviewer, Marissa. "I suppose Marissa will be replaced by some intern who does reviews of video gaming." I said, disgusted with the whole thing.

Jeff shook his head. "You're not far off actually."

"Not Marissa, not really?" I couldn't stand it, so I put my hands over my ears, "La, la, la, la. I can't hear you."

He chuckled. At least I'd made him smile.

"How's the Happiness class?" He asked.

"It's fine." I wasn't going to tell him that I'd skipped class last night because my friend is a murder suspect. I changed the subject instead. "That feature on dementia that we talked about. Turns out a woman in the Happiness class is caring for her father. I'd like to write their story."

"Sure," Jeff said. Though I didn't think he was hearing me. Now he changed the subject: "What's your plan for the video?" he asked.

"Thought I'd talk about that new program in California. How long should this be?"

"Three minutes tops."

"I'm not sure I can say anything worthwhile in three minutes."

"You can learn. It's where the future is. Have Poppy edit it and then I'll look." Jeff's cell rang, and he pulled it from his pocket. "Gotta take this," he said, turning to leave.

The video session went well. We even had some fun with it thanks to Poppy – she can loosen anyone up. We were stiff at first, which was exasperating for Jeanine behind the camera until Poppy started doing her schtick, mock imitations of me feeding Lindy the most boring questions, with a totally flat affect.

"You forget how to smile, Ann? We're talking positive here! Innovation! Get down with your inner bubbly, girl!"

Once we laughed, it got easier. Maybe there was something to this Happiness thing. Pretend to be happy and you will be? Still, we spent an hour filming a piece that would end up no longer than three minutes.

I began collecting my things around four o'clock, hoping to get home a little early so I could continue packing up my house.

I took the long route out of the newsroom to avoid walking past Jeff's office, hoping he wouldn't notice my early exit. I knew I should be working late, proving my worthiness for this job since Jeff's comment that my job was safe *for now* had gnawed at me all day. Instead, I'm out of here.

I checked my cell in the car and saw a missed call and voicemail from Alex. I clicked on it.

"Ann, call me back! I'm in trouble!"

CHAPTER THREE

"If we want to find meaning in our own lives, we have to begin by reaching out." – *The Power of Meaning: Finding Fulfillment in a World Obsessed with Happiness.* - Emily Esfahani Smith.

"They told me not to leave town," Alex said when I called her back. She sounded like herself – more pissed off than afraid.

"They really said that?" I asked. "It's such a cop show cliché! What changed?"

"Janet Cooper told them she heard Matt arguing with a woman the night before he died— said she sounded like me."

"Who's Janet Cooper?"

"Look, can we talk in person? Where are you right now?"

I told her I was just leaving work and she suggested I stop by her office – just a straight shot downtown to the One Union Square building.

I checked my watch. "I need to get some packing done tonight. I should really head home."

"Please? I could really use someone to talk to – a friendly face."

I left the *Times* and pulled into a parking garage off Fifth Avenue a couple of blocks from Alex's office. As I walked down the busy street, I tucked in my scarf and buttoned my trench coat against the wind. Once inside the building, I took the elevator to the twenty-fifth floor where I found the reception area of Turnbull, Proctor and Samson, LLP.

"I'm here to see Alexandra Rhodes." I told the young blonde receptionist. "She's expecting me."

While she rang Alex, I looked around the lobby. It smelled like it had recently had an upgrade – fresh paint and new lights maybe. The color scheme left me cold though. We have enough gray in Seattle without painting interiors that color. The space featured the obligatory seating area with some sort of mid-century modern vibe, beyond which appeared a glass-walled conference room where several men in suits were meeting. I sat briefly in one of the molded plastic Eames chairs. Finding it uncomfortable as well as hideous, I stood and walked over to the sideboard to get a closer look at three decorative orbs set on top. Strangely attractive, they resembled iron skewers which had been bent then welded together and painted gun metal gray. Weird. I picked one up to examine it, surprised at how heavy it felt in my hands. At the sound of the conference room door whooshing open and a loud, agitated male voice, I turned.

"I've had enough of this bullshit! If you guys can't keep the SEC, the IRS and the U.S. Attorney's Office off my back with three lawyers charging me five hundred dollars an hour for the last six months, I'm going to find someone else who can!"

A red-faced and corpulent middle-aged man stomped past me and out to the elevator bank where he slammed the *down* button with his open palm, immediately pulled out his cell phone and began fiddling with it while he waited. I watched as he got into the elevator. As the door closed behind him, the receptionist quietly left her station, walked to the door of the conference room, and asked, in a hushed tone, if the three stunned lawyers needed anything.

"More coffee, water? No? Why don't I just close this door for you." She smiled at me in passing and picked up the next incoming call as if what we'd just witnessed was all in a day's work.

"What a zoo, huh?" I hadn't even noticed Alex appear at the opposite end of the reception area. "Come on back," she said. "My office is this way."

We walked down a hallway, offices on the exterior walls, and cubicles on the interior. "Who was that guy?" I asked.

She shrugged. "One of the firm's more colorful clients."

"He sounded pretty unhappy," I said.

"Yeah – par for the course. He fires us periodically. Then he comes back the next time he gets a grand jury subpoena."

"And you? How are you doing?"

"I've been better. This is me." She directed me into her office. I sat in a small club chair while she closed the door and dropped into a maroon leather executive chair behind her glass-topped desk. I looked around and noticed the lack of anything personal— no photos, no artwork, just her law school diploma – Harvard – propped up against a low bookcase under the window.

"We just moved into this space; I haven't had time to do much with it yet," she said, as if reading my mind.

I nodded. "Okay, where do you want to start? Tell me about the police? Or start with Janet Cooper?"

"Janet Cooper is the wife of Tim Cooper, one of the partners here at the firm. Tim and Janet live next door to Matt Downey. Apparently, Tim liked Matt's McMansion so much that, when Matt sold off part of his lot, the Coopers bought it."

"Yuk. I sure wouldn't want to live next door to anyone from work."

"Right? Anyway, the police were doing their routine questioning of Matt's neighbors – asking whether they heard anything suspicious that night. It was Halloween, you know, and there were lots of parents and kids out and about. Janet told them she heard Matt arguing with a woman who sounded like me."

"You do have a distinctive voice."

"Yeah, yeah, I know, New Yawk meets Bawstun."

"Were you at Matt Downey's house?" I asked.

"Ann, you know I did not like Matt Downey, but I did not kill him! Do *you* think I killed him?"

"I asked you if you were at his house."

"I did not kill Matt Downey!" She paused, looked defiant. "No. I was not at his house."

"Okay. Have you hired a lawyer?"

"I have a call in to Richard."

"Richard Reopelle?"

"Of course! If I'm going to hire a criminal defense lawyer, I'm going to hire the best."

"I know Richard."

"You mean you *know* him, or you just know his reputation."

"I know him. He represented the sleazy guy who pushed Julia Comstock of the Aurora Avenue Bridge a couple of years ago."

"Oh yeah, you told me about that." We sat with that between us for a moment.

"I feel like Richard only represents people who are guilty," I said.

"Come on, I didn't know you were so cynical – in this country, an individual is innocent until proven guilty, right?"

"Right. Okay. Now, tell me about your relationship with Janet and Tim Cooper. Friends?"

"No. Tim is the most blatant sexist in this firm. Now that Matt is no longer with us that is." She snorted. "May he rest in peace."

I ignored her black humor. "Explain."

"So, Tim was Managing Partner before Dennis. During his tenure, last year, five lawyers left the firm and started their own shop. It's no coincidence that three of them are women. Now I'm the only one left."

"Wow! Sexism is alive and well in some of the most respected Seattle law firms. Maybe I should write about that."

"It's true. Tim made their lives miserable with unrealistic expectations, buried them in all the dog cases, and claimed they weren't pulling their weight, stuff like that. After they left, Tim hired three lawyers right out of law school – Stanford, Michigan, Yale – all men. He's working them into the ground, expects two hundred billable hours a month. It's good for the firm that law schools are churning out record numbers of eager new lawyers and jobs are fewer and farther between. Anyway, guy's a prick." That seemed to be one of Alex's favorite adjectives to describe men. I'm pretty sure it's the same way she described Matt Downey.

"And his wife, Janet, why would she lie about you?"

Alex stood up and walked to the window, gazing out at the view of the city with her arms crossed. "Janet knows Tim had the hots for me before they started dating; tried to get me into bed when I first got here. I'm sure Janet saw Tim tripping over his dick whenever I was around." She turned back to me and said, "Janet's never been my biggest fan."

"Did you date Tim?"

She turned back to me. "No, of course not. I told you I never date anyone I work with. It's not professional." She returned to her executive chair and leaned my way over her desk. "Tim and I worked together quite a bit when I first started out. I did most of his research, second chaired on a couple of trials, that kind of thing. When I realized his interest had nothing to do with my brilliant legal mind, I established very clear boundaries before he made a total fool of himself."

"Okay, good. So, Janet's a lawyer?"

"No. She worked here as a legal assistant – dated half the single lawyers in the office before she found one who would marry her. She left as soon as he put a ring on it. Now she plays house in Clyde Hill."

"That gated community in Bellevue?"

"Yes," she said. "Very posh."

"Those places give me the heebie-jeebies—all those perfect houses in perfect *cul de sacs* with perfectly barked flower beds."

She laughed.

"Okay, I get that Janet is not your BFF," I said. "But still, she must have heard someone arguing with Matt. The police just need to figure out who she is. Is he dating someone? You have any idea?"

"I'm pretty sure he and Gina, our receptionist, have hooked up a couple of times. Doubt she'd have it in her to kill him though. Probably had more than one bimbo he was schtupping. *Hell hath no fury*, and all that. I'd be looking for a scorned woman if I were investigating instead of wasting time on me." Alex shook her head and rubbed her temples, pressed her lips tightly together and looked down at her desk. In that moment, I could feel the fear radiating beneath her bluster.

Looking up into my eyes, she said, "I did not kill Matt Downey." Her voice wavered as she continued, "I'm annoyed that I have to hire a lawyer to prove my innocence. You're right about the justice system Ann, it's backwards—guilty until proven innocent."

"Did I say that?"

When the phone buzzed, Alex snarled at the receptionist. "Gina, I asked you to hold my calls."

"Sorry, Alex, but its Richard Reopelle. Said you'd want me to interrupt."

"Right. Put him through." Alex thanked Richard for calling back promptly and told him she had me in her office with her and that we were on speaker phone. She also gave him a brief synopsis of her situation, Matt Downey's death and the Seattle police detective's warning her not to leave town. Richard said hello to me, made a polite comment about my latest journalistic success with the education blog—always the charmer. Then he said he'd be happy to meet with Alex.

His voice boomed into the space between us. "My first recommendation, however, is don't talk to the press. Why do you have a *Seattle Times* reporter in your office? No offense Ann. Alex, call me back when she's gone. From now on, say nothing to no one. Nothing to other members of your firm, nothing to your friends, and especially nothing to Ann Dexter. You got that?"

"Hey, Richard!" I blurted. "Don't hang up! I'm not writing about Matt Downey's death. Alex and I are old friends. I'm here as her friend."

"All right, I hear you. But, Alex, my advice still stands. Call me back after Ann leaves, okay?" He hung up.

"You know I'm not going to write about this, right?"

"Well, it just now occurred to me that *prominent lawyer's legal associate suspect in murder investigation* might be a juicy story that your employer may want to splash across the front page of the local section."

"Right. I'll see if I can get that stifled. Certainly, *I* won't write it. Remember, you asked me to come over here? You wanted a friendly face. Nothing has changed." I stood to leave, feeling awkward.

"I'm sorry Ann. I know you won't write about this, but I suppose Richard's right. Talking to a newspaper reporter right now is a bad idea for me. Let me walk you out."

We walked past the kitchen break room where three women were gossiping over coffee. I caught just a snippet of their conversation. "You think she got him drunk, waited for him to pass out and held him under?"

I nudged Alex and stopped at the open door.

"What?" Alex asked.

The three women got quiet.

"Just wondering if I could get a glass of water before I leave?" I wanted a visual on the office gossips; I also wanted to stop them.

"Sure." Alex and I walked into the kitchen, and she took a glass from the cabinet, filled it with filtered water from the front of the fridge and handed it to me. I gave the three women the once over — an extremely thin brunette in her mid-fifties, a tall dishwater blonde who looked like a Midwest farmer's daughter and a striking African American woman.

"Better get back to those interrogatories." The anorexic said, standing up. I recognized her voice as the gossip. "Yeah, I've got to file a motion," the Midwest girl said.

"Hey, Alex." The black woman nodded at Alex as she got up to leave. "How you doing?"

"Hey, Ashley."

"I'm sorry about what's going on," she said.

"Yeah, me too. Thanks."

Ashley trailed the other two out of the room and I noticed how great she looked in a tight black skirt and red heels and felt a twinge of jealousy that I could no longer get away with that look. Probably, I never could have. I finished my glass of water and made my way to the elevator, glad that Alex seemed to have at least one sympathetic co-worker. One is always better than none. We said our goodbyes.

"Stay in touch." I said.

"Sure. See you soon." Alex replied. But I felt like something had changed in our relationship. Like her lawyer had poisoned it somehow.

I walked myself out of the office and through the lobby to the elevator thinking about Janet Cooper's accusation, wondering if Alex had talked with Tim Cooper about it. I hesitated, then went back to the receptionist's desk.

"Gina, I'd like to talk with Tim Cooper. Is he in?"

Gina checked her computer. "Mr. Cooper is in court for the rest of the afternoon. Would you like to leave a message?"

"I'd like to speak with him tomorrow morning if possible. Is he available?

"Let me check with his assistant." I waited. "Ashley, is Mr. Cooper available tomorrow morning? Ann Dexter would like to speak with him." Gina looked up at me, "How much time do you need?" she asked.

"Half an hour, tops," I replied.

"Okay," Gina smiled. "He can see you at nine."

Driving home in the blustery dark rain that is pervasive here in November, the cruelest month, I realized that my Seasonal Affected Disorder was settling into my psyche for a long winter's nap and knew I'd have to find the SAD light before I could move into full steam ahead packing mode. Pooch went nuts when I got home, jumping around, and nosing her tennis ball at me. Why hadn't I asked my neighbor to come by and walk her today? There was nothing for it but for me to head out in full rain gear: rain pants, raincoat, rain hat, wellies, and gloves. Nevertheless, the rain was dripping off my nose by the time we had made one lap around the baseball field at Shoreview Park. I didn't feel great about walking around up here in the dark with only that one eerie yellow light glowing from the far side of the park. Anyone could be hiding there. Okay, now I was creeping myself out. Time to get back home. Boxes and packing seemed like a fine way to spend the night now that I'd experienced the alternative and found it extremely unpleasant.

I pulled on some yoga pants and my favorite wool grandpa sweater while I searched the fridge for something edible. Grabbing a chunk of Beecher's Flagship cheddar, I found a pan and buttered two pieces of Tall Grass bread, sliced the cheese, and placed the sandwich in the pan to toast while I rummaged around in the cabinet for some tomato soup. Preparing my favorite homey meal made me feel a little better. As I bit into the gooey sandwich, my spirits began to lift. Pooch put her big furry golden head in my lap, and I scratched behind her ears distractedly while I flipped open my laptop and clicked onto the *Seattle Times* website to check if there was anything interesting in the news. Nope. I checked my horoscope instead.

You're being tested over the next two days. There are professional benefits, so suck it up and focus. Hold your temper. Don't push personal beliefs on others. Prepare thoroughly and explore new ideas. Find unexpected resources. Follow intuition.

Sounds about right. Hold my temper and prepare to be tested. That bit about pushing my personal beliefs on others was funny. That's what I do, along with preparing thoroughly and following my intuition. My intuition told me it was time to pack the garage, but I couldn't face that now. I would be too cold in there. I went into the guest room—recently Nancy's room—instead. The bed linens were easily thrown into the washer, but the closet was a different matter altogether. That's where I keep those boxes of photos I mean to sort, purge, and send off for scanning. I decided for now to simply round up all the photos and put them into matching banker's boxes marked "photos" and pile up the boxes in the corner of the guest room. I'd send them to that scan-my-photos place later.

After an hour, I had five banker's boxes filled with random photo envelopes and stray snapshots and two boxes filled with albums that I really didn't want to look through now. But I couldn't help myself. I reached for the most tattered, oldest album, the one my mother had put together for me that first Christmas after I'd left for college.

I flipped through the photos capturing my childhood— birthday parties and days at Lake Minnehaha near our family home in Minneapolis. In them, I was rarely alone. Next to me, usually with her arms wrapped around me, was Nancy, grinning into the camera. I searched through until I found the one I'd been looking for—the one of Nancy and me at the cabin in northern Wisconsin that our family rented every summer. The shot is grainy and neither of us is smiling. I recognized the trace of terror lingering in my six-year-old eyes and noticed the bright yellow air mattress propped behind us on the deck. I remembered paddling out into the deep water where the bigger kids were goofing around. I'd hoped they would play with me. A boat must have zoomed too close, roughed the water, making it impossible for me to stay on the float. I fell in. I remembered the feeling of helplessness, the gasping for air and sucking in water instead. I couldn't swim. I thrashed around for the surface while getting deeper and deeper until at last I grabbed onto something solid. Onto Nancy. What if Nancy hadn't spotted me and pulled me out? I didn't want to think about the *what if*. I slammed the album shut, but it was too late. The Pandora's Box had already been opened. All those emotions were swirling around the room threatening to overwhelm me. So, I did what I'd been avoiding for the past several weeks. I called Nancy. I listened to the phone ring and ring while I paced the room, worried about hearing her voice, wondering what to say. When the call flipped to voicemail, I felt relieved.

"Nance, it's me. Sorry I haven't returned your calls. Um, we should talk, Also, I'm putting my house on the market soon so, maybe you could come by and pick up your stuff? Well, call me back?" A voicemail was so much easier than talking face-to-face.

CHAPTER FOUR

"One friend said that in his office, whenever crisis strikes, he tells everyone, "this is the fun part!" Gretchen Rubin, *The Happiness Project*.

I woke up Friday morning and let Pooch out, surprised to see frost on the grass. The sky was low and looming. I sniffed the air, plunging my hands deeper into my fleecy robe as Pooch bounded around the yard. My nose told me it might snow, but I dismissed that thought as absurd. It never snowed in Seattle in early November. I checked the weather app on my phone: thirty-five degrees and cloudy right now. Beginning around five o'clock this afternoon snowflake icons showed up in the forecast. I doubted that.

Before I left for my meeting with Tim Cooper, I called his wife, Janet. I wanted to hear her version of the night Matt Downey drowned before I spoke with her husband. I didn't think I should make that phone call from the office. At first, Janet was reluctant to talk with me. When I told her I was fact-checking for a *Seattle Times* article, she got curious.

"You're putting this in the newspaper? I'm sure Tim wouldn't want the firm to look bad in the press," she'd said.

"I have an appointment to speak with your husband later this morning," I told her. "I'm just researching the circumstances around Matt Downey's death. Nothing will appear in the paper until someone is charged. But I wanted to speak with you directly since you're the person who heard Alex in Matt's backyard that night. Is that correct?"

"It is."

"You said that you recognized Alex's voice right away. You don't have any doubt about it? It's important, of course, because it

26

places Alex there the night that Matt drowned, implicating her if they decide his death was not accidental."

"I understand that. Tim didn't want me to say anything about it, but I just thought the police should know. I didn't see any reason to lie about it."

"How can you be certain it was Alex you heard?"

"Alex has a pretty distinctive voice, right? – All east coast abrasive Jew. Sorry, was that inappropriate?" I didn't dignify her comment with an answer.

"Anyway, I could tell they were arguing about the office. She kept calling him an asshole – one of Alex's favorite terms by the way – and saying something was inexcusable, no woman should have to put up with it. Then she said, *I'm not going to put up with your bullshit anymore!*" She lowered her voice conspiratorially. "The woman, you know, is a real ball-buster."

I let that go too. "Then what happened?" I asked.

"Matt kept telling her to calm down, suggested they go inside, so they did."

"This does not sound like a conversation they were having in the hot tub."

"No."

"Do you remember the time?"

"It was early, about seven, I'd say. Tim and I were in our outdoor room having a glass of wine in front of the fire before dinner. We were hiding from the trick or treaters, if I'm honest." She shrugged. "We put the bowl of candy on the front porch for the kids to help themselves. I mean, Halloween is crazy busy in this neighborhood. I'd already seen enough costumes for one year."

"Okay. Did your husband recognize Alex's voice?"

"He didn't want to. As soon as he heard them arguing, he went inside to start dinner. He's a great cook."

"Nice." I said, thinking Janet Cooper sounded convincing, wondering why Alex would have lied to me.

"Of course, Tim is furious that I talked to the police. He'll be annoyed that I talked to you too. He doesn't want me messed up in this whole thing. It has been pretty disturbing for the firm."

"And, extremely difficult for Alexandra," I reminded her. "I understand that you used to work at Turnbull, Proctor. Did you work directly with Alexandra?"

"No. I mostly worked with Tim, did some work for Matt too."

"I thought Matt and Alex worked on cases together."

"They do now. Or they did, I guess. That all happened after I left." Her voice cracked, and I thought she might cry. "I'm sorry. I still can't believe he's dead."

"It must be difficult. You were friends," I said, always ready with the platitude, casting about for something else to say while Janet collected herself.

"Do you work outside the home now?"

"Oh, that's just perfect. You think I'm a little stay at home wifey jealous of Alexandra Rhodes and her big-time career. Well, you've got that wrong. I'm very happy with my life. Thank you very much."

Something about protesting too much crossed my mind. "I'm sorry. I believe you misunderstood my question. I just wondered if you'd moved on to something else."

Silence on the other end.

"Thank you for your time," she said. Then hung up without saying goodbye.

I checked my watch. I had just enough time to get to my meeting with Tim Cooper. Hopefully, Jeff wouldn't miss me. When I walked into Turnbull, Proctor and Samson, the receptionist greeted me by name. I barely had a chance to look around and pick up those weird decorative orbs that so attracted me, when Alexandra's colleague made an appearance.

"Ann Dexter?"

"Yes, hello."

"Tim Cooper," he said by way of a greeting, briskly gripping my hand. He followed that up with an unconvincing, "Nice to see you." He led the way to his office, and I had an opportunity to give him the once-over while we went through the preliminaries.

I placed Cooper in his early forties, the kind of guy who might be considered good-looking in an uptight, white bread kind of way. His features were regular but his small, gray, deep-set eyes, and his habit of furrowing his brow while listening made him look constantly worried. He wore a dark gray suit, expensive and conservative with a clubby tie. He kept his brown hair cut short and either used some sort of scented hair product or was one of those rare heterosexual men who still wore cologne or aftershave. My nose twitched at the woodsy scent, and I thought I might sneeze.

"The firm has given a press release to the *Seattle Times*. Why is it that you want to talk with me?"

Apparently, he hadn't been listening to me at all—the occupational hazard of a stressed-out lawyer interrupted from his work. I reminded him that I wanted to help Alex, and he apologized.

"Right, right. Sorry. How can I help you?"

"As you know, Alex has been questioned by the police. I know you and your wife were interviewed as well. I spoke to Janet earlier this morning."

"What? You talked to Janet? I told her not to discuss it." His face reddened, and he began to tap his pen on the desk, giving me an unwanted flashback to the Armory last Spring. I quickly suppressed the memory and tried to focus on Tim Cooper instead. "It's bad enough that one of our partners died under suspicious circumstances, it's another thing altogether that our colleague is a suspect. This whole thing puts the firm in an awkward position." He rubbed the sides of his head, a nervous tic which released more of the woodsy scent into the room.

"Of course." I said, affecting an empathetic look. "Just to clarify, Janet is fairly certain she heard Alexandra and Matt arguing. What about you? Did you hear Alex in Matt's backyard that night?"

"No. That is, as soon as I heard what sounded like an argument, I went inside. I do not like to eavesdrop, Ms. Dexter. In fact, it annoyed me that I could hear Matt at all. When we bought the lot, I tried to talk him into re-orienting his patio – the property's big enough. But he never got around to it."

"Did you hear a woman's voice?"

"It may have been a woman's voice. I believe Matt had a date that night, someone he'd just started seeing; he seemed to be looking forward to it."

"Do you know her name?" I got excited.

"I think it was Jacqueline. Can't remember the last name. Matt met her at some nonprofit fundraiser."

"Okay." I noted down the name.

"Look, I've told the police everything I know." He glanced at his watch then over my shoulder at some commotion in the hallway. His eyes grew wide, and I turned to see what had surprised him. Through the glass panel next to his office door, I just caught the backs of what looked like two uniformed police officers.

"If you'll excuse me, I need to see what's going on here." He stood and walked out the door, leaving me alone.

I sat facing the open door for as long as I could stand it, then tiptoed over to the doorway and peered around, unprepared for the scene unfolding in the hallway. One cop steered Alexandra down the hall holding onto her arm while the other one followed behind with a plain clothes detective.

"How dare you come in here and arrest an associate of this firm!" Tim Cooper's angry voice echoed through the hallway. "Ms. Rhodes is a respected member of the Washington State Bar Association and she has the right to a lawyer. In fact, I believe you know the name and phone number of her lawyer. You could have had the courtesy of calling Mr. Reopelle. Alex would have come in voluntarily. You can bet I'll file a complaint with the police department over these unnecessary and highly inappropriate tactics!"

"We have an arrest warrant here Mr. Cooper. It's all perfectly legal – even if it doesn't fit in with your plans for the day."

"Alex!" I stepped in front of the threesome coming my way. Alex looked up at me and shook her head, uncharacteristically quiet. "What's going on? Officer, may I see a copy of the arrest warrant, the affidavit?"

"Not unless you're her lawyer."

"I'm with the *Seattle Times*. This is a matter of public record."

"The officer turned to me. "I guess you can go to the courthouse and get a copy then. Sounds like you know the drill.""

"Alex, I'll call Richard. See if he can meet you at the jail." Then, to the cop, "Are you taking her to the King County Jail?"

"Yes, Ma'am. That's where the bus stops today."

Dazed, Alexandra stared straight ahead as the officers led her through the reception area with Tim Cooper and me following behind. "I'll call Richard now," I said to Cooper, still fuming and muttering about outrageous police tactics and the potential for bad press.

"You're not going to write about this, are you?" He asked me.

"No, I'm not going to write about this," I said. "I'm going to call Alexandra's lawyer. I think you should be more worried about what's happening to your colleague than whether I'm going to write about it."

"If you'll excuse me," he said, and left me standing there while he charged back down to his office.

The receptionist continued to field incoming calls with a calm, upbeat and musical tone. "Turnbull, Proctor and Samson! May I help you?"

I waited for her to put a call through, then asked, "Gina, do you know the last name of a woman Matt Downey was dating – Jacqueline something. Someone he'd met at a fundraiser?"

"Jacqueline Forte? Were they dating?" Gina's eyes widened. "She called a few times about the Art with Heart fundraiser. I think Matt supported that organization. I don't think they were dating." She shook her head. "Were they dating?"

Gina looked stricken and I remembered that Alex had named Gina as one of Matt Downey's conquests. I thanked Gina and got out of there before she could ask any more questions or start crying.

I called Alex's lawyer as I walked to my car. When I explained how Alex had been arrested, he let loose with a string of expletives, railing on about the Seattle Police Department's tactics. "They've been getting so much bad press about racial profiling that they see Alexandra as *The Great White Defendant*! Bad for us."

I appreciated Richard's allusion to *Bonfire of the Vanities*, one of my favorite Tom Wolfe novels. The scene of the Wall Street executive's humiliation while he's booked into jail with packing peanuts stuck to his expensive suit rushed vividly to the top of my brain. I didn't want Alexandra to experience anything like that.

"Can you meet her at the jail, Richard? Get her out of there?"

"Are you writing about this?" He asked – the second person to ask me that in the last few minutes.

"No, Richard, Alex is my friend. I want to help her. I want you to help her. Can you do that?"

"She's my client. I'll make some calls, get a copy of that affidavit. The police must have some evidence connecting her to the guy's murder."

"Oh, one other thing," I said, wondering how to tell him I'd spoken with Janet Cooper, that she'd sworn she'd heard Matt and Alex arguing the night before they found him dead in his hot tub. I just told him straight out.

"You are investigating! Jesus, Ann, you assured me you wouldn't write about this."

"I'm not writing about it. I'm just concerned for my friend."

"Let me handle it from here," he said. "I'll make some calls and find out what other evidence they've got. One woman saying she thought she heard Alex arguing with Matt is not enough for a warrant."

"Can you get her out of jail?"

"I'll do the best I can." He hung up.

I considered heading down to the jail myself, but I had a deadline looming and had to be sharp. I needed Jeff to believe he needed me on staff. Those layoffs continued to haunt me. Still, I couldn't leave it alone. As soon as I got to the office, I called my friend and Seattle Homicide Detective, Erin Becker, to see if she could tell me anything. Erin promised to check and call me back later. I had no excuse but to sit down in my cubicle and get back to my real job, the one that paid the bills.

Erin called after five.

"It's not good news about your friend Alexandra," she said.

"Tell me."

"We got a print off a water glass at Matt Downey's house."

"Oh no," I said. Thinking, *she lied to me.* "Alex's?"

"Bingo!"

"Now what happens?" I asked.

"The detectives on the case are questioning Alex now. They'll take a statement, hear what she has to say. There'll be an initial appearance, bail hearing. She should be released quickly. We'll keep investigating."

"Why the drama? Why not just have Alex turn herself in? She's a professional. She's not going anywhere."

"It's not my case. I'm guessing they want to talk to her before she gets lawyered up and her statement is all neat and tidy – practiced. You know what I mean?"

"Yes, but Alex *is* a lawyer and *has* a lawyer. It seems like a cheap shot to me."

"You're welcome," Erin said, before hanging up on me.

"Shit," I said aloud. I could not afford to alienate my one friend in the police department.

CHAPTER FIVE

". . . people, young and old alike . . . need love and care. They need to belong to someone." Emily Esfani Smith, *The Power of Meaning*.

I left the building while the first snow of the season began falling around me. The flakes were heavy and wet, the temperature hovering just around freezing. I couldn't remember the last time it snowed in early November. I couldn't forget what Erin had just told me about Alex's fingerprint at Matt Downey's house. She'd lied to me! What was she doing at Matt's house that night and why had she lied about it? The police thought she'd killed him. I couldn't believe that. There must be a logical explanation. But I wouldn't get to hear it until Richard got her out of jail. There was nothing I could do about it now.

I pulled up the collar of my raincoat, leaned into the wind and walked through the parking lot to my car. I cleared the windshield of snow and worried a bit about my balding tires on the icy roads. Bracing myself for the long drive home, I turned on the radio and listened to the snow coverage, changes to bus routes and cancellations. The snowy landscape reminded me of Minnesota, which reminded me of my sister. Those photos I'd flipped through continued to haunt me. I hoped Nancy would call me back soon, even though I dreaded the conversation. Let's face it, I was still holding onto a lot of anger about her relationship with Victor. I mean, *thou shalt not date thy sister's boyfriend*, right? I simply could not pack Nancy's things away and move them to storage without a conversation. We had to talk. Maybe it was time for forgiveness.

The cars moved slowly along the Aurora Avenue corridor. Snow mixed with rain until I reached the Seattle city limits and entered what meteorologists call the "convergence zone." This area just north of Seattle, from my Shoreline neighborhood north to Everett, usually got cooler temperatures and more precipitation. This afternoon it meant the snow falling in full force, no more rain mixed in. I gripped the steering wheel and focused on the road. Only twenty-five more blocks to go. I could make it. I had to make it. Pooch was at home waiting for me, expecting dinner and a romp around the park. She so loved the snow.

As I headed down the hill and past the Seattle Golf Club toward my neighborhood, the snow played tricks with the light. With few streetlights along this stretch, the darkness usually intensified. Tonight, with the snow clinging to the branches of the evergreens and blanketing the grass, it was brighter here, so beautiful. I was lost in thought when my tires locked in a skid and began sliding sideways. Pumping the brakes did nothing. I picked up speed and careened downhill straight for the telephone pole on that last curve before my turn. I pulled the steering wheel hard to the left and the car fishtailed. I pumped the brakes again and pulled right, swerving around the corner, and slowing down at last. My heart pounded as I slid into the driveway, my tires making fresh tracks. I clicked the garage door opener, and it didn't respond.

"Shit," I said aloud, knowing the thing had frozen shut. It had happened before.

I collected my laptop and bags from the backseat and made my way to the front door, noticing that both the front porch and front hall lights were on. That seemed wrong. I never leave the lights on. My feet were soaked and freezing by the time I got the key into the lock and walked in, expecting my usual furry greeting. Instead, Pooch was MIA and the door to the basement stood open. Lights were on down there too.

"Pooch?" I called, and the dog came bounding up the stairs. "Sheesh, you worried me girl. What were you doing down there?"

"It's me, Ann. I came over to get my stuff."

At the sound of her voice, a jolt of adrenaline ran through my body. I looked down at my sister standing at the bottom of the stairs wearing jeans and a sweatshirt, hair pulled back. For a moment I felt like I'd seen a ghost. Like I'd conjured Nancy with all that thinking about her and Victor on the drive home. No, it was really my sister, in the flesh, standing at the bottom of the stairs.

"Jesus, Nancy, you scared the shit out of me!"

"Sorry, Ann. I got your voicemail. When my yoga class got cancelled this afternoon, I decided to come by for my stuff. I thought I might be finished before you got home." She looked at her watch. "Of course, it's taking me longer than I thought it would."

"It's snowing like hell out there, or didn't you notice? Where's your car? I didn't see it parked in front."

"Oh, it's in the garage. I still have your garage door opener. Sorry."

The rage welled up in me. "Sorry? Sorry you still have my garage door opener and now your car is stuck in my garage, or are you sorry for anything else?" I didn't like the way I sounded. I was being mean, and I knew it. Forgiving her in theory was way easier than forgiving her in fact.

Nancy walked up the stairs towards me and I turned away toward the fridge.

"I'm having a glass of wine." I pulled out a bottle of Pinot Gris with shaking hands. All the adrenaline from the drive home in the snow and the shock of seeing Nancy had me amped up. Fight or flight? I could feel Nancy standing in the doorway, but I couldn't bear to look at her. Instead, I reached into the cabinet for a glass, then took two. I turned.

"You want a glass?"

Nancy stood there looking like she might burst into tears. Her shoulders were already shaking a bit.

"Don't cry! Stop it! Don't make me feel sorry for you! I do not feel sorry for you!" I turned away and back to the task at hand, pouring two generous helpings into the glasses, my mind racing with all the things I wanted to say to Nancy, how I wanted to hurt her. I took a sip and turned to face her, but she was gone. I heard water running in the powder room and figured she'd gone to collect herself. Good thing. I took both of our glasses to the living room, then remembered the last time the two of us faced each other in that room, with her in Victor's arms. I returned to the kitchen, set the glasses down on the table, pulled out a chair for myself and took a deep breath. How could I possibly start this conversation?

Nancy walked into the room, looking nervous but determined. "Look, Ann. Maybe I should just go. Maybe you aren't really ready to talk to me."

"Have you looked out the window? They're predicting a lot of snow tonight. Your car is stuck in my garage with the door frozen shut. Good luck getting an Uber. It's nuts out there. I'm afraid you're not going anywhere."

Nancy went to the window and peered through the blinds. "It doesn't look that bad to me," she said.

"Toto, we're not in Minnesota anymore," I said.

Nancy smiled. "Right? This whole city shuts down when there's a trace of snow. It's crazy. The news coverage always cracks me up. Guys standing around in giant parkas, a half- inch of snow at their feet talking like it's the blizzard of a century!"

She giggled. Soon she escalated into full throttle laughter, and I couldn't help myself. At her first snort, I started laughing too. Pretty soon we were both laughing uncontrollably – our nerves and emotions running high. We laughed and laughed. Nancy snorted and got us going all over again. Finally, I grabbed the box of tissue, wiped the tears streaming down my face and Nancy did the same.

"It's not that funny."

"I know."

"So, you're moving," she said. "I think it's a good idea. I know you've been considering it for a while."

"Yeah. It's time to move on. Time for me to get a different life. There have always been too many ghosts here anyway, especially now." I gave her a look. "But I don't want to talk about Ben now. I'm not even sure how to talk to you."

"Look, Ann. Let's start with an apology. I'm so sorry about what happened with Victor. Here, I mean, you walking in like that. It was difficult."

"Difficult? You're saying it was difficult?" Suddenly, her apology didn't feel right. "How about wrong?" I said. "It was wrong Nancy, wrong! After all I'd done for you, all we'd been through, you repay me by taking Victor from me? I still cannot believe it. How could you?"

"I didn't *take* Victor from you Ann. You practically handed him to me on a platter. I mean, you never seemed to care for him very much. That's how it looked to me anyway. But I didn't *intend* to." She started talking in non-sentences. "I mean, Victor is so . . . And you're, well . . . Let's just say I knew you were ambivalent about your relationship with Victor. That time I started teaching him to tango. That was only because you were an hour late for your date. An hour! You never called, never even apologized. Then he and I were having such fun with our tango lessons. That kiss? It was our first kiss that you walked in on. It was spontaneous, fun, like Victor. We never meant to, I never meant. Oh shit, I'm not making any sense. Let me start over."

"It may have been your first kiss, but not your last, right? Don't you know how much that hurt me? I'll admit that Victor was not the love of my life, but that's not the point!"

Please, Ann. Can you let it go? Can you forgive me?"

I looked into her pleading eyes. "No. I don't think I can forgive you, Nancy." I was still being mean, but I couldn't help it.

I took another sip of wine and Nancy did the same. I watched her like Pooch watches a squirrel. She began to feel it. I saw her squirm. She opened and closed her mouth, at a loss for words.

"Please?" She asked in a whisper. "You're my only family. I love you more than anything. You saved my life. Say you forgive me. We can get beyond this. I'll stop seeing Victor if that's what you want. If you want me to choose, I choose you." She reached for my hand, but I pulled it away and put it in my lap.

I stood up and paced around the room. Pooch stood up and walked beside me for the first few steps then stopped and looked confused. I scratched her head, beginning to calm down. Dogs are better than Xanax that way.

"Oh, I don't know. Who cares if you stop seeing Victor?" I said.

"That's not the point. The point is, the point is it doesn't change anything. Don't you see that the damage is done? You betrayed me, betrayed my trust, then deserted me when I needed you. How can I ever forget that?"

"Deserted you? That's not fair! You kicked me out of your house, literally left me with nowhere to go. I didn't desert you. You did what you always do, Ann. You pulled away from me. You've spent the last six months ignoring every phone call, every email, every effort I've made to talk to you and explain. I want to get past this, Ann. I really do. The question is, do you?"

I returned to the kitchen table and sat facing Nancy, the pain in her eyes reflecting at me. "Oh, Nancy. This is shit. I hate this!"

Nancy sat still while I went back to the fridge for the wine bottle. After refilling my glass, I tipped the bottle at Nancy. She nodded. I poured, put in the stopper, and set the bottle on the table between us.

"I agree," she said. "This is shit. How can we get beyond it?"

"I don't know, Nancy."

"I think the first thing is we both agree that we want to get beyond it. Then we start to rebuild, brick by brick." She paused, checking for my reaction. "I don't love Victor, Ann. I love you."

At the sound of those three words, I lost it. The tears welled up and overflowed. Nancy reached for my hand and this time I held on to it.

"I love you too," I whispered. Pretty soon we were both sobbing. We cried for a long time, until Nancy chuckled.

"What's funny?" I asked.

"We're not in Minnesota anymore, Toto."

I smiled, but still needed reassurance.

"You're sure you're not in love with Victor?"

"I'm not in love with him."

I looked at her closely. "I believe you. There is something about him, right? Something attractive."

"He's totally empathetic," she said. "That's why he's such a good psychic. You always found that creepy. That's why you and Victor were never going to work out."

"But you liked it, right? You believed in that stuff."

"So did you. You just didn't want to. Let's not go there either. We're finished talking about Victor." She got up and walked to the window, pulled up the blinds. "Let's go play in the snow!" At the excited pitch of Nancy's voice, Pooch got up and wagged her tail, looking from Nancy to me.

I went to the window. "It's still coming down." I looked at Pooch. "Pooch loves the snow, don't you Pooch?" The dog barked and we both laughed. "Okay, let's go!"

Nancy and I dug around in the closet trying to find enough warm clothes and boots and gloves for both of us. Once we were dressed, we headed over to Shorewood Park with Pooch, who didn't need a leash or a tennis ball. She bounded around in the snow, biting it, tossing it up in the air with her nose, running laps around the baseball field while Nancy and I egged her on.

"Go Pooch go!" We shouted at her. We chased her around until the wet snow seeped into our boots and soaked our gloves. We went back home and made popcorn for dinner. Over cocoa, she told me how she'd rented an apartment in Fremont near the yoga studio where she taught classes. She invited me to stop by any time and gave me a spare key. I told her about the happiness class, and I told her about Alex.

"I remember Alex," Nancy said. "Do you think she killed him?"

"No, I don't. But I'm worried about her. And I'm pissed at her for lying to me."

"Of course you are. Just don't get pulled in. Like you usually do." She said.

"Don't worry. I won't. I've learned my lesson. Alex has a lawyer and I trust the truth will out. She'll be fine." I said, trying to reassure myself, though I doubted Alex would be fine. She sure was not fine right now. She was in jail, but there was nothing I could do.

I changed the subject. "Let's watch something funny on TV. Have you seen this series called *The Good Place*?"

"No. But I've heard of it. Isn't that the one where Kristin Bell dies and goes to heaven? Ted Danson is God, or Saint Peter or something? It's supposed to be very funny."

"That's the one," I said. We watched a couple of episodes, and we laughed a lot. Then I had to find the sheets for her bed which I'd already packed away. We hugged goodnight and I slept well for the first time in a long while. We'd both needed this nurturing night. It would be a long time before I had another one like it.

The next day the temperature rose to the low forties and the snow melted. It always amazed me how this happened in Seattle. Unlike Minneapolis, where the snow begins to fall in November and lasts through March, here the snowfall comes quickly and leaves the same way, snow turning to rain and a distant memory in twenty-four hours. School kids would be disappointed that this happened on a Friday night. No snow day.

Nancy and I spent the morning packing up my house. I enjoyed her company and needed her help. Every couple of hours we checked the garage door and finally by mid-afternoon it had thawed enough to respond to the click of the opener.

"Halleluiah!" I said.

"Had enough quality time with your sister?" Nancy suggested.

"No, no. I'm so glad you were here. I could never have made this much progress without you. Really, our talk last night was way overdue. I've missed you," I said. Nancy smiled.

"Also, I have an appointment at four with a couple on Capitol Hill who need a house and dog sitter while they're out of the country. Wish me luck. If this works out Pooch and I will have a free place to stay while my house is on the market."

"If it doesn't work out, you could always stay with me." Nancy said. "Except I'd have to check with the landlord about Pooch. I think there's a no dog over twenty pounds clause in my rental agreement."

"That sort of thing always annoys me. If I ruled the world, only dogs over forty pounds would be allowed in rental properties. Thanks for the offer anyway. Keep your fingers crossed that these folks like us."

"I'll say a prayer to the Cosmic Muffin for you."

I laughed at the little joke we shared about our Lutheran upbringing. Nancy was even more rebellious against the evangelical church of our youth than me.

"Thanks, Nance." I said. "We're golden."

We finished loading up Nancy's car with several boxes of her stuff, and hugged goodbye. I watched her car disappear down the street with mixed emotions – bittersweet. I knew she would not visit me here again. There was no going back, and I felt like it was all happening too fast. Today I would see the Saltons, tomorrow the movers would come to give me an estimate. It was hard to imagine storing most of my worldly possessions for an unknown period to be unpacked at an unknown place. I took a deep breath. I could do this. One step at a time.

CHAPTER SIX

"Be Serious about Play * Find More Fun * Take Time to be Silly * Go Off the Path" Gretchen Rubin, *The Happiness Project*.

Once Nancy was gone, I turned to Pooch.

"We need to get ready, girl." At the sound of my voice, she looked up at me, cocked her head and wagged her tail. The Saltons, Tanya and her husband James, wanted to meet both me and Pooch, to make sure I'm acceptable and that Pooch and their chocolate lab, Doozie, would get along. Knowing that a tired dog is a good dog, my plan had been to take Pooch for a quick run in the neighborhood then head over to Capitol Hill with a well-exercised and well-fed dog. Since it was still a little slushy out, I took Pooch back over to the park instead and let her chase a tennis ball for ten minutes while I thought about how much I wanted this gig. It seemed perfect: the Saltons need a companion for their dog and someone to stay in their beautiful house in a fabulous neighborhood and we need a place to stay for a while. I didn't have much time. Betty had scheduled the staging for next week, which meant I had to be out of the house by then. If this didn't pan out, I suppose I could always move in with Nancy temporarily. What would I do with Pooch? I could never leave her.

I rubbed Pooch down with a towel before settling her into the backseat of the car.

"This is important, girl." I told her. "Be your best doggie self today." Pooch licked my face and handed me her still-damp paw. I closed the door, got behind the wheel and looked in the rear-view mirror at the dog. I swear she winked at me. I think she understood.

I found a parking place around the corner from the Salton's on Prospect near Eighteenth East. This is one of the supreme neighborhoods in Seattle, all large old stately homes inhabited by Seattle's liberal elite. It's also just a few blocks from Volunteer Park and Lakeview cemetery, known as the burial place of Seattle's most important pioneers. The big draw, though, is Bruce Lee. I was already planning my future runs around the park with Pooch. The power of positive thinking! I laughed at myself but repeated something from the Happiness Class anyway – "Just say yes to joy!"

At the stairs to the Salton's corner house, we were greeted by a bronze sculpture of four people moving forward. I recognized it as one of those African sculptures made by artists in Zimbabwe. I sat on the steps to talk to Pooch. "You know, girl, you need to be on your best behavior tonight." She looked at me with serious eyes, cocking her head at the tone of my voice and, in her doggy way, trying to make sense of things. I grabbed her leash and led her up to the front door.

As soon as I rang the bell, the door opened. They were waiting.

"Hi! I'm Tanya and this is James," the woman said, indicating the man standing next to her. As we introduced ourselves and shook hands it struck me that with their fair hair and skin, great posture, and perfect teeth, they looked like Norse gods. Well, Norse gods dressed in the usual Seattle style, flannel and fleece for each of them over designer jeans. Pooch stuck her head between my legs like she always does when she's feeling a little unsure. Meanwhile, James held Doozie by the collar while the dog wagged and whined, pulling to be freed.

"Before we go inside, let's see how they get along out here on neutral turf. Okay with you?" James asked.

"Sure." I nodded, and he let go of Doozie's collar. The dog sprinted down the stairs and did a few laps around the front yard while Pooch watched, a tentative wag starting up at her backside. She looked up at me. "Okay, Pooch, go play."

I unclipped Pooch's leash and she approached Doozie in the yard with a play-bow. Doozie gave Pooch's rump a good sniff and

Pooch returned the favor. Soon the two of them were off running and wrestling in the grass. When Doozie began barking, James called her. "Here Doozie! Enough! " But Doozie just kept on running, barking gleefully. "Doozie!"

Time to show these folks how a well-trained dog behaves. I called Pooch's name and, once she'd looked at me, gave her the hand signal to come. She bounded up the stairs and sat at my feet panting and smiling.

"Doozie! Get over here!" Embarrassed now, Tanya made excuses for the dog while James ran after Doozie, trying to corral him. Doozie responded in the way I expected, running around the yard now with James as his playmate rather than Pooch. Eventually James caught Doozie's collar and dragged him up the stairs and into the living room. The dog took off into the kitchen where we could hear him noisily drinking from his water bowl.

I looked around the comfortably furnished living room, taking in the tasteful decor and amazing art, then sat down on one of two neutral sofas and settled Pooch at my feet. Tanya chose the opposite sofa, while James folded himself into the overstuffed leather chair next to the fireplace. He kicked off his loafers and put his huge stockinged feet up on the matching ottoman. I gestured to the gorgeous baby grand piano across the room.

"Do either of you play?" I asked. "It's beautiful."

"I do," said James. "I played jazz piano in high school, dabbled around some more in college, considered a music major but didn't really have the chops." He shook his head. "What about you?"

"No." I shook my head. "I had the obligatory lessons as a child, but that was it. I love music though – both jazz and classical." I didn't want to mention my love of opera in case they knew about Franco Albanese and my experience last year. I changed the subject instead. "Your home is beautiful," I said. "It looks like you've done a lot of traveling."

"Thank you," Tanya said. "We have. Travel is our passion." She pointed out the dancing stick they'd purchased in Australia and described the huge pointillist piece of aboriginal art hanging on one large wall. "It's meant to be an aerial view of the countryside, with the circular areas representing cultivated fields. That's the river that runs through the region," she said, pointing out the azure wave through the middle of the painting.

"It's beautiful," I smiled. "I'd love to do some more traveling."

"You should," Tanya replied.

"It looks to me like the dogs get along well," James said. Then, "Hey, Pooch!" At the sound of her name, Pooch went to James, sat at his feet, and looked up at him. He reached down and gave her a pat. "What a great dog!" Pooch's tail thumped twice against the glossy hardwood floor.

"She's had a lot of training." I said, "almost made it to seeing eye dog."

"Nice. Maybe you could try your hand at training Doozie. We'd even pay you for that." He smiled over at Tanya, and she nodded.

"Do you have any questions for us? Now that you've met Doozie?" Tanya asked.

"Yes. You know I work full-time. I'm wondering if Doozie is used to being left home alone, and for how long."

"Actually, he's not." Tanya said. "Doozie goes to daycare three days a week and then we have a dog walker the other two days. On the weekends we like to take him to Marymoor or hiking. Does that sound like a schedule you could live with?"

"Yes! Well, I can't really afford daycare for Pooch, but I could take Doozie for you."

James and Tanya made eye contact. "We could pay for Pooch. That way the dogs will become good buddies. I'm sure she'll love the place. It's called Central Bark."

"Really? I mean, I'm sure Pooch would like that." At the sound of her name, Pooch came over to me and looked into my face. I scratched behind her ear and her tail thumped. It sounded like they were going to offer me this gig. My stomach did a little flip as the two of them looked at each other again. Tanya nodded at James.

"We checked your references and feel sure that our house and Doozie would be in good hands with you. We'd love for you to take care of Doozie and our home while we're gone. Are you up for it?" James asked.

"Yes! Thank you!" I couldn't believe my luck. Imagine me living in this fabulous house in the best neighborhood in the city. "Thanks!"

Doozie bounded back into the room and play-bowed at Pooch, who pretty much ignored him, so he jumped over the coffee table and onto the loveseat where Tanya sat. "Doozie, off!" The dog just wagged his tail and sat down next to her, offering her his paw. "Oh Doozie, you're such a charmer." The dog laid down and, panting in our direction, appeared generally pleased with the situation.

Clear who was boss of the household, I asked, "Is Doozie allowed on the furniture?"

"We know he gets up here while we're at work," James said. "It seems foolish to enforce the no furniture rule while we're at home. It's annoying when we have guests though, especially guests who have no use for dogs. We usually send Doozie to daycare when we have dinner parties."

Doozie needed some training. After my initial euphoria, I now saw the downside of this gig, and his name was Doozie. I smiled and assured the Saltons that we would all get along just fine. They gave me the particulars of their itinerary and explained that they were leaving next week.

"I know it's soon. If you can't start right away, we'll just board Doozie at Central Bark until you're available," Tanya said.

"Next week is perfect," I replied.

Tanya promised to email me the details, their contact numbers out of the country, and everything to do with the house as soon as possible. We shook hands and I walked out the door with Pooch at my side and an enormous smile on my face.

Once we were out of there and rounding the corner to our car I let out of whoop. "Woo-hoo! Pooch, you charmer. We did it! Free digs for six months. Yes!" I knelt and faced her, "High five!" Pooch raised her paw to my open hand and gave it a touch, a trick Victor had taught her, but I tried not to think about that.

* * *

I spent the rest of Saturday night continuing to pack. The job seemed endless. My appointment with the moving and storage company had originally been set for that morning, but since the snow had messed with everyone's schedule, they cancelled, then tried to change my time to Monday. After much cajoling, the guy took pity on me and agreed to come out on Sunday instead.

First thing Sunday morning, I headed to the den with a roll of tape and several book boxes. The books in there were what I thought of as *second tier*, my favorites filled the shelves Ben built for them in the living room. My plan was to keep only the books I loved, the ones that *sparked joy*, as that tidy Japanese author would say, or the ones I hoped to read again or simply needed to keep nearby for frequent consultation. I would give the rest of them to the Seattle Public Library. Since the storage facility charged fees based on weight, it would be best to let go of some books.

After an hour I had a pile to donate and had filled three book boxes for storage. Unfortunately, I'd gotten drawn into re-reading *Travels in Siberia*, one of my favorite travel odysseys by journalist Ian Frazer. Why didn't I take exciting trips to Russia, write a series of articles for the Atlantic about them and then morph that into a best-selling book? Oh, right, I took trips to Seattle School Board meetings. No vodka-drinking characters one could hire to drive through the Siberian winter landscape there. No filthy restrooms or giant mosquitoes either. There were some benefits to my job, I reminded myself.

I jumped when the doorbell rang, and Pooch let out a series of loud barks. The guy from the moving company had arrived. I went to the door while Pooch did her usual routine: woofing once, then finding a tennis ball to present to whomever my guest might be. Hope springs eternal with this canine. Everyone is a potential fetch partner.

"Tony Boraccini," the guy at the door announced as he held out his large hairy hand for me to shake. His name fit. Tony had steel gray close-cropped hair, like a military buzz. He was short and stocky with smiling dark eyes and a rough complexion. He dropped my hand, and his eyes went to Pooch, who was sitting next to me wagging her tail and still holding a tennis ball in her mouth. Tony got down to doggie level and scratched behind Pooch's ears.

"You'll have to find another pal for fetch, buddy." He said. "I'm here to talk with your human." Then he stood up and looked around. "Looks like you've got everything pretty much under control here. Your move out is next week. Still on schedule?"

"Sure." I said, thinking, *You've got to be kidding, I'll never get this stuff packed up by then.*

He pulled out his tablet, opened a program, apparently a room-by-room inventory and began tapping away. When he opened the door to the front hall closet, I cringed at how much junk was still crammed in there.

"I haven't gotten to this yet. I'm planning on getting rid of some of this stuff."

"Right. I'll just include everything in the estimate. Our guys can pack up anything on the day of the move. Just in case you're not completely ready for us."

"I'll be ready. I'm actually a highly organized person."

Tony smiled again, and I followed him through the house with a growing knot in my stomach wondering why I felt so crummy now that moving had become a reality. Now that I could finally let go.

We were upstairs in the guestroom, the room which Nancy had helped me box up completely, when the doorbell rang. Pooch woofed and scurried downstairs. I followed her down, told her to sit and grabbed her collar as I opened the door expecting a person. Instead, a small box addressed to me had been placed on the doormat and I just caught the taillights of a FedEx truck turning out of my cul de sac. I picked up the package and shook it like a Christmas gift, trying to glean its contents. I checked the return address but that offered no clue; it had been sent from one of those generic mailbox places. I set the package on the hall table and went back upstairs to Tony. He'd cruised through my bedroom and was opening the doors to the bathroom cabinet when I walked in.

"Sorry," he said, though he didn't sound like he meant it. "I have to check inside every cabinet and drawer. Want to be as accurate as possible."

"Right," I said, wondering if he'd been through my underwear drawer too.

Tony suggested we finish up by going through the garage and I cringed. "Just a warning. It's crammed full. I'll be selling and donating some of those things before next week."

"Sure," he said, tapping away on his tablet and ignoring me.

Tony was getting on my nerves. Where did he get off suggesting I wouldn't have the house totally packed up, each box with a complete inventory of its contents affixed to the side and every room as clean as a whistle. That was my plan, and I would do it. For sure.

When I finally closed the door behind Tony, I felt relieved that he'd left but panicked that I still had so much work to do to get the house ready.

"We'll get it done, right Pooch?" I turned to see the dog pushing the box around the hallway with her nose. She'd clearly knocked it off the table.

"Pooch! What's that you've got? Let me see." I took the package into the kitchen, retrieved the scissors from the top drawer and opened the box while Pooch sat at my feet expectantly. "This box is addressed to me, not you Puccini." At the sound of her name, the dog swept the floor with her tail and looked up at me. I opened the box. Inside was an old dog toy of Pooch's and a bag of her favorite doggie treats, the dried lamb liver kind, along with a card. The card had a picture of a Golden Retriever on the front with a tennis ball in its mouth. "Best day ever," it said. Inside, in handwriting I recognized, a brief note. *Found green monkey under my bed and thought Pooch might be missing him. Hope you're well. - Victor*

"Really?" I said under my breath. Did he hope I was well? Or did this have something to do with Nancy breaking it off with him? I felt a pang of something I didn't want to acknowledge. Regret?

mom died, almost three years ago now, my dad kind of shut down, seemed lost."

She shook her head, looked at her hands then up at me. "My parents lived over in Wenatchee, that's where I grew up."

Wenatchee is a small town in a picturesque valley between the Wenatchee and Columbia rivers, about a hundred and fifty miles east of Seattle. It's known for apple growing and is nicknamed *The Apple Capitol of the World*. I had a fond memory of driving through it one summer on my way to a resort town on Lake Chelan, a little further east, with Ben.

I nodded, and Emily continued.

"After mom died, I took a couple of weeks off to deal with things and spend some time over there with dad. I wanted him to come back with me for a change of scene, hoped he would spend some time with Madison – that's our daughter." She paused and smiled at the mention of her daughter, an obvious bright spot in her life. "But Dad didn't want to leave, said he'd be fine." She trailed off, lost in her memories.

"When did you suspect that your dad had dementia?" I asked, to get her back on track.

"Typically, I'd call Dad a couple of times a week after mom died and check in with the neighbors. Sometimes he wouldn't even answer the phone, or he seemed confused, like I'd just awakened him from a deep sleep. Then one day dad's next-door neighbor, Sally Johnston, called me. She said dad hadn't recognized her when she went to see him and that he'd shouted at her for disturbing him. She'd pushed into the house and found dirty dishes in the sink, clothes on the floor, and some ridiculous show blaring on the television. I could hardly believe it."

Emily dabbed at her eyes with the tissue disintegrating in her lap. I encouraged her to continue.

"I couldn't ignore it any longer," she said. "You know how we do that? Pretend things are not as bad as they seem, holding onto some twisted hope that messes with your rational self until you just can't possibly ignore the truth any longer?"

"I do." I thought about how long I held onto the idea that Ben would be fine, that the doctors were wrong about his diagnosis.

"I took more time off work, went over there to see things for myself." She shook her head.

"That's when you decided to bring him back to Seattle with you?" I asked.

"I don't like Seattle!"

I jumped at the sound of his voice. Neither Emily nor I had noticed her dad enter the room. He wasn't even in the room really, just lurking in the archway between the living and dining rooms.

"Who are you?" Mr. Clark asked nervously, pointing at me. He rushed to Emily, real panic in his voice now. "You said you wouldn't leave me with anyone I don't know. Who is she?"

Mr. Clark pointed his bony finger at me, and I stood to greet him, extending my hand. "Hello Mr. Clark, I'm Ann Dexter, a friend of Emily's."

Instead of taking my hand, Mr. Clark stared at me until I dropped it. "I'm here to talk to your daughter for a bit," I said, as gently as possible. "I'm not staying long and she's not going to leave."

"My daughter isn't home right now!" he said forcefully. "She's at school."

"Dad, I'm right here. You remember. I mentioned this morning that my friend Ann would be coming by this afternoon before dinner."

"I'm hungry," he said. "I want dinner."

Emily patted her father's arm. "It's not yet dinner time, Dad. We'll have dinner later. Do you want a snack? How about some crackers and cheese?"

"Okay."

Emily looked from her dad to me. "I'll be right back." She took her father's hand, like a child, and led him out of the room. After a few awkward minutes on my own, I followed. Mr. Clark sat at a marble counter dividing the dining room and kitchen watching Emily slice some cheddar.

"I love your house." I said, searching for a neutral topic. Emily looked up and smiled. "Yeah, we just finished the kitchen remodel last year. Took out the wall. It made a huge difference."

I pulled out the second chair at the counter to sit, but changed my mind when Mr. Clark looked at me suspiciously and leaned away into the wall.

"It looks like it's always been this way. I hate it when people remodel kitchens with no sense of the house's history."

"Me too. These are the original cabinets. Dan and I painted them and got new hardware." She picked up the plate of cheese and crackers. "Want to go back and watch *Friends*?" she asked her dad.

"Are you leaving?"

"No, dad. We're going to talk for a little bit longer. Do you want to sit here while we chat or go back into the TV room?"

"I need to go to the bathroom," he said, standing up.

"Okay, I'll come with you." Emily answered.

"I went," he said, looking sheepish, as a foul odor assaulted my nostrils.

"Okay, Dad," Emily replied. "Let's go and get you cleaned up." Emily took her dad by the hand again and led him down the hallway to the bathroom. "Be right back," she said over her shoulder at me. I was moved by her patience.

I went back to my earlier seat on the sofa, picked up my notebook and jotted down *Tough duty*. Then *understatement*. I included a quick summary of what Emily had told me about her dad and what I had observed. I had a few more questions. But when Emily came back into the room and apologized, I wanted to bail. I'd seen enough.

"You see how it is." Emily said. "And it's not getting any better." She shrugged and lowered herself into an overstuffed armchair.

"This is tough, Emily," I said. "I really had no idea."

"Yeah," She shook her head. "I think it's worse than having a parent die, watching him deteriorate like this. I mean, this isn't my dad, not really. When mom died, it happened suddenly. She'd been so healthy, only sixty-four, rarely had a sick day in her life. Then one day she fell at work on her way back from her coffee break, hit the floor. She never regained consciousness. They took her to the hospital, and she died a couple of hours later."

"I'm so sorry," I said — that overworked phrase that pops out of most everyone's mouth in the face of death.

"You said your mom was at work. What did she do for a living?" I asked, hoping to fill in some family details.

"Secretary at Tree Top, the apple juice company. Eventually she became office manager, then human resources manager. That's where she met dad. He worked in the plant, and she sat at the front desk for years. Dad only retired the year before Mom died. She swore she'd retire too but could never seem to do it. She loved that place."

Emily pulled a tissue from the pocket of her cardigan, dabbed her eyes, and then twisted the tissue into a ball and made a fist around it, clasping one hand over the other before looking back at me.

"I miss my mom every day. And every day I watch my dad getting farther and farther away from himself. It's terrible. A kind of torture."

"Who takes care of your dad while you're at work?"

"Three days a week he goes to a daycare center for people with memory loss, which is how I've been able to go back to work part-time. Good thing too, because of the financial strain we've been under. Mary recommended it, actually."

I took that in. "You're lucky the library has been so accommodating," I said, thinking about all those little pink slips at *The Seattle Times*. "Have you considered putting your dad into full-time care? This is so hard, what you're doing here."

"It is. But no, I could never put Dad into one of those places. Couldn't live with myself if I did. Waiting to die, that's what those sad old people look like in there. Have you ever been to one, seen it for yourself?"

"Not for years, not since I left Minneapolis. I used to visit my Grandma. She died a long time ago." What I didn't say was how

I avoided those places like the plague. "What I remember most about her place is the smell – chicken soup mixed with some kind of disinfectant."

"Terrible, aren't they?"

"Yes," I said. "But I like to think there must be some good ones."

"Maybe for the rich." Emily shook her head. I returned to my questions.

"What strategies have you developed? To help you cope, I mean."

"I started taking yoga classes just after Madison went off to WSU last September. That helped. I got a little time for myself, time to breathe. That's where I first met Mary."

"Oh, right. I remember that Mary teaches yoga. My sister's a yoga instructor too. I've never really had the patience for it myself. I have a hard time sitting still."

"That doesn't surprise me." Emily smiled.

"Yeah." I chuckled.

"And you're dealing with an empty nest too, now that your daughter is off at college. How are you feeling about that?"

She shrugged. "We moved dad right into Madison's room just a week after she left for college. Our nest is not really empty after all."

"And the happiness classes? Are they helping you cope?" I asked.

Emily looked thoughtful. "Maybe. But I think going out for drinks after the class has helped even more. You know that Courtney, Jennifer, Winkie and I all met in Mary's yoga class, right? I'd say we've all gotten closer since we extended the happiness class to include happy hour. I've really enjoyed getting to know you and Alex, too," she said.

"Even though Alex spends most of her time making fun of the class?"

"She's entertaining."

"She is." I agreed.

"I heard about Matt Downey," she said. "That's something. The guy who made her life miserable is dead."

"Yeah, but his death is making her life even worse now."

"How so?"

"The police think he was murdered. And they've taken Alex into custody for questioning."

"Oh my god." Emily looked at me, wide-eyed. "They don't think Alex had anything to do with it?"

"They do. But they're wrong. She has a good lawyer and he'll figure it out."

"Wow. Is there anything I can do?"

"Not unless you can give her an alibi. Still, I think it will work out," I said, fearing that it would not. I looked down at my notes. "I just have one more question."

"Shoot."

"How's your husband coping?"

She grimaced. "Not well. Last week we had our first date alone since Dad moved in. What a disaster. Dad wandered out the door when the caregiver thought he'd gone to the bathroom. Luckily, my neighbor found him playing with her dog in her front yard and brought him home. It terrifies me to think what might have happened."

"Yeah."

"Dan's been supportive, mostly. But after what happened last week, he wants us to revisit one of those facilities." Emily twisted the tissue in her lap again, worrying it for a while. "I just can't do it." She looked at me.

"I'm sorry." I didn't know what else to say.

She nodded. "Dan's been working a lot of overtime. He's an engineer, works at Boeing. Sometimes I think he puts in more hours than he really needs to because he doesn't want to come home to dad."

As if on cue, Mr. Clark appeared in the doorway, and I stood to leave.

"Thanks for your time Emily, I really appreciate it." I turned to her dad, "Goodbye Mr. Clark," I said, and the old man glanced at me briefly, puzzled, as if trying to remember something about me. With a sudden spark of recognition and an enthusiastic smile and wave, he said, "Bye Karen! Enjoy the show."

CHAPTER EIGHT

"Rebels seek to follow their own will, yet they're often undone by their own willfulness." – Gretchen Rubin, *The Four Tendencies*.

On Monday morning, at our weekly meeting with all the education reporters (the numbers were dwindling) I listened as Lindy talked about a new law that Governor Inslee had signed.

"The law requires school districts across the state to create community truancy boards by the end of the next school year — like the one we featured on the blog a couple of months ago about Spokane," she explained.

"I remember," I said. "Their truancy board had some good results working with families to keep kids in school. They had some awesome social worker heading it up, right?"

"That's right." Lindy said. "Instead of arresting kids who've missed a bunch of school and sending them to court, they get help from their community, their teachers and social workers."

"Sounds great. What about funding?" I asked, always looking for the cloud behind the rainbow.

"There's no funding yet," Lindy explained. "Still, I think it could happen."

"Let's write a follow-up," Jeff suggested. "Ann, can you talk to some of the counselors in the Seattle District? I'm thinking we need a piece that highlights how many kids a program like this could help in Seattle."

"Sure." I said. "But I'll have to put off the article on dementia."

He furrowed his brow. "I don't want to do that," he said. "Lindy, can you take this on? Check in with Ann if you need any help."

"Sure, Jeff." Lindy chirped.

"Great!" Jeff stood up, signaling the end of the meeting.

I went back to my cubicle happy that I had one less story to write and hoping Lindy could write it without much help from me. Then again, what if Lindy didn't need my help at all? Did that make me redundant? No. I'd just changed my focus. Jeff wouldn't include me in the next round of layoffs if I wrote the best story possible about Emily and her dad. I knew I could do it. I'd started writing Emily's story at home after our interview yesterday afternoon, struggling with how to capture the emotion of their situation – how Emily loved her dad desperately, but how he'd changed into someone unrecognizable and the toll that had taken. If you couldn't count on your brain, what then?

My own brain was a mess. There were just too many things going on in there. First, I was moving. I felt both excited and sad about that – a roller coaster of emotions. Panicked thoughts kept surfacing about being homeless. Ridiculous, I know. I had a great place to stay, but that was temporary. Second, my job felt precarious, third, my writing felt stale, and finally, my friend was a liar. What the hell was she doing in Matt Downey's house? I couldn't puzzle it out. Why lie about it if she had nothing to hide? I checked my watch and wondered if her lawyer would get her out of jail today.

I found Richard's office number in my phone contacts and hit the call button. His receptionist told me that Richard had a court appearance this morning and then a meeting out of the office. She didn't expect him until late afternoon. When I asked to speak with his assistant, she said that Cheryl had gone to court with him. Frustrated, I refocused my attention on the task at hand and made some progress on Emily's story. Then I made my way downstairs for some lunch at the Starbucks we shared with the Amazon crowd, another group of young enthusiasts. I didn't aspire to their work though, didn't even understand it really. They never seemed particularly excited to me, mostly just tuned in to their devices. I checked my own device but found nothing new.

Late in the day, I had an email from Alex. Subject line: *I'm Out - Can we Meet?* Appreciating the wisdom of hiring a good lawyer,

I clicked on the note and typed in a quick reply. I wanted to see Alex face-to-face and hear her explain herself. I could spare an hour before I headed home and continued the seemingly endless task of packing. We agreed to meet again at Oliver's Twist. It would be sort of on my way home.

I spotted Alex sitting in the far corner of the neighborhood bar, staring into her cocktail glass. The drink looked festive in its stemmed glass with sugary rim. Alex did not. She got up to hug me and I felt the tension in her shoulders and back. Even in the dim light I saw that her bloodshot eyes were swollen, void of makeup and underlined with dark smudges. I wanted to ask her what it was like spending a night in jail, but that seemed wrong.

"I won't even ask how you're doing." I said, as the waitress arrived to take my order. "Diet coke please." The waitress nodded and left us alone.

"Not drinking?" asked Alex.

"I've got too much to do tonight."

Alex nodded but didn't ask about it. "Yes. I am feeling as shitty as I look," she said. "And no. I did not kill Matt Downey."

"You lied to me about where you were on the night he died."

Alex avoided my eyes. She took a sip from her drink and shook her head.

"Why did you lie to me and to the police?"

"I was terrified! Everyone knows I hated Matt Downey. I told anyone who would listen that I wished he were dead. Then I was stupid enough to think no one would find out I'd confronted him that night."

"Confronted him about what? Why did you go to his house?"

"Look, Ann, I'm sorry I lied to you. I really am, but I was scared."

I nodded. "Why don't you start at the beginning. Tell me what happened."

"Right. Matt left me at the office that night to finish up the PowerPoint for our presentation to Jefferson Stone, which you already know. We were pretty much ready to go so I didn't really mind. Anyway, after he left, I went into his office to find something I knew Corey Adams had sent to us in an email."

"Who's Corey Adams?"

"CFO at Jefferson Stone. Doesn't matter. It's just that I couldn't find my copy of the email and I know Matt keeps every email he's ever received, so I went to his office to look for it. His email was up, as always, but before I searched for what I was looking for, I noticed the last email he'd received, from the partnership committee, about me."

I flinched. Not only was my friend a liar but also someone who snooped in other people's email.

"I know, I know. I shouldn't have looked at it." She took another big sip of her drink. "I knew Matt had sabotaged me before and I thought, I really thought, that this time he would support me for partnership. He'd hinted as much during our prep for Jefferson Stone." She continued to stare into her drink. "Prick," she said. "Ironic, isn't it, how he's still making me miserable, even from the grave."

Alex picked up her red Kate Spade bag, took out a cigarette and lit it. I looked around, feeling guilty, same as I did when Debbie and I sneaked our first cigarette behind her parents' garage when we were in eighth grade, and it wasn't even my cigarette. The waitress appeared immediately. "I'm sorry, Ma'am, but there's no smoking in here. Not in any Seattle bars or restaurants."

"Oh shit. I always forget." Alex took another deep inhale and then dropped the cigarette into her glass of water. "Sorry. Could you get me another glass of water?" The waitress picked up the glass as if it contained a urine specimen and scurried off behind the bar. I felt embarrassed to be with sitting with someone so rude, but I let it go. Alex had spent the weekend in jail. I could cut her a little slack.

"You were going to tell me about Matt's email." I reminded her.

"Right. So, I looked at the whole email thread, the initial one from Dennis Proctor reminding Matt of the partnership meeting and including a list of associates up for partnership this year."

"You were on that list."

"Of course. He rated all the associates up for partnership with his own kind of star system. I couldn't believe it! He'd given me two stars – one because my billables are *right up there* and one because I'm *smart as hell*. His words," she said, almost smiling.

"I'm guessing two stars is not enough?" I asked.

Alex shook her head. "Asshole. He went on to say that I had a bad attitude and poor rapport with clients. He ended his email by saying, quote, *I think it's unlikely that Alexandra will ever bring in any clients. Therefore, I do not recommend her for partnership.* Then he said he'd be happy to discuss this in more detail at the meeting."

"You were angry." I said.

"You bet your ass I was angry! I was mad as hell! I called him, but he didn't pick up, so I decided I'd just go over there. I had to confront him before our presentation in the morning. I did not want to go into that meeting with this on my mind." She paused. "I'm sure he just hit *ignore* whenever he saw my name as the caller."

I thought about how the police would have Matt's cell phone records, how they would add the calls from Alex as evidence of something. "How many times did you call?" I asked.

"I don't know. I tried several times."

"What time did you get to his house?"

"I left the office around five forty-five, but traffic was a bitch. I probably didn't get there until close to seven. His neighborhood was swarming with little kids – trick or treaters."

"Right," I said. "Was he alone?"

"Yes, but he was expecting someone for dinner. He'd been in the kitchen preparing food, had the table set for two, all very cozy. He wanted to get rid of me as soon as possible. I followed him out into the yard where he had something ready for the grill. I suppose that's when that nosy bitch next door heard me."

"Tell me about your conversation." I said. Alex waved at the waitress, who didn't look too pleased to be serving us after the cigarette episode. Alex ordered another Old Sally cocktail, something with bourbon and blackberry liqueur, and I declined.

"I told him I knew he planned to trash me at the partner's meeting, and I demanded that he explain why. He said the thing about client rapport again and I totally lost it. I started out fairly rational, but before long I was yelling and swearing, the whole nine yards."

"Apparently, he got you a glass of water?"

She raised an eyebrow at me. "How'd you know that?" She thought for a moment. "Oh, affidavit for the arrest warrant."

"Doesn't matter." I said.

She shrugged. "Anyway, I actually thought I might change his mind."

"You thought you would change his mind by yelling and swearing at him?" I asked.

She ignored my comment. "He suggested we go inside. He got me a glass of water and I calmed down." She said. "I reminded him of how he'd told me earlier that day what a great job I'd done on the presentation we were working on. He thought about that, and said he'd give me the lead on the presentation with Jefferson Stone in the morning. If I could land them as clients, he'd recommend me for partnership. He also suggested I write a memo to all the partners, outlining why I deserved to make partner, paying particular attention to the concerns he had outlined. He reminded me that he had just one vote and I might be able to persuade the other partners of my qualifications."

"You left happy?"

"No. I left worried. I realized as soon as I got out of there that Matt had just said what he needed to say to get me out of his way, so he could continue with his dinner for two. Then the next day, when he didn't show up for the client meeting, I thought maybe he had decided to let me take the meeting all by myself – sink or swim, so to speak."

"Bad analogy," I said.

"Right."

We sat quietly sipping our drinks as the bar filled up and the aroma of popcorn surrounded us. "Want to get some of that?" I asked. "This place is known for their truffle oil popcorn."

"Not hungry. You go ahead." Alex said.

I considered Alex's story. The only way out of this mess for her would be to identify the other woman who Matt was expecting for dinner. She was the last person who saw him alive.

"What about Matt Downey's date that night?" I asked. "Did the police talk to her?"

"No. When I told them he was expecting a woman for dinner, they said there's no evidence that anyone else visited Matt that night. They think I'm that woman."

"What does Richard have to say about this?"

"Richard says I can't talk to you about it." She shook her head. "Look Ann, I know you're good at this. Can you help me? Somehow? Please?"

I'd never seen Alex so frightened, so vulnerable. "I will, but you've got to promise me something."

"Anything."

"No more lies."

"I promise."

I left Alex finishing off her drink and took some of the popcorn to go which I wolfed down on my drive home.

CHAPTER NINE

"Questioners question everything. . .. others may find their constant questioning to be tiresome, draining, or obstructive." – Gretchen Rubin, *The Four Tendencies*.

The next morning, I woke up thinking about Alex and Matt Downey. Possibly they had made it into my dreams, my brain working overtime trying to solve this puzzle, like it always does when I know in my gut that something is wrong. Like a dog on a bone, I just keep working it. Yes, Alex had motive and opportunity, but I believed her. She had not murdered Matt Downey. I knew enough to know that any human being is capable of murder given the right (wrong?) circumstances. This was not that circumstance for Alex.

There were just so many questions. Had the police found Jacqueline Forte – Matt's presumable dinner date that night? If so, why had they dismissed her and arrested Alex? I knew I should not be interfering in the police investigation, my relationship with the Seattle Police Department was precarious enough, especially after my last conversation with Erin. I couldn't even write about this mess. To keep my job, I had to keep working away on whatever article Jeff wanted me to write – stress, dementia, happiness, whatever. Still, I knew I had to find and talk to Jacqueline Forte. How hard could that be?

I began making phone calls as soon as I got to the office. I called Turnbull Proctor first. I knew Gina had been upset about Matt's death and that she had fielded at least one phone call from Jacqueline Forte. Maybe Gina could give me a number for Forte, or maybe Gina knew more than she was letting on. I needed to talk with her.

"Turnbull, Proctor & Samson," Gina's voice, perky in my ear, surprised me a little.

"Hey, Gina, it's Ann Dexter, Alex's friend, from the *Seattle Times*."

"Oh, hi there. I'm sorry but Alex is not in the office today."

"Actually, I was hoping to talk with you. Do you have a minute?"

"Well."

"I know you have to man the front desk. But I was hoping I could buy you a coffee on your break? Meet you at the Starbuck's downstairs? You name the time."

Reluctant at first, Gina caved after a little more cajoling from me. At eleven, I stood in line at Starbucks when Gina came through the door. I waved her into the line with me.

"I don't really know anything about Matt's death," Gina said, as we waited for the barista to draw the espresso. "No one at the firm thinks Alex had anything to do with it. I can't believe the police arrested her in the first place. It's outrageous."

"I agree. Though they let her go without charging her. That says something."

"Yeah," Gina smiled. "She had a good lawyer."

The barista placed our lattes on the counter, and we took them to a table in the back.

"What's bothering me," I said, "is that the police were so quick to arrest Alex. If Alex didn't do it, then there's someone else out there who did. Someone the police haven't found or haven't even thought of yet."

Gina raised an eyebrow, nodded.

"Do you know if Matt had any real enemies, anyone who might want him dead?"

"No, of course not. That's ridiculous. The problem with Matt is the opposite. Everyone loved him. He got along well with everybody in the firm, except Alex, I guess. He is, I mean was," a shadow crossed Gina's face and she paused to take a breath. "He was the biggest rainmaker," she said. Then followed that up with: "one of the top producers," in case I didn't know what *rainmaker* meant. "We all miss him very much." Gina's voice cracked, and I thought she might cry.

"You and Matt had a thing, right? You dated him?"

She blushed. "No, not exactly *dated*," she said. "We had a thing, like he had with many women, a sex thing. God, he was hot! I guess you never met him?"

"No. I'd only heard about him from Alex."

"Maybe she was the only woman who didn't think he was hot."

"Right." I sipped my latte. "I'm wondering about another woman who Matt may have been expecting for dinner the night he died. Dennis Proctor told me he thought Matt had a date with a woman he'd met at a fundraiser, Jacqueline Forte. Do you remember taking any calls from her?"

"I do," she said. "I took a call from her several weeks ago when Matt was out of the office. I remember because she rambled on about how she needed to remind Matt about a fundraiser coming up – something about Art and Heart. I guess a bunch of art galleries sponsored an art walk and some percentage of the profits go to the Heart Association or maybe something to do with art programs for kids. I can't remember the exact details. I think she was involved with the organization."

"How so? Like on the board, or a volunteer?"

"I can't remember anything specific. I know he donated every year to the American Heart Association, has heart problems in his family."

I thought about that for a bit. "Since Matt died, no call, no contact from Jacqueline Forte?"

"I haven't taken any calls from her since."

"Would you have a phone number for her? From when she called Matt about the fundraiser?"

"No. I just put her through to Matt's voicemail. It could still be there, I guess. If he didn't erase it. The police would have that information already, of course. They've been all over his office and computer."

I nodded. "Right."

We said our goodbyes standing in the wind in front of One Union Square, Gina's blonde hair whipping around her face, cheeks already rosy from the cold. "Stay warm," she said.

I walked the two blocks to my car wishing I'd worn a hat or gloves. It had been a long time since I'd lived in the Midwest where freezing temperatures were common. Now, even though it was in the low-forties, I felt it.

Back at the *Times*, I called Alex to see if she could check Matt's office voicemail for Jacqueline Forte's number.

"No can do," she said. "I can't show my face in the office until I'm cleared of all charges in Matt Downey's death. I've been forced to take a leave. How do you like that?"

"I thought the firm was behind you. Dennis Proctor went ballistic when the police arrested you. I witnessed that."

"They say they believe me. But the party line and the way they're treating me are two different things. I guess it doesn't look good to clients."

I thought about those clients who'd rushed out of the office when the police were escorting Alex out the door.

"You're really going to do it?" Alex asked. "Look for Jacqueline Forte I mean?"

"Of course. I need to talk to her. If Matt had a date with her the night he drowned, then she was the last person to see him alive, not you. I mean, why aren't the police looking for her? How did she just disappear?"

I waited for Alex to respond. After a long silence, I said, "Alex?"

"Sorry, I'm here. It's just. I'm so glad you believe me, that you're willing to help."

"I told you I would. I keep my word if you keep yours, remember? I'll see you at Happiness Class tomorrow."

"Nah. I'm finished with Happiness Class. I don't know what I was thinking when I signed up. Happiness Class? What a joke."

"You did it for me. And I can't quit. Mary is a friend of Jeff's. My editor, remember? I'm in it for the duration. But, hey, tomorrow's class is all about the four types," I said. "Don't you want to know what your type is?"

"Oh, I know my type all right."

"Rebel?" I guessed.

"Unemployed." She replied.

After I hung up, another call came in. The caller ID flashed, *Turnbull, Proctor.*

"This is Ann Dexter."

"Ann, it's Gina. Hey, I was thinking about what you were saying about Jacqueline Forte. I doubt she's a murderer and maybe I'm just doing this out of jealousy or something since Matt never invited me over for dinner, or even out for a real date. Anyway, I just checked his old voicemails. I've got her number."

"Hey, thanks Gina. I appreciate it."

I immediately called the number Gina gave me. No answer, no voicemail either, just ringing and ringing. How would that happen? Don't all phones have some automatic voice messaging service? Even if it's a robot, the phone wouldn't just ring *ad infinitum*, would it?

I finished up my work for the day and headed home, thinking I might start my evening with a run. I couldn't get up early enough on these dark mornings to run with the dog but sometimes after work I latched on Pooch's lighted collar and ran around my soon to be former neighborhood. These runs had two positive aspects. First, they got me tired enough that I could sleep at night instead of staring at the ceiling as the anxiety machine started up. Second, they reminded me why I wanted to get out of this place. The neighborhood is dark and remote, nothing like the Salton's Capitol Hill neighborhood. I couldn't wait to move.

Pooch was ecstatic when I hooked on her leash.

"Want to go for a run?" I asked. The dog bounded around the front hall and woofed at the door. That made one of us. "I love running!" I said aloud to Pooch, trying to convince myself that this was a good idea. By the time we got to the top of the hill, my heart rate was up, and the endorphins were kicking in. I could do this. We took our regular three-mile route around the community college without seeing another soul.

After a quick dinner of whatever I could find not rotting in the fridge, I went down to the garage. Time to start the task of tagging things in there and deciding what to sell on Craig's List. When the doorbell rang, I looked at my watch: eight o'clock – a little late for solicitors and I wasn't expecting anyone. Pooch went into full protective mode, barking all the way up the stairs to the front door. I followed her into the hallway, grabbed her by her collar and opened the door to two police officers. After flashing their badges, they asked if they could ask me some questions.

"What's this about?" I asked.

"We're here to ask you about your friend Alexandra Rhodes."

"Alex?" My brain went round and round with questions as I looked from one officer to the other. "Far as I know, Alex was arrested and released. Not charged."

"May we come in? We just have a few questions."

"Sure." I let go of Pooch's collar and she sniffed each one of them in turn. I showed them into the den, apologizing for the state of things.

"Moving?" The officer who'd introduced himself as Markos asked while seating himself on the edge of the gray leather loveseat. Dark and solid, Markos exuded confidence and strength in his very posture. Pooch sat at his feet recognizing the alpha in this duo.

"Yeah. *Never again* I said last time I moved. And yet, here we are." Knowing nods all around.

"Hey girl!" The other one, Detective Baker, said to Pooch in a high-pitched tone, trying to engage the dog, who simply looked up at Markos instead.

"Good looking dog," he said. Blonde and baby-faced, Officer Baker reminded me of a Labrador puppy while Markos seemed more like a Rottweiler.

"She is."

Failing at breaking the ice with the dog, the good cop picked up the Ian Frazer book I'd left on top of the otherwise packed book boxes and asked, "Any good?"

"I liked it," I said. "But I know you guys aren't here to ask me for book recommendations."

"Right." Officer Markos fixed me with his unblinking dark eyes. The guy clearly had years of interrogations under his belt.

"As you may know, Ms. Rhodes was possibly the last one to see Mr. Downey alive."

"Except for the woman who got into the hot tub with him." I suggested.

"Now what do you know about that?"

"I don't know anything except what Alex told me. She left Matt shortly after seven as he prepared to entertain someone for dinner. He couldn't wait to get rid of her, so he could get on with it."

Markos scratched his head, then shook it slowly back and forth with a frown. "Thing is, there are no other fingerprints except for Ms. Rhodes and Mr. Downey's anywhere in the house or around the patio."

"The cleaning lady found him, right?" I asked. "I imagine she'd done some cleaning before she looked out the window and spotted him in his hot tub."

"Seems like you've done a lot of thinking about this."

I responded with a shrug.

"Did Ms. Rhodes ever tell you that she wished Matt Downey dead?"

"What? Well, sure. But we all say that about people we hate. Dislike, I mean. Matt Downey pretty much made Alex's life hell at work. But I'm sure you know all this. Why ask me?"

"Do you happen to know where Ms. Rhodes is right now?"

"Home? Binge-watching episodes of Law and Order?"

Officer Baker grinned, but Markos just drilled into me. "We haven't been able to get a hold of her."

"What? I talked with her earlier today. She didn't say anything about going anywhere. Said you told her not to, in fact." Wished I hadn't said that as soon as it popped out of my mouth.

"We did. Do you have any idea where she might have gone? A relative or friend she would go to?"

"No." I realized I didn't remember much about her family. Were they still alive and well and living in New York somewhere? I had a passing thought about that spa she'd been to in Arizona but didn't mention it.

"When you last spoke with Ms. Rhodes, did she mention her plans?"

"She told me the firm had informed her that she would be taking a leave of absence until the investigation into Downey's death had eliminated her as a suspect. She was not at all happy about that." The conversation came back to me now. "She said she had no idea what she would do all day now that she couldn't go to work. She's a bit of a workaholic."

"Right. You featured her in that *Times* article you wrote about stressed out executives last month. You writing about Matt Downey's death?"

A little flattered that he'd read my article, I looked down at Pooch so Markos couldn't read my face. "No, I'm not."

"All right." Markos stood up and so did Detective Baker and Pooch, both waiting for direction. "If you hear from Alexandra Rhodes, do let us know."

"Pooch!" I called the dog to me, reminding her who's boss around here, as my cell phone bleeped once from the back pocket of my jeans with a text message. Markos and Baker stopped in their tracks and looked at my backside. I ignored it and opened the front door with a smile. "If I hear from Alex, I'll tell her to call you?"

"Thanks. And thank you for your time."

I closed the door after them and pulled out my phone – just a reminder for a dental appointment I'd made six months ago. Better cancel that. While I had my phone out, I texted Alex: *Where are you? The cops have just been to my house asking!*

No response. But I couldn't worry about it. I'm sure Alex hadn't left town without telling me. No more lies. We had a deal.

CHAPTER TEN

"Sometimes loving kindness comes in the form of compassion, the stirring of the heart in response to pain or suffering – our own, or that of others." Sharon Salzberg, *Real Happiness.*

Early Wednesday morning, I drove into the office through the cold, dark drizzle, determined to get into the *Times* before most of my colleagues were out of bed. I needed to finish the article on Emily and her dad today. I sat clicking away on my computer when I sensed the presence of someone approaching. I looked over my cubicle's half wall where one of the interns stood, looking tentative. "Hey, Brandon, what's up?"

"You're writing that feature on family's living with dementia, right?"

"I am. It's almost ready to go. Why?"

"I just finished looking through the police blotter. Like I do?"

"Yeah?" I nodded the encouragement he needed to go on.

"I saw that some old guy drowned in Lake Union, near the Northlake tavern. You know, bottom of Wallingford?"

"Okay."

"Right. Sorry. Well, the guy had dementia. It turns out he went missing last night, walked right out of the house in the middle of the night. Must have walked off the end of the dock, maybe hit his head. Anyway, thought you'd want to know."

I thanked Brandon and clicked off the document I'd been working on and switched to the police blotter where I found the piece: *Body of Elderly Man Found in Lake Union. Seattle Police are investigating the death of an elderly man found drowned in Lake Union near Gasworks Park. The man, identified as Robert Clark . . .*

"Oh no!" I said out loud as the name sunk in. This wasn't just some old guy, this was Emily's dad, Robert Clark. His voice was still in my head, *Bye Karen!* I read the rest of the piece. *Mr. Clark wandered away from his residence sometime between 11:00 p.m. Thursday night and early Friday morning. If you have any information, saw, or heard anything unusual in that area last night, please call the Police tip line at . . .*

"Oh my God," I muttered to myself, then re-read the piece. He must have walked out of the house while Emily and Dan were sleeping. Emily's worst nightmare. I picked up the phone to call Emily and then thought better of it. I'm probably the last person she'd want to talk with right now. Instead, I headed for Jeff's office to tell him about Mr. Clark.

I explained how I'd interviewed Emily and her dad over the weekend and that I was just finishing the article about dementia when I learned about Mr. Clark's drowning.

"I'll have to go down there." I said.

Jeff shook his head, ran his hands over his thighs like he does when he's thinking something over.

"Okay," he said. "I'll need to send someone to the scene. Might as well be you."

Not exactly the resounding endorsement I hoped for, but I'd take it. I jumped into my Camry and tried to figure out the fastest route to the north end of Lake Union, turning right onto Westlake Avenue and then cursing myself for my choice. The other way would have been faster. Should have used Google Maps. Of course, I never really listen to that voice inside my phone, being stubborn and always thinking I know the better route anyway.

The police were still at the scene where Mr. Clark was found, yellow tape and all. It made my stomach lurch. I knew they'd taken the body away, but I couldn't help wondering about it. Were his watery old eyes open when they found him? Was his skin pale and blue? I imagined his sad grandpa sweater and baggy pants soggy, stuck to his body. Had his old brogues weighed him down? I wondered what his confused last thoughts might have been. I didn't want to think about whether Emily had been to the scene or whether, right now, she might be identifying her father's body in the cold concrete basement of Harborview.

With these things rolling through my mind, I parked the car in a lot across Northlake Way and pulled the hood of my raincoat up over my head. The rain came down in earnest, pelting the street, dripping off the front of my hood and onto my nose. I pulled out a tissue and wiped my face as I approached the scene. A small crowd had gathered just off the Burke-Gilman trail which paralleled Lake Union along this stretch. I assumed that these were people just out for a walk with their dogs or on their morning run who'd happened upon a disaster – the train wreck they couldn't turn away from.

A young female police officer, asking people to leave, saw me approaching.

"Please, head back to where you all came from," she said, looking pointedly at me. "Unless you witnessed anything here, please go home."

I pulled out my press ID. "*Seattle Times*," I said, trying to sound like that gave me the authority to be there, rather than the effect it usually had. She frowned in response.

"Can you tell me who's in charge?" I asked.

"Detective Costello." She nodded to a dark-haired cop taking a statement from a young woman in lime green rain gear at the end of the dock. The woman was gesturing as the detective wrote in a notebook.

I stepped onto the wooden dock, the loud clack of my boots propelling me forward. The boats bobbed in the water as I passed, while the wind roughed the lake and whistled through the covered slips. It reminded me of the other time I'd been here several years ago. We'd been invited out on our friend's sailboat for the annual Fourth of July bash. It was quite the scene – a unique Seattle party lasting all day and into the night, culminating with the fireworks display around 10:00 p.m. I remembered the great potluck dinner we shared – everyone contributing something seasonal to add to the huge amount of lemon chicken which our friends John and Angie had served deliciously cold. Ben and I had baked his favorite strawberry rhubarb pies for dessert. We'd had lots of food, great conversation and a few too many beers by the end of the day. Because of the traffic jam that always happens afterwards, we didn't get home till the wee hours of July fifth. I let the wave of memory roll over me while I continued walking toward the homicide detective. I thought about that day and how happy we were – laughing and full of life. Then I thought about the fragility of life. Ben is gone just as Emily's dad is gone, both leaving loved ones in their wake.

I stood lost in these thoughts at what I hoped was a respectful distance but still within earshot of Detective Costello's interview. I made eye contact with a boat owner in the next slip polishing the wood railings on his boat who, like me, appeared to be straining to hear snippets of their conversation.

Detective Costello shut his notebook and tucked it into the pocket of his trench coat. He shook hands with the witness.

"Thank you for your help, Ms. Skolnik. We'll be in touch if we need to ask you any follow-up questions." The woman nodded and turned, practically knocking me down in her hurry to get out of there. Detective Costello looked my way, then fixed his dark eyes on me, rubbing the stubble on his chin and raising his eyebrows in a question before I could even open my mouth.

"Ann Dexter, *Seattle Times*." I extended my hand for him to shake, and he grasped mine tightly, his gaze steady, intimidating. The guy was good-looking in the way I always liked, tall, dark, and handsome. He had excellent posture and nice teeth, though I'd only caught his smile briefly as he sent the witness on her way. He exuded confidence. I liked that too.

"Mr. Clark's daughter is a friend of mine." I said. "Also, I'm writing an article about families living with dementia. I interviewed Emily and Mr. Clark over the weekend. I was shocked to find out about his accident this morning. Can you tell me anything about what happened?"

He remained stone-faced. "Our investigation is ongoing," he said.

"Ongoing?" I asked. "It was an accident, right?"

"Looks like an accident. Haven't done an autopsy."

"Will you though? Do an autopsy, I mean?"

"Routine procedure in a suspicious death," he said, looking over my head.

"Were there any witnesses? Anyone see Mr. Clark last night?"

"No one has come forward. Just the boat owner who found Mr. Clark in the water this morning."

I glanced over at the man still polishing the wood.

"Not him. Guy from the *Miss Vicky*." He nodded to the sailboat on our right. "He didn't stick around—seemed pretty shook up. Took off right after we questioned him."

I nodded.

"I don't think you'll find anyone to interview about it now. I'm heading out of here myself." He shook his head. "Sad situation. The family probably won't want to re-live it by reading it in the paper tomorrow."

"Thanks." I said to his back as he hurried away.

My conversation with Detective Costello had gotten me nowhere. The guy was easy on the eyes but not so easy to talk to. I wanted to do something, so I got into my car and drove to the Clarks' house. I wasn't planning to intrude and didn't know what I'd do once I got there. I drove slowly up Wallingford Avenue listening to the slap slap of the windshield wipers. A car was parked in front of Emily's bungalow, so I continued to the corner and turned around, idling for a few moments across the street. The house looked dark and impenetrable – every blind pulled down tightly on all the front windows. I tried to draw out the courage to go in and talk to Emily in person, but I was frozen in place. I knew that nothing I could say would make any difference. Just as I thought I'd leave, the front door opened, and a woman emerged, pulled up the hood of her cobalt blue raincoat, and made her way down the porch steps to the sidewalk. I got out of my car.

"Excuse me?" I said, and the woman looked up startled, her eyes red rimmed and bloodshot. "Sorry, I didn't mean to frighten you. It's just that I heard about Mr. Clark's accident and thought I might stop in to see how his family is doing. They're not expecting me though." The woman looked at me, curious now, the fear gone from her eyes. I extended my hand.

"I'm Ann Dexter."

"Carlene Broderick." We shook hands, both at a loss for words.

"I'm a neighbor, just down the street here. Poor Robert. He wandered down to my house occasionally. He liked my dog."

"Oh, right. Emily told me about that. Mr. Clark ended up in your front yard a few weeks ago while she and Dan were out. "

"Yes," she said. "I'm not sure if I imagined this or not – because the storm was so loud last night – but something startled me awake around five o'clock this morning. I thought I heard someone at the door. By the time I got up and went to peek out onto the porch, no one was there – nothing but the wind blowing branches up against the side windows. After I heard about Robert, Mr. Clark, I wondered if maybe it was him at my door. Oh." Carlene teared up and wiped her face with the back of her hand. "Maybe I could have stopped him."

"Don't blame yourself. It was probably just the wind. No reason to imagine the worst. Nothing to be done about it."

"Thanks." Carlene took a deep breath. "Well, I'd best head home. Rudy will be expecting his walk. Dogs don't care about the weather, you know." She tried a weak smile.

"I do know. My dog? Rain or shine, better take her out."

Carlene nodded. "Bye now."

"Wait! One question," I said. "How are the Clarks doing? Do you think they'd mind if I went in? I'd like to say how sorry I am, see if there's anything I can do."

"Emily's pretty shook up, of course. Blaming herself. She'd arranged for a locksmith to come today to put in some sort of fancy locking system so her dad couldn't get out. A day too late, she keeps saying. Poor thing. I think it might help her to see a friendly face."

"Thanks." I watched Carlene walk down the street and searched for something more than platitudes to offer Emily – came up empty.

I knocked on the door and waited. A man, about six feet tall and stocky, with a kind face and tired eyes opened the door and looked at me closely.

"Yes?" he said.

"Hi, you must be Dan. I'm Ann Dexter, a friend of Emily's. I heard about her dad and just wanted to come by and offer my condolences, see if there's anything I can do?"

Dan rubbed the stubble on his chin and opened the door for me to enter. "Emily!" He raised his voice in the direction of the kitchen. "Someone here to see you."

"Nothing you can do of course. Unless you have a time machine," he said, with an awkward smile. "Sorry, not funny."

Emily appeared in the doorway, looking tiny and frail, diminished by her grief, like she'd aged in the few days since I'd last seen her. I put my arms around her. "I'm so sorry about your dad."

She gulped back a sob. "Oh, Ann. The locksmith was coming today. Today! This wouldn't have happened if I'd done it sooner. How can I ever forgive myself?" I hugged her closer and then pulled back to look at her.

"Emily, please. Don't torture yourself. This is not your fault. If the front door had been locked, your dad might have gotten out some other time, some other way."

Emily shook her head. "I can't see how."

"Have you two eaten breakfast?" Dan and Emily looked at each other, as if the question stumped them both.

"I guess not. We noticed dad was gone first thing and then the police were here and now."

"Now I'm here. I'm pretty good at breakfast. Let me make you something. You need to eat. Have any eggs?" I walked to the kitchen and opened the fridge, found some eggs in the door and a wedge of cheddar in the drawer, also butter and English muffins.

"Ann, you don't need to."

"I want to. And it's important that you eat. It's too easy to forget those things at a time like this. You have coffee?"

"I'll get that." Dan said, opening a cabinet and retrieving a canister with coffee. He made coffee on autopilot while I whipped up the eggs and Emily sat at the counter staring into middle distance. Death will do this. I recognized it and wished I could fix it but knew I could not. I could attend to the survivors though. I busied myself with the omelet.

"Your daughter, Madison? Will she be coming home?" I asked.

"Yes. She's coming in tonight. She was planning to come home in two weeks anyway. For Thanksgiving."

"Right." I'd been trying to forget the upcoming holiday. Holidays were not my favorite things these days. Alone again. Alone and homeless, I thought, then kicked myself mentally for the self-pity in view of Emily's situation.

"They'll be doing an autopsy." Emily said quietly. "I just hope he didn't suffer. But how is that even possible? Drowning is a terrible way to die." Emily sobbed, and Dan rubbed her shoulders.

I spooned eggs onto two plates, buttered the English muffins and placed the plates at the counter where both Emily and Dan were now seated. When Dan put his arm around Emily and she leaned into him, I realized that my utility here had passed.

"Looks good, Ann. Thanks." Dan picked up his fork and looked at his wife. "Honey, you do need to eat. Can you try some?"

Emily nodded and picked up her fork. They ate in silence while I cleaned up the mixing bowl and pan and wiped my hands on the kitchen towel.

"Do you have a doctor you can call?" I asked. "Maybe get something to help you sleep tonight?"

"We'll be fine, Ann. Thanks for making breakfast. You've been kind. Everyone is so kind." she said, putting down her fork and turning to me. "Courtney called me earlier, to see how I was doing. Heard it on the news, I guess. Sweet of her."

Surprising, is what I thought. Bad news travels fast.

CHAPTER ELEVEN

"Laughter is a physical expression of humor and joy that has numerous protective qualities. It's one of the best ways to manage perceptions of stress and to develop resilience and improve psychological sturdiness as it strongly correlates with happiness." - Kavita Khajuria, MD, *Psychiatric Times*, August 17, 2018, Vol. 35, Issue 8.

Back at the *Times* I met with Jeff to brief him about Mr. Clark's death and updated our online piece about it. At times like this, I wished I had an office I could lock myself into so no one would bother me. I did have a "do not disturb" flag that I set on the wall of my cubicle when necessary and everyone knew to leave me alone when they saw it. I plugged into some classical music, Bach's *Brandenburg Concertos*, and spent the rest of the day reworking the piece about Emily and her dad. The horrible ending made it almost impossible for me to finish. I could have worked on something else, but writing had always been its own sort of therapy for me, which reminded me of the happiness class and the Four Pillars we'd talked about last week. Maybe writing was my Transcendence Pillar, as Mary had suggested. It's why I became a journalist. Looking at my notes and bringing Robert Clark to life on paper somehow made it possible for me to move forward. Writing it down got it out of my head. At least for now.

When my phone alarm went off to remind me it was time for Happiness class, I considered taking a pass. Certainly, Emily would not make it. Alex was MIA and I didn't relish the idea of pretending to be happy knowing how unhappy Emily was right now. At 3:30 I changed my mind and decided to head over to the Phinney Neighborhood Center anyway with the plan of letting

Mary know about Emily's dad and maybe talking with a few of the other class members I'd wanted to interview.

When I arrived at the class, Mary was at the white board. I looked around the room at the unusually small group today. A young guy waved at me, and I waved back, trying to remember his name. I approached Mary and she flashed me a smile.

"Hello Ann! Please take a seat. Class is about to start."

"Can I talk to you for a minute?" I asked. "Something has happened that I think you should know about." Mary checked her watch.

"Can this wait until after class?"

"No, it can't. It won't take too long."

"What is it then?" she asked, the annoyance clear in her tone.

"I think it's best if we talk in private," I said.

Mary frowned and shook her head, so I followed up with: "You need to know this."

Mary shrugged then smiled broadly, apparently using her own happiness tactics to get herself back on track. "Let's meet in the classroom across the hall."

I headed out the door while Mary wrote something on the white board and told the class she would get started in a few minutes. I sat in one of the wooden chairs lining the perimeter of the room while waiting for Mary, idly wondering what kind of class happened in here.

Mary breezed into the room, her long skirt brushing the dusty floor as she hurried to sit beside me. "This must be terribly important," she said.

"Emily Clark's dad wandered away from their house this morning and drowned in Lake Union," I said straight out.

"Oh!" Mary's eyes opened wide, and she pulled back from me as if I might strike her. "That is terrible news, Ann."

"I thought you should know. I stopped by to see her this morning." I said. "She's taking it pretty hard, feels responsible."

"You were right to tell me," Mary said, fidgeting a bit and looking down at her hands folded in her lap. She began to twirl one of the rings on her right hand, a silver band with three black pearls. Her other rings were less remarkable, a turquoise on her pinky finger and a yellow amethyst on her pointer. "Thank you. I'll give Emily a call to express my condolences later this evening." She stood. "I'd best get back to class."

I nodded. "One other thing," I said. "Do you know what's going on with Alexandra?"

The frown reappeared on Mary's face. "I read about that. How is she doing? Have you spoken with her?"

"I have. But since then, she seems to have disappeared. That is, the police can't find her."

"Really? Well, perhaps we can discuss this another time. The class is waiting for me." She made her way to the door.

"It's weird, don't you think?" I asked, following behind her. "Two suspicious deaths, just a week apart, connected to people in this class?"

Mary stopped and turned to me. "Things happen," she said. "Bad things happen all the time. People die."

"It bothers me," I said. "Two possible murders, both drownings too."

Mary flinched. "It bothers me too, Ann," she said, something flashing in her eyes. "But we best get back to class."

I had trouble with Mary's reaction. She seemed dismissive, too quick to move on, yet holding back, afraid of facing the truth. I wanted to pass on the class. Not only was I saddened by Robert Clark's death and worried about Alex's disappearance, I was also exhausted and facing the movers on Friday. I had so much left to do. Still, I wanted to tell the others about Emily's dad, and I needed to hear their individual expectations and experiences with the class for my article. That deadline was also looming. I followed Mary into the room and found a vacant seat between Jennifer and Courtney.

Jennifer was the mother of two elementary school aged girls, married to a cop, and Courtney was a Resident at the UW Medical Center, though I couldn't remember her specialty. She usually looked tired. Not today. Today Courtney smiled brightly at me as I settled into the chair next to her and I smiled back automatically. Only after I shrugged off my coat and looked around the room did I notice that everyone had broad smiles on their faces. Mary stood next to the whiteboard at the front of the room on which she had written SMILE in bold block letters, while flashing her happiest smile at the class. When Winkie entered, she immediately began laughing.

"Isn't this fun!" she said loudly, as she found a chair and beamed her very white teeth around the room.

"You all look so happy tonight!" Mary said. Awkward tittering moved through the group. "Somehow just putting a sign in the front of the room that told you to smile, made you all do it. From where I'm standing, you all *look* a lot happier tonight than you usually do at five o'clock in the middle of the long work week."

Mary surveyed the room, making eye contact with each of us. I couldn't help but wince at her fashion choice tonight: she'd taken off the flowy cardigan and was wearing a white t-shirt with that awful and pervasive yellow smiley face emoji stamped across her chest. It didn't fit. Then, neither did this silly smiling business.

"Tonight," she said, "we're going to continue with the idea that when we pretend to be happy, we can actually increase our happiness. We're going to begin with some laughter exercises. Before you dismiss this as silly or awkward, I want you to know that way back in 1995 a doctor in India did a study on laughter. He discovered that our bodies cannot tell the difference between fake laughter and authentic laughter. We're going to experiment with this now. I want you to push your chairs against the wall and come into the center of the room.

"Give yourselves enough room. First, we're going to do some deep breathing. Inhale deeply through your nostrils while raising your hands above your heads. On the exhale, I want you to lower your hands while laughing. Like this." Mary demonstrated, and we all chuckled awkwardly at her "hahahaha!" exhalation. By the third repetition, we were all laughing convincingly.

"Good," said Mary. "Now, we're going to add some clapping in a two/three rhythm. Like the cha cha. Clap twice on the left side, ho ho and three times on the right side, ha ha ha! Great! now let's move around the room like a conga line, clapping and laughing and moving. Ho, ho, ha, ha, ha!"

By the time we'd made one complete turn around the perimeter of the room, I was laughing hysterically for real, and it seemed like the entire class was doing the same. We looked ridiculous.

"We're going to try one more exercise and then we'll finish with my personal favorite. This time, I want you to clap and stomp your feet like you're completely delighted by something while saying *very good, very good*, then raise your hands and shake them up high while saying *yay*! If it's painful for you to raise your hands above your heads, then just give two thumbs up with a stirring motion on *yay*!" Mary demonstrated the stirring motion with a waggle of her hips, and we all cracked up and followed her lead.

Very good, very good, yay! rang out around the room, along with raucous laughter.

"You're all so good at this! Did you know that on average a child laughs naturally three hundred times a day while the average adult only laughs around thirty times? Tonight, we're feeling the laughter. One last exercise. I want you all to pretend you're holding your cell phones to your ears. Got 'em? Now I want you to laugh as if you've just heard the most hilarious story from the person on the other end of that phone."

No need to demonstrate this time. The entire class held up their fake phones and laughed uproariously, bending over in laughter. Occasionally someone would catch my eye and raise an eyebrow or shake their head, but the laughter kept on coming.

"Okay." Mary said after a while. "How did that feel?" She asked.

"Silly," said Jennifer. "I haven't laughed that hard in ages."

"I feel great!" Mary said. "I just got the entire class to laugh uproariously without telling a single joke. Anyone else want to talk about how they feel?"

"I felt awkward at first," said Courtney, "but then I just couldn't stop laughing because everyone looked so ridiculous. Laughing for no reason, clapping, and stomping and laughing at fake jokes."

"How do you feel now?" Mary asked again. "Happier than when you walked into this room?"

Nods all around. I realized that I, too, felt better. I'd walked into the room feeling terrible about Robert Clark's death and worried about Alex. Now I felt different, not exactly happy, just more energized.

"This really isn't very practical though," Courtney said. "I mean," she continued "we can't just walk out of some terrible meeting or family situation and start laughing our heads off."

"Of course not." Mary replied. "But you can take laughter yoga classes whenever you want to – there are several in the Seattle area – or take one online."

As we were stacking our chairs, I asked Courtney if she'd like to go for coffee, talk with me about the class.

"Sure," she said. "I have the night off."

I helped Jennifer lift her chair into place. "Jennifer? Want to join me and Courtney for coffee?"

"Not drinks?" Jennifer asked. "I mean, coffee is fine. Ryan is picking up the girls and getting pizza. I told him I'd probably be home a little later."

Did I hear something about a girls' happy hour?" I turned to see Winkie behind us. "That's the best idea I've heard in a while. I'd love to join," she said.

"It's coffee, not drinks tonight," I said. "I've got too much to do tonight to start out tired. I'm moving tomorrow. I need some caffeine."

We walked over to the Starbucks across the street. I know lots of Seattleites who believe that a friend wouldn't take a friend to Starbucks – when Starbucks moves in, small independent local coffee shops are shut down. But, hey, Howard Schultz is local. He just hit on an amazing coffee shop model. I love that I can walk into a Starbucks and know what to expect. The decor is warm and welcoming, the baristas are always friendly, and the aroma of coffee does something to bring out my endorphins. Kind of like fake laughter.

We dashed across the parking lot and pushed into the warmth and familiar ambiance. I inhaled, smiled, and got in line with the others already talking about the class.

"Weird, right?" said Jennifer. "But I do feel pretty good right now. All that laughing."

We all agreed. Then Courtney repeated what she'd said earlier and what we all knew intuitively. "Too bad it won't last."

We gravitated to the comfy seating area—all leather cushy chairs surrounding a small round table—and sipped our drinks. I knew I would immediately kill the good vibe, but I charged ahead.

"Has anyone else heard the terrible news about Emily Clark's dad?" I asked, glancing at each woman in turn.

"I read about it," Courtney said. "And I called Emily earlier to check on her."

"What happened?" Jennifer asked, eyes wide. "Did he get lost again?" She looked from Courtney to me.

"It's much worse." I shook my head. "He let himself out of the house and wandered down to Lake Union in the middle of the night. He drowned."

"Oh my god, no!" Jennifer clapped a hand over her mouth.

"I know," I said. "I came to class to let Mary know. And I wanted you all to know."

"Poor Emily," Jennifer said.

"How's she doing?" asked Winkie.

"I saw her this morning," I said. "She's in shock. Blames herself."

A few nods, a few head shakes. No one knew what to say. We sat quietly for a few minutes with the bad news hanging over us.

"I don't think I ever asked you all why you signed up for this Happiness Class." I said, hoping that moving into interview mode would break the tension. I turned to Jennifer. Jennifer Tompkins is petite and naturally fair-haired, blue eyed and pale. She blushes frequently, which seems odd to me in a woman her age – I'd place her in her early forties – but maybe that just relates to having a light complexion.

"Oh," she began, with that deer in the headlights look she has most of the time. "I don't know. I feel like I have what seems to be the perfect life—a good husband, two healthy, great daughters, and a job I like." She shrugged. "I still feel like something is missing."

"I get that," said Courtney. "I have a great career, but that means I don't have the energy for a serious relationship right now. I guess I'm trying to develop inner happiness rather than waiting for the perfect man to ride in on a white horse. Also, I'm drawn to those happiness lists."

"Really?" I asked. "Those seem superficial to me. Like this laughter thing. I agree that one needs to find happiness within, but I think it can be kind of narcissistic and lonely, all that wool-gathering."

"I was never lonelier than in my marriage," said Winkie, with a frown. Her comment surprised me. In fact, the depth of this conversation surprised me, like our laughter therapy had opened these women somehow.

"I feel that." Jennifer said. "I'm lonely because my husband is gone so much." Courtney piped up.

"He's a police officer. Courtney said. "He works a lot."

"Right," Jennifer continued. "When he's not working, I know he's thinking about work. Most of the time, he doesn't talk about his work, especially around the girls. He sees a lot of bad stuff in Seattle, which makes him surly and overprotective of the girls."

"I can see how that would happen. It's a tough job," I said.

Jennifer nodded. "Like last weekend. Brooke was invited to her first sleep-over birthday party, but Ryan said no. Oh, the tears and the drama."

"Why wouldn't he let her go?" Courtney asked.

"Oh, he was fine with her going to the party, just not the sleepover part. Thinks she's too young." She shook her head. "She's nine years old."

"I'm pretty sure I went to sleepovers in third grade. They were fun." I said.

"Yeah." Jennifer said. "But, once Ryan decides, it's written in stone. No amount of cajoling, begging or tears will change his mind. We spent the whole night arguing about it. He picked her up at eight-thirty, but she wouldn't speak to him all the way home. She ran into the house, wouldn't acknowledge me, then slammed her bedroom door behind her. I could hear her crying in there.

When I tried to talk with her, she was inconsolable. I worry that his protectiveness *is* a little over the top. I want the girls to have normal experiences. It's normal to have sleepovers, right?" Nods all around.

"Jenny," Courtney said. "Maybe you need to assert yourself. Ryan sounds like a real control-freak. That's not good for you or the girls. Girls need their mothers to be strong."

"No offense, Courtney, but you're single and don't even have any kids." I interjected. "I personally think that childless women like us should not give advice on child-rearing."

"I hear what you're saying," Courtney nodded. "I'm not a mom, but I was a young girl with a controlling father. My dad made my life miserable, and I always blamed my mom for not standing up to him."

Courtney eyes welled up and I figured there might be some baggage here. I wasn't the only one feeling awkward and tongue-tied. We sipped our coffees and avoided Courtney's eyes.

"I'm just saying," Courtney continued, "that it's a mother's responsibility to be strong for her girls. You have just as much, actually, even more to say about how they're raised than your husband does."

"Why would I have *more* of the responsibility?" Jenny asked.

"You're a woman. You know more about how to raise a girl. You have experience *being* a girl. All Ryan knows is how to be a controlling male."

"That's a little harsh. You don't even know him. Ryan does the best he can. It's just. He just wants to keep the girls safe is all. I'm sorry I mentioned it." Jennifer said.

"No, no. My bad." I interjected. "I just fell into interview mode. Wanting to know why we all decided to take this happiness class. I'm sure we all have baggage, things we're not happy about."

Jennifer gave me a half-smile, then asked. "What about you, Ann, why did you sign up for this class?"

"I'm writing about it," I said. "My editor knows Mary. He thinks an article about Happiness will interest our readers."

"You're not going to write about this conversation, are you?" Jennifer asked.

"Of course not. I'm just writing about the class."

"You mean, you don't want to be happy?" Courtney asked.

I shrugged. "Sure. But I don't think this class will do it for me." I looked at each woman in turn, expecting someone to disagree.

"I don't know if I should mention this," We all turned to Winkie. "One time, at a sleepover in fourth grade? My friend's brother come in after their parents were asleep and offered to show us all his wee-wee, if we, you know, showed ours."

"Jesus, Winkie," said Courtney, "Wee wee? We're all old enough to recognize the words for male and female anatomy. Can't you just say penis and vagina?"

"Didn't everybody play doctor growing up?" I asked. "Were you harmed in some way Winkie?"

"Well, no, Annie, not then, but boys were always bothering me. Especially my friends' brothers."

"No one calls me Annie," I said.

"Sorry. I just wanted to say that I understand the concern, is all. Pretty girls are in constant danger of being taken advantage of. Until you get to my age, that is. Then you become invisible."

Groans all around. "Now that's the hot topic in the news these days," I said. "Toxic masculinity. Every man in power seems to have had episodes of abusive behavior to women." A brief thought of Alex and Matt Downey flashed into my consciousness. I shrugged it off.

"I don't want to talk about that right now," Courtney said. "Because that feeling of well-being I got from class has totally evaporated."

Nods all around.

"Hey, let's get it back," she suggested. "Pull out your fake cell phones and imagine you've just heard the funniest joke from your friend on the other end." She put her thumb to her ear and pinkie in front of her mouth to demonstrate. "Hahahaha," she fake-laughed, bending over in her chair.

Winkie followed her lead and soon we were all laughing hysterically into our air phones. The other customers looked at us like we were lunatics. Maybe we were. Or maybe it was just a hint of how desperate this quest for happiness could become.

CHAPTER TWELVE

"Moving doesn't change who you are. It only changes the view outside your window. You must *choose* to be happy, grateful and fulfilled." Rachel Hollis, *Girl, Wash Your Face*.

I got home and finished the last of the moving tasks with Pooch following close on my heels. The dog had always been a canine empath and tonight she clearly felt my ennui.

"It's going to be okay girl. Don't worry." I got down on the floor to scratch her furry head and wondered who needed reassurance more – me or the dog? There was not much for either of us to do but wander around the place having second thoughts. It was much too late for second thoughts. I heated up some leftover Chinese food I found in the mostly empty fridge and fell asleep on the sofa watching re-runs of *Law and Order*. When I woke up somewhere around midnight, startled by a loud commercial on the television, Pooch lifted her head from where she was sleeping at my feet and looked up at me with a sleepy and confused face.

"Need to go out?" I asked, as I opened the front door. She obediently went out and sniffed around on the grass while I stood in the doorway watching her through the yellow beam of the lone streetlight between my house and the neighbor's. I inhaled deeply, appreciating the scent of the clear air, with its hint of cedar and earthy dampness. Living on Capitol Hill would be different. Urban. In a good way, I reminded myself.

First thing in the morning, I took Pooch for a walk, suddenly nostalgic for the park, the *cul de sac*, even for the quirky neighbors who usually drove me crazy with their tidy lawns and uptight politics. On our way back, I stopped next door to say an official goodbye to Nicole, my favorite young neighbor and dog-walker, and to drop off Pooch. I knew it would be confusing for Pooch to watch all our stuff being moved out of the house, so I'd asked Nicole to take her to Central Bark – the daycare that the Saltons used for Doozy. Both dogs would be waiting for me later this afternoon, once I was all moved in.

Nicole invited me in, and Pooch wagged her entire backside with joy when she suggested they go out into the backyard for a game of fetch. I watched them play for a while glancing over at my back deck, empty now of furniture and scrubbed clean of moss. The facing windows were sparkling but dark and for a flash I saw a shadow there, a ghost, some trick of the light. My heart leapt, fooled me into conjuring Ben. He'd loved the view from those windows, the huge cedars across the ravine, the private path to Puget Sound that we'd trespassed on with Pooch many weekends in the summer – nothing but a mess of mud and fallen branches this time of year. In my mind's eye I saw Ben standing there with a cup of coffee, as he did most mornings. I shook off the memory, packed it away like I'd packed up my stuff, came back to the here and now with Pooch nudging her tennis ball at my feet. I picked it up and tossed it to the far corner of the yard, smiled as she ducked under the rhododendron to retrieve it and bounded back to me, dropping it at my feet. Nicole picked it up and gave it another throw.

"Last one, Pooch," she said, looking over at me. "Are you okay?"

"I'm fine," I replied, swiping the back of my hand across my cheeks. "The cold is making my eyes water, is all."

We went back into the house and Nicole gave me a hug. Pooch tried to get in on it like she always does, pushing her big head between us. We laughed, and I gave the dog a pat.

"Thanks for taking Pooch," I said.

"No worries," Nicole replied.

I opened her front door and heard the downshifting gears of the moving truck turning off Innis Arden Drive and onto our street. I ran back to my house and stood in the doorway as the large moving truck pulled up in front. The rain fell steadily, and I hoped they'd come prepared with something to keep my worldly belongings dry. I felt a flutter of excitement as two men jumped out of the truck, one with clipboard in hand.

"Good morning, Ma'am. I'm Jesse, I'll be the lead for your move this morning." He shook my hand. This is Octavio. Mark and Justin are right behind us." I looked out the open door and saw two other guys pulling out tarps and rolls of plastic. I needn't have worried about protecting my stuff from the rain.

"I'd like you to walk me through the house, so I get a sense of how ready you are. Then I'll plan the order we take things out of here." Jesse said.

"Sure." I replied. "I've got everything boxed up, packed and ready to go. Except the TV. And the computer is still hooked up for the wi-fi. I didn't unplug any of that stuff. "

"No worries there. We can leave that for last. We have special cartons for electronics. We'll make sure to keep the cords bagged and included in the box for each piece."

"Sounds good."

Mark and Justin got busy wrapping my sofa completely in plastic while I lead Jesse upstairs. He explained that they would tag every item with a barcode identifier so that we would have an inventory of every item that would go into storage today.

"Good plan." I said. "If only I could see the future and where and when these things would be unpacked." I said. "Also, I have my own color-coding system on the boxes. A different color for each room."

"That will come in handy for your move-in." He smiled, reassuring.

After we finished the walk-through upstairs, I followed Jesse back down and gasped to see that my living room was completely empty.

"Wow," I said. "You guys are fast."

"The living room is always pretty quick. Lots of big pieces. It slows down when we get to hauling the boxes."

I doubted that when I saw their system. One guy would pick up a couple of boxes and load them onto another guy's back, the carrier reaching behind while his partner stacked the boxes in twos or threes depending on size.

"Doesn't that kill your back?" I asked Octavio. He just smiled. "No, not at all. It's much easier on the back this way."

Things were moving out of the house so quickly that I felt slightly nauseous. So many years of my life moved out in a couple of hours. It seemed best for me to stay out of the way, so I busied myself in the kitchen, doing the last wipe down of the fridge and inside the cabinets. I poured myself another cup of coffee and went out to the garage. They hadn't started in here yet. The memories were still intact: bicycle, skis, camping gear, an old set of golf clubs I hadn't used since Ben died. It all seemed part of another person's life. Why was I storing this stuff anyway? I hadn't used most of it in years. I had to get a life. A new life. All this throwing myself into work, pulling back from relationships, it had to stop. Why was I here on moving day all by myself? Masochism. I pulled out my cell and called Nancy. Straight to voicemail. She was probably teaching a class right now. I thought about calling Alex, wondered if she was still MIA. I scrolled through my contacts and called her. Voicemail again. Where was she? I tried not to worry. I returned the phone to my back pocket and took one last look at the garage before heading back into the house.

The living room, dining room and kitchen were all empty now. I could hear the movers upstairs joking with each other, their footsteps overhead. I started to head up but backed down when Octavio and Justin appeared at the landing, boxes on their backs. I watched them move out the door. The rain had stopped. The sky was lightening up.

I found my laptop on the kitchen counter and turned it on to check the headlines. *What you need to know about Seattle's homeless crisis*. Homeless tent camps have sprung up under freeways and overpasses. They are pervasive in the city. I was deeply engrossed in the story when Jesse interrupted.

"Ma'am?" I looked up at him standing in the doorway with his clipboard. "I think we're pretty much ready to go," he said. I just want to make sure that we have everything we're dropping off at the Capitol Hill address on the truck last, so we can off-load it first. Would you come check?"

I'd been thrilled when the movers said they could make a stop at my new temporary home to drop off the few things I was taking with me. I had some clothes, my suitcase and a small two-drawer file cabinet which held important papers and files with bills, notes, letters, my passport, and other miscellany of life. I also had one box of books. I couldn't put all of them into storage. Without some of my favorite books, I would be completely adrift.

"Looks good to me," I said.

Jesse handed me the paperwork to sign, the inventory of stuff going into storage, the amount of time he and his crew had worked this morning. Arrival 8:15 a.m. Departure 11:35 p.m. Just over three hours for four guys to clear out my entire house. I was amazed at how quickly they'd worked. But then, that's what I'd paid for. I wouldn't know exactly how much I'd pay until they sent the final accounting. Apparently, they weighed the truck empty and then weighed it once they got it back to the storage facility with my stuff. I would be charged for the weight rather than the volume. I should have gotten rid of more stuff.

As the movers left, I jumped into my car to follow them to my new address on Capitol Hill. I glanced over my shoulder at the house while I pulled out of the driveway, feeling odd, a little queasy. I reassured myself that I didn't need to say goodbye quite yet. I'd be back. The stagers would show up tomorrow and who knows how long the place would be on the market. Hopefully, not long in this real estate climate. I didn't want to get overly optimistic.

The moving truck was parked in the alley behind the Saltons' house with the back open when I arrived. I found a spot down the block and fumbled around in my purse for the keys, unlocked the door and went through to the back. The guest room where I'd be living was on the first floor at the back of the house, just off the kitchen. I wondered whether it had been the servant's quarters at one time. I had Mark and Octavio put the wardrobe in the bedroom, along with the small file cabinet. The box of books they left in the kitchen. The whole process took them less than fifteen minutes. Amazing. I spent a minute looking around my new bedroom—very Pottery

Barn. Painted white headboard and chest of drawers, blue and green striped duvet cover and too many pillows on the queen size bed. I wondered vaguely whether I would be comfortable here but tucked that thought away as I busied myself moving my clothes from the wardrobe box to the closet which, though not overly large, had been tricked out with some kind of closet system. Everything fit nicely with space left over.

My stomach growled, and I went into the kitchen. The fridge was empty except for condiments. I opened a cabinet and found a glass, poured myself some water from the dispenser in the door of the fancy stainless steel fridge and sat at the marble kitchen counter, feeling out of place around all this opulence. Then I remembered I'd soon have the company of two dogs. For now, I could either head to the grocery store or walk to one of the many restaurants just a few blocks from the house. I decided to walk and get to know my new neighborhood. I could pick up the dogs and settle into my new digs later.

CHAPTER THIRTEEN

"Fortunately, there are still ways to cultivate meaning-building friendships." Emily Esfahani Smith, *The Power of Meaning: Finding Fulfillment in a World Obsessed with Happiness.*

Walking the few blocks to the retail area on Fifteenth would have been more pleasant on a warm, sunny day. Today, even decked out in a raincoat, rain hat and my favorite grass green wellies, the drizzle dampened my spirits. I felt a little lost and out of place in this mostly unfamiliar neighborhood. Oh, I'd been to visit Victor at his nearby office several times, but I didn't want to think about that. The thought of running into Victor, especially after my last conversation with Nancy, filled me with anxiety. I pushed those thoughts out of my mind, crossed Fifteenth and spotted a place called *Bakery Nouveau*. That sounded promising.

Once inside, I inhaled the warm comforting aroma of buttery pastries and steaming espresso. My stomach rumbled as I viewed the sandwiches on display. So many savory choices: ham, turkey and roast beef, roasted veggies and caprese, on as many different breads: baguettes, sunflower rye, sourdough, challah, multi-grain fougasse with olives. I picked a ham and cheese on a crusty baguette and a latte, then moved past the pastry case filled with macarons, shortbread, madeleines, breakfast pastries with fruit, a huge chocolate layer cake, and finally the handmade chocolates: salted caramel, hazelnut praline and coconut ganache. I hesitated only a second when the young woman asked, "Anything else?" I simply could not resist a salted caramel for now, and a small package of freshly baked chocolate shortbread cookies wrapped in cellophane and tied with a yellow ribbon for later.

I found a table for two near the back and facing the front windows, hung my raincoat on the extra chair, sat down and took a large bite of the sandwich. It was perfect – salty shaved ham and sweet creamy French brie on deliciously crisp and chewy bread. What a find – an authentic French bakery within walking distance of my new house.

I finished the last bite of my sandwich, ate the salted caramel, and began unwrapping the cookies when I saw Detective Costello walk through the door and head to the display case. What was he doing here? I didn't think he was stalking me. I did wonder whether to turn toward the window, suddenly become very interested in my cell phone, or keep staring at him so he would notice me and maybe say hello. I decided to watch him. He was about six feet tall, had great posture, and looked confident. I'd noticed that before. He wore gray slacks topped with a black raincoat. His shoes were black and shined. It was hard to tell much more from this distance, but I remembered his intense brown eyes from our last encounter. The memory of that made me sad and I wondered how Emily was holding up. Meanwhile, Costello selected a meaty sandwich and topped off his order with a large slice of chocolate cake. While waiting for his coffee order, he turned to find a place to sit and caught me staring at him. He looked surprised at first but then smiled and headed my way. He looked even better when he smiled.

"Fancy meeting you here," he said.

"Nice to see you. I've never been here before. You?

"Are you kidding? "It's a favorite of mine. Best chocolate cake in town! Have you tried it?"

I laughed. "No. But I have got myself a whole package of cookies for later." I lifted the cellophane package to illustrate.

"Nice."

"Mind if I join you?" he asked. "I'll give you a taste of this," he said with a nod toward the chocolate cake.

"I'd like that," I said.

He smiled, set down his sandwich and the huge slice of chocolate cake on the table. Before he could sit, the barista called out his name and he went to get his coffee. I hadn't known his first name, Greg. It suited him. Greg Costello. I liked the way that sounded—solid somehow. He nodded at the barista, picked up his drink and returned to the table.

"You live around here?" he asked.

"I guess I do," I said. "I just moved into a place a few blocks away. I'll be here for the next six months."

"Why six months? Seems short."

I explained the situation and he nodded. "Good time to sell I hear."

"Yeah, but a bad time to buy, right?" I shrugged. "It's the old Catch-22."

"Maybe you'll get lucky," he said. I liked his optimism.

"Maybe. What about you? You live nearby?" I checked his left hand for a wedding ring and saw none, surprised at how pleased that made me feel.

"I do. I bought a condo on Sixteenth, an old apartment building turned condos back when that was trending a couple of years ago. Unlike now when apartments are going up all over the city and the condo market has declined. Just my luck."

I smiled.

"But back to you. When did you move?"

"This morning."

"Seriously? And you're just having a little walk in the rain for lunch? Nice." He took a large bite of his sandwich, a huge grilled panini with several thick layers of meat and melted cheese. The flaky crust left crumbs on his upper lip which he licked before dabbing them with a napkin and taking another bite. I watched him eat, amused.

"What? Do I have something in my teeth?" he asked.

"No, no." I said. "I just enjoy watching anyone eat with such gusto."

"Gusto? Is that a polite way of saying I'm inhaling this sandwich and my manners are atrocious? Sorry but I can't remember the last time I ate. I'm starving. Wait till I get to the cake if you want gusto." When he smiled his whole face lit up and his eyes sparkled.

He worked on finishing his sandwich and I sipped my latte.

After he'd swallowed the last bite, he asked, "How's your friend doing?" His face was serious now.

For a minute I thought he might be talking about Alex and got flustered, the guy's a cop after all. Then I realized he meant Emily.

I shrugged. "It's rough. She feels responsible for what happened."

"How so?"

"Her dad had wandered away before, just last week when they had a caretaker for him. Apparently, he'd walked out the door while she was in the other room and ended up at the neighbors. Emily had a locksmith scheduled to come in the day after he died to install some fancy lock system to keep him safe." I shook my head. "One day too late."

"That's tough." He said. "Poor old guy."

"Yeah." I looked past his left ear and out the window where the sun had made a welcome appearance.

"You still investigating his death? Or did the autopsy prove it was accidental?" I asked.

"Don't have the full autopsy report yet," he said. Then, changing the subject, he asked,

"How'd your move-in go? You facing a sea of boxes when you head back there?"

"Nah, not so much."

He raised his eyebrows.

"Since I moved into a place that's completely furnished and only brought some clothes and books, it makes things easier. Though I do feel a little adrift," I said, slightly embarrassed that I'd talked about my feelings. This was not my usual way.

"I'll bet."

Suddenly uncomfortable, I figured it was time for me to get back to it.

"I should probably go pick up my dog." I said. "And my new landlord's dog too. Did I tell you this gig comes with a chocolate lab named Doozy?"

He chuckled. "Sounds like you'll have your hands full. I love dogs, miss having one. Only bad thing about my condo is their policy on dogs. Can't have one over twenty pounds."

"That's annoying," I said. "I imagine the place is overrun with yippy ankle biters?"

"Yes! There's a Chihuahua, a couple of Frenchies, a Yorkie and a Pug."

"Ugh. Real dogs are all over forty pounds, as far as I'm concerned."

He laughed. "I agree."

"It was nice to see you." I said, pulling my raincoat from the back of the chair where I'd hung it to dry. I stood to put it on.

"Hey, you can't leave yet," he said. "You haven't even tasted the cake!"

"Okay." I sat down as he cut a large forkful and lifted it to my mouth. I wasn't going to let this strange man feed me in public, so I took the fork from his hand and fed it to myself.

"Mmmm." The deep chocolate and perfectly moist texture of the cake had my taste buds springing to attention. "Wow. That is delicious. You weren't kidding."

"Sure!" I pulled out my phone. "Go ahead. I'll note them in my phone, so I don't forget."

He looked confused. "Oh. Uh, I meant maybe I could take you to dinner sometime. Introduce you in person."

"Oh!" I felt the color rush to my face. It had been a long time since anybody asked me for a dinner date. Unless you counted Franco Albanese, whom I did not want to think about right now. I must have looked skeptical at best.

"No worries," he said. "If you're too busy. Or married. Or something."

I smiled at his sudden loss of confidence.

"Nope. Neither married nor too busy." The words just popped out of my mouth without any forethought. He smiled. *What the hell*, I thought, reaching for the pen in the pocket of my raincoat.

"Here's my cell." I wrote the number on a napkin and handed it to him. He looked so pleased that I didn't know what to say, so I fell back on the one thing we had in common.

"You said you didn't have the full autopsy report on Robert Clark. What did the preliminary report show?"

He furrowed his brow at me. "You really know how to kill a mood," he said.

"Sorry." I replied. "Just curious."

He nodded. "Poor guy had a large contusion on the back of his skull, probably hit the edge of the dock when he fell in. Official cause of death was drowning."

I nodded. "Terrible way to die," I said.

"I've seen worse," he said. I let that go.

"I guess you're still investigating because of the blow to the back of his skull. In case he got it before he fell into the water."

"We have to make sure we've eliminated that possibility, yes."

I looked at Greg differently now, aware of just how easily I'd sabotaged the good feelings between us. I must be a master at that.

"Surely, the man didn't have any enemies. Who would possibly have any motive to kill him?" Just as those words left my mouth, I realized that the police would be investigating Robert Clark's family. It wasn't easy living with a man in the late stages of dementia. Certainly, Emily would never harm her father. They'd be more interested in Dan.

"You can't possibly think that anyone in his family would do such a thing?"

He shook his head, fixed me with an impenetrable look. "You know how investigations work, Ann. You're an investigative journalist, right? We follow all the leads until we're satisfied that we have all the answers. There are just a few more questions we're working on. That's all."

"I see," I said, though I didn't really understand what questions might have come up. Now things felt awkward. "I guess I should go," I said, standing. "I have a lot to do."

"Of course," he said. "Good luck with the new place and the new dog." He picked up the napkin with my number on it and shoved it into his pocket. He didn't say he'd call me.

I tried a tentative smile. "Thanks." I said, heading to the door while he sat down again. I noticed a slant of sunlight on the floor and turned to look at Greg with my hand on the door.

"The sun came out!" I said, with a real smile this time. He gave me a thumbs-up with a nod and a mouth full of cake.

With the cloud cover gone, the temperature had gone down a few degrees and I shivered in my still damp raincoat. The cold didn't bother me too much. Give me cold and sunny over cool and rainy any time. I picked up my pace to raise my heart rate and felt warmer with each block. I walked north on fifteenth, heading toward the grocery store with the plan of making myself a cozy dinner in my new place. The store seemed small and cramped compared with the more suburban Central Market I was used to in my old neighborhood. I filled my cart with the ingredients for an easy skillet beef burgundy recipe that I loved to make for cold nights. I also liked to share it with someone. Maybe I'd call Nancy, or I could try Alex again. Instead, I'd probably just enjoy the solitude and freeze the rest. Old habits die hard.

The walk to my new place toting a large bag of groceries felt longer than the trip to the bakery. I set the bag on the front porch while rummaging around for my house key. When I slid it into the lock, I felt like an intruder. I wondered how long it would take before this place felt like home. Probably never. Six months was not a long time. But as I looked around the nicely furnished rooms, I didn't have any doubt that this would be a great place to stay for a while.

I wandered about the Salton's house room-by-room wondering about their story, what their lives together were like. It reminded me of a novel, *Outline*, which I'd been reading. In it, the author describes marriage as a merely a system of beliefs, a story which is ultimately a mystery. She also suggests that marriage manifests itself in things that are real, especially the house in which the couple lives. With this in mind, I saw the house in a new light, not just a collection of things, things purchased in good taste certainly, but as a reflection of the owners' relationship. This only got me so far. I could see that one of them liked jazz, there was a large collection of jazz CDs in a cabinet with the sound system.

I couldn't tell if this was a shared interest. There were African artifacts and photos from their travels. These things seemed more a reflection of their shared lives. I didn't want to think of this place as quite so personal. I wanted to feel comfortable here. If this house was a manifestation of their marriage, that made be an interloper inserting myself into the mystery of their relationship. Also, following that logic, I'd just given up the one manifestation of my marriage to Ben. Of course, I'd needed to sell my house, to let it go completely to move forward. I knew I'd always have the mystery of our relationship locked up in my memory. I would never let go of that.

After I'd made the rounds of all the other rooms, I returned to my own and began unpacking my toiletries and placing them in the medicine cabinet and drawers which were clean and empty, just waiting for me. Which reminded me that Pooch and Doozy were also waiting for me at Central Bark. Time to pick them up and start this new phase, wherever it would lead.

I had a little trouble finding the doggie daycare as it was tucked onto a side street just a block off Rainier Avenue in a semi-industrial area. I drove past what looked like a group of homeless people hanging out in a parking lot. A couple of trucks were parked against a building, five or so down-and-out individuals were sitting on backpacks or wooden pallets. A few were smoking, a couple were talking with each other. They all looked hungry and hopeless, and I thought about the mayor's plans for solving the homeless problem, how long it would be before those plans impacted these folks. I wondered where they would all sleep tonight, another wet and cold Northwest autumn evening. Life could be very different, I reminded myself.

When I finally spotted the squat building painted green with the Central Bark logo on it (a smiling black and white dog against the backdrop of the Space Needle) I pulled into the parking lot. The door into the building was on one side and the other side housed an indoor/outdoor space filled with small dogs running around and yipping. I entered a hallway with stairs leading down to the large dog area (evident by the loud barking) where a sign directed me to check in at the desk in the small front office to my left. There, a young woman with pink hair – Samantha according to her name tag – sat behind the counter at a computer. She stood as I walked in and greeted me with a big smile.

"Hi there! Who are you here to pick up?"

When I told her Pooch and Doozy, she nodded.

"Right!" she said. "Tanya told me you'd be coming for Doozy today. Great! Also, your dog, Puccini? What a sweetheart! She did very well today." Samantha handed me a piece of paper with notes on it about which dogs Pooch had played with and how well socialized she is. It ended with an enthusiastic, *We can't wait to have Puccini back again!* I smiled, imagined this is how moms feel when picking up their children after the first day of kindergarten.

"Thanks," I said. "Also, I never use the dog's full name. She answers to Pooch."

"Right! I'll make a note of that," she immediately jotted it down.

"We'll be back in a couple of days, I guess. I'm not really sure of Doozy's regular schedule, though I know I have an email about it." I took out my wallet and placed my credit card on the counter.

"Oh, no. We don't need that. The Saltons have a credit card on file, and you are authorized for as much daycare or boarding as you need for Doozy and Pooch over the next six months. It's all been arranged. Also, Doozy's schedule, and I'm assuming Pooch's now too, is Monday, Wednesday, and Friday for all-day care, and drop in as needed, of course."

I couldn't help thinking that these dogs were better taken care of than those people I'd passed in the parking lot. I shook my head as I put away my credit card and Samantha retrieved the dogs' leashes from a cubby behind her desk then pushed a button on a microphone. "Doozy and Pooch are going home!" she said. I heard a muffled reply on the other end. "Got it." Samantha handed me the leashes and gestured to the door. "Kayla will meet you with the dogs at the top of the stairs. Have a nice night!"

As I opened the door to the noise of many barking dogs, Samantha called to me. "Oh, and I wanted to mention that we have a doggie cam in case you'd like to see what's going on in the main room whenever your dogs are here!"

"Seriously? Like a nanny cam for dogs?" I asked.

"You'll love it!" she said. "Once you start watching them it's hard to stop!" Before I could reply, Doozy had bounded into the small hallway and jumped on me, nearly knocking me off my feet.

"Doozy! Down!" I said, to no avail. The dog simply ran circles around me, nosed my crotch, then nosed her way into the office and jumped up so that her front paws were on the counter, tongue lolling and tail wagging.

"Hey, Doozy, you want a cookie?" Samantha asked as she took a dog biscuit from the jar Doozy had almost knocked to the floor. "Here you go!"

"Seriously?" I asked. "Don't you think he should sit for his treat?"

"Oh, he's too excited right now." She said, then gave Doozy a pat. "You're such a good boy!"

"He has terrible manners!" I said, and Samantha frowned at me.

"He just has trouble with transitions. He's really a great dog."

I told Doozy to sit, and he looked at me like he'd never heard that command. "Doozy, sit!" I repeated, while tapping his backside. Still, he looked at me with gleeful eyes and wagged his tail. I pulled a biscuit from the jar and used the most basic training strategy to get the dog to sit, showing him the treat while lifting it up higher than his head. This would ordinarily prompt a dog to sit while watching the treat. Instead of sitting, Doozy leaped up and grabbed the treat from my hand. Samantha snickered.

"Doozy!" I scolded, turning to Samantha. "Has this dog had any training at all? I mean, the sit command is puppy training 101. All dogs can be taught to sit."

"Why don't I hold him while you clip on his leash?" She suggested as another dog parent came through the door and Doozy leaped at the guy.

"Hey, hey, buddy, how you doing?" The guy patted Doozy's head. Sheesh, the dog got nothing but positive reinforcement for his bad behavior. Once I had Doozy on leash, I turned to Pooch, who'd been sitting patiently at the top of the stairs this whole time and attached her leash. When I finally got both dogs into the backseat of my car, I took a deep breath and looked at their goofy faces in the rearview mirror.

"It's going to be a long six months," I said, as they thumped their tails in response and grinned expectantly back at me.

CHAPTER FOURTEEN

"Death scares us. And because it scares us, we avoid thinking about it, talking about it, sometimes even acknowledging it, even when it's happening to someone close to us." Mark Manson, *The Subtle Art of Not Giving a F*ck.*

I arrived at the office on Friday earlier than expected. Even with feeding and dealing with two dogs, including dropping them off at daycare, the drive to the *Times* was so much easier— no more long slogs down Aurora Avenue or worse, the perma-clogged I-5 with its never-ending traffic. I pulled into my parking space before eight, greeted the guy at the front desk with a quick wave before making my way up the stairs. The newsroom was humming along as always, but there seemed to be something particularly interesting going on in Lindy's cubicle. She and Poppy were watching Lindy's computer screen and cracking up. I headed their way.

"Hey, what's so funny?" I asked.

"Oh my God, Ann, you have got to see this video. It's a rap music video made by a student teacher in Chicago welcoming his students to fourth grade. Hilarious!"

I scrunched up my face. "Sounds like a hoot," I said, unconvinced.

"No, no, seriously, it's fabulous! Come over here, we'll start it again."

I walked around Lindy's desk, so I had a good view of her computer screen while she queued up the You-Tube video and made it full screen. The music starts, a quiet, *yeah, yeah, yeah* while the camera scans around a typical elementary school classroom, landing on a very young black man, in white shirt and tie sitting at the teacher desk with his sneaker-clad feet propped up on it. He looks into the camera and sings, *Welcome to the fourth grade!* (holding up four fingers) *I'm happy to meet you!* (points at camera) *I can't wait to see you!* (points to his eyes, then back at the camera) *We'll have a good tiiiiiime!* (does a little happy dance with his arms.)

I was immediately drawn in and smiling at the young teacher's enthusiasm and energy. As the teacher continues to sing this simple song, he appears in different parts of the classroom: dressed as Einstein in front of a white board filled with equations, looking through beakers, in the gym bouncing a basketball and sitting again at his desk with his feet propped up reading a book, *Captain Underpants*, of course.

"This is hilarious! You're right!" I say to Lindy and Poppy when the video has finished.

"It went totally viral on You-Tube," Poppy says. Lindy has a call in to him. We've got to interview this guy for the blog!"

"It's perfect." I agreed. "Great that it's a young black man getting into teaching. How rare is that?"

"Exactly. I left a message at his school and hope he gets back to me today."

"Keep me posted," I said. "I'd better get to it." I picked up my bag. "You know how it is. You can take a day off, but your work is still waiting for you when you get back." I said.

"Oh, right," said Poppy. "How'd the move go?"

"The move was easy. It's the dog that I get to spend six months with that's the problem."

"You love dogs! He and Pooch get along, right?"

"Well, yes. But this dog, Doozy?" I emphasized his name.

Poppy snickered, "Great name."

"Yeah, well, he embodies it." I said. "The dog is three years old and has no training. He jumps up, doesn't even know the sit command and he's completely food driven. Last night I made my favorite beef burgundy recipe and while I ate, Doozy sat next to me drooling all over my lap until I finally banished him to the kitchen. When I heard a crash in there I ran in and saw he'd knocked the pot off the stove and was wolfing down my leftovers."

"Nice restful evening, in other words." Poppy said.

"Right." I replied. "I do love the house, and the neighborhood is fabulous. I can't wait to run the two of them down and around Volunteer Park. That is, when it stops raining long enough."

"I hear ya." Poppy headed to the technology pod, and I settled into my cubicle, fired up my computer and pulled up the article I had to finish. Just reading through the draft depressed me. The picture in my mind of poor Robert Clark in Emily's living room, the scene at Lake Union. His memorial service was this afternoon at 1:00. I wasn't looking forward to that either.

I put on my headphones to drown out the buzz and got back to work. At lunch time, I got up to take a break, pick up a latte and some protein before the memorial service. I sipped my latte and finished a breakfast sandwich while checking my personal email. Tanya Salton had sent a note saying they'd arrived in Cape Town, hoped my move had gone well and that Doozy was being a good boy. *Right*, I murmured under my breath, *a real good boy*. I decided to answer that one later. My sister had also emailed saying she'd like to stop by, help with unpacking. Nice of her. I typed a quick response and finished my latte with just enough time to make it to Robert Clark's memorial service at the University Unitarian Church.

* * *

I sat near the front of the church waiting for the Celebration of Life service to start, thankful that there was no casket surrounded by funeral flowers on the altar. Instead, I studied the carved wooden chalice hanging on the wall, the symbol of Unitarian Universalism. The chalice was about the same size as the hanging Jesus in the Lutheran church I grew up in, but the flaming chalice reminded me more of an old-fashioned martini glass, the flame like an olive stuffed with pimento sticking out the top. Ridiculous how my mind wandered during emotional situations. I felt the heat in my face. At least no one could read my mind. I watched as Mr. Clark's friends and family arrived, quiet and respectful, hardly anyone dressed in black. Their attire seemed like what Seattleites wore to the opera, everything from dresses and suits to blue jeans. Most of the mourners had hung their raincoats in the vestibule and sat quietly as a woman played something classical on the piano. I didn't recognize the piece, Mozart maybe, upbeat for a funeral but good for a celebration of life.

A few minutes before the 1:00 p.m. start time, Mary and Jennifer arrived. I waved and they took the open seats next to me. When the minister made his way up the center aisle in his crimson robe, I turned to see Winkie and Courtney sitting a few rows behind. I craned my neck to see if Alex had made it but didn't spot her. Greg Costello was sitting in the back row. What was he doing here? I quickly turned away, so he wouldn't catch me staring. Dan and Emily sat in the front on the other side of the aisle, Emily holding hands with her husband and a young woman I assumed was their daughter, Madison. I watched, fascinated as the minister lit the smaller chalice set on a table at the front of the altar then climbed the few steps and took his place behind the podium. The Reverend Turppa, according to the program, a tall man with a warm smile, opened his arms wide as he looked around the room.

"Welcome friends to this church as we gather today to remember Robert Clark, beloved grandfather of Madison Ross, father of Emily Clark and Dan Ross, members of this congregation. Let us begin with a reading from the poem *In Blackwater Woods* by Mary Oliver:

I listened as the poem began with a description of trees turning into pillars of light and giving off a scent of cinnamon. I closed my eyes and imagined those trees, but I felt my chest tighten as he read the last few lines: *To live in this world you must be able to do three things: to love what is mortal; to hold it against your bones knowing your whole life depends on it; and, when the time comes to let it go, to let it go.*

An audible sob came from the family's row, and I kept my head down and my eyes squeezed shut trying to keep my own emotions in check. I wondered again about Greg Costello sitting in the back of the church. I turned to sneak another look and found him staring directly at me. With the eye contact, the scene of Robert Clark's drowning on Lake Union came back to me unbidden – his cold watery death. Probably because Greg, as I'd come to think of him, had shown up in his official homicide detective capacity rather than friendly neighbor. Was he looking for suspects? Did he think that someone at the funeral had murdered Robert Clark?

During the next musical interlude, my brain mulled things over. One suspicious drowning among people I cared about was one too many. Two seemed pathological. I had to believe that Robert Clark's death was tragic, not intentional. It simply made no sense. Maybe Greg had another reason for being here. I looked at the program hoping that the service would be brief. After the music, a middle-aged man got up to speak, Todd Meeker, according to the program. Todd talked about how he'd met Robert Clark when they both worked together at Tree Top in Wenatchee and had remained friends for thirty years. He described Robert as his mentor, a great guy who had taught him a lot about work and about life. I thought about my colleagues at the *Seattle Times* wondering if any of them would choose to speak at my funeral. Maybe Jeff?

My mind continued to wander until Madison stood up to honor her grandfather. Pale and shaky at first, the young woman regained control of her emotions once she got going. She talked about the happy times she'd spent with her grandfather, how he'd taught her to ride a bike and taken her camping in the Cascades. When she talked about his dementia, how they'd been missing him for some time now, I felt my own tears welling up. I hadn't expected this to be so emotional for me, but it was impossible in this setting not to think about loss, about Ben especially, but also my parents, and the near loss of my sister Nancy.

Madison ended her tribute by saying, "I will always miss you Papa, but I will always remember you and I will always love you." I looked over at Emily smiling with tears streaming down her face.

Death sucks. Even when it's time for someone to go, it sucks. After Madison's words, the minister stood up and read what Emily had written about her dad but was too emotional to deliver herself. He then gave a brief homily, sprinkled with more poetry and not one bible passage as far as I could tell. He ended with a prayer. At least I think it was a prayer, though it did not begin in the usual way. There was no *Dear God*, or *Father* or *Lord*. He simply launched into it, calling for us to remember Robert Clark and the love we felt today surrounded by family and friends in this community and invited us to spend a moment with our own thoughts, a moment of silent reflection. After some quiet time, he said *amen*. There was a last hymn, one I thought I'd remembered, but the words had been changed. While we sang, the minister extinguished the chalice and made his way down the center aisle and into the meeting room where there would be coffee and time for paying our respects to the family. I sat for a moment with my own thoughts about Emily's dad. Even though Mr. Clark had lived a long life and was suffering from dementia, his death seemed wrong. Maybe it was the tragic circumstances but maybe it's just that death is so final. Letting go is so hard. Mary Oliver was right. When death comes, there's nothing we can do but *let it go*.

Mary, Jennifer, and I stood, along with everyone else, and made our way directly into the meeting room.

I turned to Mary, feeling awkward after how we'd left each other on Wednesday. Before I could think of something to say, she leaned in and said, "I can't stay long." I nodded. "I have a three o'clock yoga class," She explained.

Emily, Dan, and Madison were standing near the door, a long line of mourners forming in front of them. We joined the queue along with Winkie and Courtney, who were already in line.

Courtney looked tired, as usual, and I wondered about the wisdom of our medical system, doctors working twenty-four hour shifts with nothing but a quick nap in some uncomfortable hospital bed, sometimes no rest at all. How could that lead to excellent care?

"Hey," Courtney said as we joined them. "Poor Emily," she continued. "This sucks. Nice service though." Nods all around.

"Emily seems okay, don't you think?" Winkie asked, and we all looked at Emily, smiling at whoever she was talking to now, hugging her before moving on to the next person waiting to pay his respects.

"Looks like she's got some good drugs," Courtney said. "Maybe Xanax. She's a little dazed looking, but functional. I hope she takes all she needs to get through this."

I scanned the room for Detective Costello and spotted him at the coat rack near the door. It looked like he was planning to leave without paying his respects to Emily and her family, and without saying hello to me. I excused myself from the group and caught up with him just as he pushed open the door.

"Detective?"

He turned to look at me, halfway out the door, his hand on the push bar.

"Hello, Ann." He met my eyes and held them for an uncomfortable length of time.

"Can I ask you something?" I said. "Maybe outside?"

He nodded, and I followed him out to the courtyard.

"Are you here in your official capacity? I mean, Mr. Clark's death was a tragic accident, right? No foul play?"

He raised his eyebrows but said nothing.

"I'm surprised to see you, is all." I said.

"It's routine." He said. "Until the investigation is complete, we're still collecting facts."

"The autopsy didn't show anything suspicious, did it?"

"Like I said, we're still investigating. I can't comment on the autopsy."

"But. – "

"Nice to see you, Ann." He turned and was gone before I could ask the questions that were racing around my head. I stood there watching his back, confused and disappointed. He sure wasn't as friendly here as he'd been at Bakery Nouveau. Still puzzled, I heard the church door swoosh open and Mary rush out.

"Weren't you going to say something to Emily?" She gave me a look of disapproval. "Our group is with her now. Hurry or you'll have to wait in that line again."

I hurried back in and saw Emily surrounded by Courtney, Winkie, and Jennifer. As Emily hugged Winkie, I noticed how nice she looked in black, from her dress to her designer heels. Then it was my turn.

"Oh, Emily," I said "It was a lovely service." I turned to her daughter, Madison. "Your tribute was perfect. I wish I'd met your grandfather sooner."

Madison thanked me, and I felt the push of the folks behind me. "I'll see you soon I hope?" I said to Emily.

She nodded but doubted she was tracking much of anything, just getting through.

* * *

When I got back to the newsroom, I saw Lindy in the tech pod again chatting with Poppy.

"Hey Ann!" Lindy waved me over.

"I interviewed that fourth-grade teacher!"

"Great!" I said, thinking, *Better you than me.* Then I said, feigning interest, "What was he like?"

"Sweet and self-effacing. He can't believe his video went viral. I told him to consider teaching in Seattle when his student teaching gig is up, and he actually said he likes rainy weather!"

"Nice." I conjured a smile. "Gotta get back at it," I headed to my cubicle comparing Lindy's enthusiasm for the education blog to my own. Quite the difference. When I started out, like that fourth-grade teacher, and like Lindy, I too had been passionate about education, teaching and then writing about it. Now? Mr. Clark's memorial had reminded me of what I'd known since Ben died. Life is short; it can end in an instant. Why am I wasting time doing something I don't love? Then that other reality hit me. I need to pay the bills, that's why. I fired up my computer and got to work. As I was packing up to leave, my phone pinged with a text. Alexandra!

Hey girlfriend, how you doing?

Where have you been? I texted back. *The police are looking for you!*

CHAPTER FIFTEEN

You should spend more time doing things that feed your spirit: more long walks with your dog . . ." Rachel Hollis, *Girl, Wash Your Face.*

Alex insisted that the cops were just messing with me, that she'd been at some place called *The Willows* in Woodinville trying to relax. She also said that her lawyer knew where she'd been the whole time. Alex suggested we go out for dinner tonight, but I worried about leaving the dogs home alone. Probably silly of me. I invited Alex over instead. It would be nice to have some company in my new place. We agreed on 6:30. She'd bring some wine and we'd get takeout for dinner. I'd been wanting to try the Thai place on fifteenth.

This time the pickup of Doozy and Pooch went a little more smoothly. The daycare manager, an authoritative middle-aged guy, called the dogs and clipped their leashes on at the top of the stairs while I waited in the office. He also helped me get them into the car, saying, "Doozy can be a bit of a handful."

I thanked him and drove the short distance to Capitol Hill feeling glad that I would have company tonight.

I found a rare parking place in front of my new place and let the dogs out, keeping Doozy on a short leash while Pooch trotted at my side. Suddenly Doozy lurched forward, wrenched the leash from my hand and ran up the stairs barking. In the shadows of the weak porch light, I could see someone sitting on the bench. Since I couldn't identify the person, I let the dog do his job.

"Call this guy off!" It was Alex.

"Doozy!" I called but Doozy kept barking menacingly until he'd cornered Alex at the front door. I grabbed his leash. "It's okay, boy, this is Alex. We like her. She's a friend." Doozy stopped barking and looked at me with his ears back and his tail between his legs.

"You big baby. It's okay." The dog's tail wagged tentatively as Alex relaxed.

"Holy shit!" She said. "I thought all labs were gentle. This guy scared the hell out of me."

"Yeah. Sorry. He needs some training."

Once inside, Doozy ran around the house and play bowed to Pooch like he was still at daycare.

"Doozy! Stop!" I said. He continued to wag at me, and I decided it was time for the crate. I'd seen a crate in the butler's pantry, but the Salton's never told me whether the dog was crate trained or if they used it.

"Time out Doozy." I filled the dogs' bowls with kibble and put Doozy's bowl into the crate. Then I closed the swinging door.

"Wow." Alex said. "Are you having fun yet?"

"I don't even want to talk about it. I had no idea what a challenge this dog would be. I should have known this gig was too good to be true. Also, you're early, right?"

"Never too early for happy hour," she said, pulling out a bottle of wine from her bag and setting it on the kitchen counter. "Where's your corkscrew?"

Alex opened the wine and poured while I called the restaurant to place our order. Then we settled into the living room with Pooch at my feet. The clock over the mantel struck six.

"I guess I am early," Alex said. "Sorry. Time seems so fluid now that I don't have a job. No appointments. Just me and this murder hanging over my head."

"Yeah." I said. "I keep wondering whether the police are trying to find Jacqueline Forte, you know, Matt's dinner date the night he died?"

"You keep harping on that Ann, but apparently, mine were the only fingerprints at the scene."

"You know that's not enough. Otherwise, you'd still be in jail. Someone needs to find that woman. I got a number for her off

Matt Downey's voicemail, and have called several times, but so far no one's answering."

"How'd you get her number?"

I told her about my coffee date with Gina. She seemed pleased.

"Thanks girlfriend. I appreciate it. It's probably more than the police are doing."

"Speaking of the police," I said, "It turns out that the detective investigating Robert Clark's death lives here in my new neighborhood. Wait. You knew about Emily's dad, right? You weren't at the funeral."

"Yeah. I got a voicemail from Courtney about it while I was in Woodinville. I drove home this morning with every intention of going." She shrugged. "I just couldn't face it."

I nodded. "I get it."

"Thanks." She said. "Go back to what you were saying about the cop investigating Robert Clark's death."

"Oh yeah. He lives nearby. I ran into him yesterday at Bakery Nouveau."

"Lucky you." Alex said.

"Actually, he seemed like a nice guy yesterday. But today, when he was lurking around in the back at Robert Clark's service, he wouldn't give me the time of day."

"What was he doing there?" Alex asked.

"I assume he was being a homicide detective. You know, noting who was there, looking for anyone who might have had something to do with Emily's dad's death, like that. He wasn't sharing with me. He just said the investigation would be ongoing until they ruled out foul play."

"Jesus. Robert Clark was an old man with dementia who fell into the lake and drowned. Fucking cops. Don't they have better ways to spend their time?"

"I don't know." I wanted to call Greg and follow up. Except that he'd basically ignored me at Robert Clark's memorial, and he hadn't called me, despite that napkin in his pocket with my phone number on it.

"How's Emily holding up?" Alex asked.

"About as you'd expect. Blames herself. Feels awful. Can't believe he's dead."

"Poor Emily," Alex said. "I know I should have gone to support her. It's just that I'm so fucked up right now. I couldn't face it."

"I get it. For what it's worth, it was a nice memorial service. If I can even use the words *nice* and *memorial service* in the same sentence, that is."

Alex raised an eyebrow at me. "You getting religion?"

"No! That's the thing about it. There was no religious mumbo jumbo about how Robert Clark is with God in heaven now. There was some poetry, some beautiful music. Friends and family said some nice things about Robert Clark. I think I like the Unitarians."

"You are getting religion!"

"Fat chance." I replied.

The doorbell rang and Doozy went ballistic barking and lunging at his crate instead of at the front door. We took the food into the dining room and once Doozy stopped whining, I let him out of his crate. I gave him a stern, "No, Doozy!" when he sat next to me begging. "Go lay down!" I said, surprised when he positioned himself under the table with Pooch and fell asleep. It must have been a big day at Central Bark.

"Let's talk about something more pleasant," I suggested.

"Good plan," Alex replied.

When neither of us could come up with anything, I grabbed my laptop and showed her the video of the fourth-grade teacher. This led to a conversation about our favorite teachers growing up, why I had become a teacher and why she'd decided on law school. Apparently her fourth-grade teacher told her she had a wise mouth and would probably end up as a lawyer. I laughed.

"Wise woman," I said.

* * *

I woke up Saturday morning with the sun shining and the temperature in the high forties – a good day to run around Volunteer Park with Pooch and Doozy. With a little trepidation, I clipped leashes on both dogs and began running toward the park.

Doozy pulled a bit at first but soon got into pace with Pooch, who occasionally nosed him back in line. I smiled and felt pleased with my dog training skills. I noticed that Capitol Hill drivers were polite to pedestrians in general and to me in particular – always stopping at uncontrolled intersections and waving me to cross in front of them. I had a pocket full of treats for Doozy which I offered to distract him whenever another pedestrian or dog came towards us. We were flying along and feeling great until we were at the intersection nearest the entrance to the park. I had the dogs sit at the curb until oncoming cars saw us and stopped.

"Let's go!" Halfway into the crosswalk Doozy lunged with such force that I fell flat onto the concrete. Both drivers got out of their cars to see if I was okay, and Pooch licked my bloody knee while I got up as fast as I could.

"I'm fine," I said. "Just a little embarrassed is all." I limped into the park and spotted Doozy barking at a squirrel perched on the lowest branch of a huge oak tree.

"Doozy! Come!" I called, and Doozy turned to look at me briefly then immediately turned back to the squirrel and continued barking.

"Don't ever do that to me again!" I scolded, pulling him away from the tree. The dog just looked at me with his dopey grin and his ears flattened. He recognized that I was unhappy with him but hadn't a clue why. We ran slowly up the path toward the sculpture and view of the city where I stopped and told each dog to sit. Pooch complied immediately, Doozy only after I offered a treat. On the slow run home, I kept the naughty dog right next to me and gave a tug on his leash whenever he started to wander. I crossed the street whenever another person approached and felt like Doozy was training me rather than the other way around.

After a quick shower and call to Nancy, I opened my computer and Googled the name Jacqueline Forte. If the police weren't going to look for her, I would have to. My search revealed three women with that name. One worked as a pediatrician in a small Texas town near Austin. I called the clinic just to make sure they kept their website current, and that this woman hadn't recently moved to Seattle and dated the late Matt Downey. While on hold, I looked at the photo of Dr. Forte on the clinic website. She did not look like Matt Downey's type. Also, her bio said she enjoyed sailing with her husband and traveling to exotic places. Traveling to Seattle for a fundraiser did not seem likely. When Dr. Forte picked up the phone, her Texas twang and sincere responses to my questions left no doubt.

"Sorry, Hon, but I'm not your gal," she'd said. I knew she was right. "I do hope y'all find her. Good luck to you."

Southern charm, I thought after I hung up, no closer to finding the right Jacqueline Forte than I'd been earlier in the day. Two other women with this name led to the same dead end. One, an insurance agent in Chicago and the other, a teacher in New York were both kind but again, not my gal.

I then pulled up the Art with Heart website and sent an email to Daphne Jensen, listed as the event coordinator, explaining that I was looking for any contact information for a woman named Jacqueline Forte who attended the fundraiser last month with Matt Downey.

Before closing my laptop, I did another Google search: "Training difficult dogs." When I found a book that looked good called, *Difficult Dogs: An Everyday Guide to Solving Behavioral Problems*, I downloaded it to my Kindle, which I kept for traveling and emergency reading like this. I spent the rest of the weekend reading it and working through some of the training suggestions with Doozy. He was not a quick study.

* * *

On Monday morning I was sitting in my cubicle dutifully writing a follow-up piece that Jeff wanted on high school truancy, when I noticed the breaking news marching around the newsroom had everyone buzzing.

I looked at the words scrolling across the reader board at the top of the room, "Police officer stabbed in University District."

Oh no, I thought. *More bad news for the Seattle PD.* They'd been having their share of negative publicity for racial profiling.

I hoped the cop hadn't shot the guy. I tried not to get sucked into the energy around that story since it would not be something I would cover. Jeff would probably send Jack, the crime reporter, out to the scene. I put on my headphones to drown out the buzz and got back to work on my article.

When I checked my personal email at lunch, I had a response from Daphne Jensen, the Events Coordinator at Art with Heart: *I'm sorry I cannot give out the names of our donors or attendees at our fundraising events. That information is strictly confidential. Our organization's professional code of conduct and privacy policy prevents me from releasing any such information to you.*

"Shit." I said out loud. "Thanks Daphne."

On my way home, I turned on NPR and got the news. "Seattle Police Officer Ryan Tompkins is in critical condition at Harborview this afternoon after suffering multiple stab wounds to his abdomen. The homeless man who attacked him this morning in the University District is in stable condition."

Oh my god! That's Jennifer's husband! I said out loud, though no one else was within earshot. Maybe I'd heard the name wrong or that the injured Ryan Tompkins was some other person with the same common name. Even so, I drove the rest of the way to Central Bark thinking about Jennifer, her girls, how traumatized they would be right now if this was their father. Oh god, please let him live. I muttered. Then I was struck by how many bad things were happening to people I knew. I did not like the thoughts that crept into my head. I knew it was time to face them, to accept them, to chase them. Who cares about high school truancy when people around my Happiness friends kept dying? There was no denying it anymore. I had to do something.

CHAPTER SIXTEEN

"There is no other topic that is written about more . . . or discussed more . . . than romantic love – the passionate attachment between two people. There is also no other topic as deeply misunderstood." Tal Ben-Shahar, *Happier*.

On Tuesday, two things happened, one bad and one good. First the bad. Ryan Tompkins died at Harborview Hospital. It made me sick to read the news as it marched across the digital ticker tape at the top of the newsroom. I'd put in a call to Jenny last night, to tell her I was thinking about her, praying for Ryan's recovery. As if that helped. I also called Mary Summers to let her know I was done with happiness classes. I just couldn't do it anymore, fake happiness in the face of all this death? No. When Mary didn't pick up, I'd left a voicemail with a request that she return my call at an early convenient time. We needed to talk. I wouldn't mention it to Jeff, though, unless he asked straight out. I'd just dutifully write the article, pretending to be the ideal *Seattle Times* reporter, willing to do whatever I needed to keep my job.

The good thing that happened, or at least what I thought was good at the time, was that Detective Greg Costello called to ask me if I wanted to try out happy hour at Smith, one of his favorite restaurants in our neighborhood.

"I know you like Happy Hours," he'd said. "Since you didn't include Smith in your feature, I knew you'd never been there."

"You read my feature?" I asked.

"Of course!" he said. Then, in an amused voice, he added, "I Googled you."

"I see," I said, a little flattered, also a little nervous. I didn't mention that I'd Googled him too and found nothing, which struck me as very strange.

"Why don't I pick you up? It's raining," he said. When I warned him about Doozy, he told me not to worry. "All dogs love me. I'm like Cesar Milan, only nicer."

I found that amusing.

I think this was a date, but I didn't know how we would avoid talking about the one thing we had in common – Robert Clark's death. Maybe it wasn't a date at all, maybe Greg was planning to interrogate me. Or maybe I could get some information from him that could help Alex. He wasn't working that case, but he had connections. Probably I should learn how to separate work and play.

"Forget it," I told myself, pushing the thoughts of murder investigations aside, and vowing to have a good time. I changed my outfit twice before settling on something I hoped was not too casual but also not trying to hard – my favorite navy cashmere V-neck sweater over skinny jeans and boots – perfectly appropriate for a neighborly get together.

When the doorbell rang at 5:25, Pooch went to the door and sat, just as she'd been trained to do while Doozy bounded to the front door and lunged at it, barking for all he was worth. I clipped on the dog's leash and told him to sit. He did, but only after I'd shown him the dried lamb liver treat I had in my hand for just that purpose. We were making progress. Baby steps, but still progress.

I opened the door and Greg crouched down to greet Doozy before greeting me.

"Hey buddy. How you doing?"

Doozy stayed sitting and sniffed Greg's hand.

"You're right, Doozy, I have a treat for you. First, I want you to stay quiet while I greet Ann. Then you can have it."

I saw him give Doozy the *stay* command, showing the palm of his hand.

I smiled waiting for Doozy to lunge at Greg. Instead, the dog remained seated while Greg stood to greet me.

"Hey," he said with a smile.

"How on earth?" I gestured to Doozy. At the sound of my voice, Doozy stood up and nosed Greg. Greg made a noise at him, like *eh*, clipped and loud, and the dog sat down again.

"Wow," I said. "You just make a noise at him, and he listens?"

"Like I said, I'm like Cesar Milan." He smiled. "I don't believe in all of his methods, he's just the trainer most people recognize." He turned back to the dog and opened his palm to show him the treat. "Here you go, boy."

Doozy took the treat, stood up and wagged his tail but did not move. Greg gave him a look and he sat down again.

"And who's this?" Greg approached Pooch, who'd been waiting patiently. As he crouched down, Pooch watched him closely.

"Can you shake?" he asked, and Pooch presented a paw. "Good girl! Here you go." Greg produced another treat for Pooch, and she accepted it gently.

"That's enough. You can tell me your doggie whisperer secrets over a cocktail."

I enticed Doozy and Pooch into the kitchen with another treat and left my laptop tuned to Jazz 24, hoping the music would have a calming effect on Doozy. Pooch was already heading to her bed in my room while Doozy stood there looking anxiously at me.

"You'll be fine, Doozy. I'll see you later."

We headed out into the drizzle and Greg gestured to the silver Audi parked across the street. "This is me," he said walking around to open the car door for me.

I settled into the passenger seat and inhaled. The car smelled good, like warm leather and clean laundry with a hint of shaving cream, masculine and lovely. I appreciated the lack of discarded fast-food bags, random papers and items of clothing which usually clutter up my car. Greg got into the driver's seat. I studied his profile in the dim light from the streetlamp overhead, his prominent nose and strong chin. Nice.

While we drove the few blocks to the restaurant, I asked Greg how he managed to get Doozy to behave. He told me that in another life, before he became a cop, he trained animals for Hollywood films.

"You're making this up!" I said.

"No, no, I swear," He replied. "I've always loved animals, wanted to be a vet when I was a kid but that didn't work out. I worked as a vet tech for a while in L.A. – that's where I grew up. A co-worker knew this guy Bud who ran a training center near LA, Bud's Animals for Hollywood. She hooked me up with him and I got the job. Worked there for several years."

"You really aren't kidding." I said.

"Nope. What about you? You always work for the *Seattle Times*?"

"No. I'm from Minneapolis, a former high school English teacher who wants to be an investigative journalist. So here I am in a job that keeps getting more precarious every day."

"How so?"

"You know that newspapers are folding all over the country in this age of digital media. We're hanging on. Barely. My employer is handing out pink slips faster than anything."

"Ah, you're worried about job security." he said, pulling into a parking place. "Here we are."

I looked up at an unobtrusive black sign on the front of an old wooden building I'd probably driven past many times. "Smith."

The place was jammed with young, happy-looking folks sipping cocktails and wine. The music was loud and pulsing. Not my favorite. Greg waved at the hostess, and she hurried toward us.

"How are you doing today?" she asked in a familiar way, with a big smile for Greg and a small nod for me. She checked the computer and gestured to the far end of the room. "Last booth in the back?" She asked.

"Sure."

We walked through the restaurant, all distressed wood and solid furniture. The many stuffed animals adorning the walls surprised me. We're talking not just deer heads with antlers but a whole wall of birds, some in flight and some simply perched there— ducks and geese and what I thought at first was a heron encased in glass.

"It's weird to see a heron displayed that way." I said.

"It is weird looking, but it's not a heron. That's a duck-billed rosy something or other."

"You're into ornithology?" I asked. "Or maybe you trained birds too?"

"No to both. I like birds, but I'm no specialist. I only know the name of that bird because I asked the waitress the first time I came in here."

We sat in the booth, and I continued to look around at the mounted animal heads, also disembodied antlers of all sizes. "Wow. So much taxidermy!" I said, Greg laughed.

"But it's cozy, right? Or do you hate it?"

"No, no, I like it. Somehow the pseudo-hunting lodge vibe works." I said. "Very hipster." I opened our menu and saw a long list of small plates that made my mouth water while Greg watched me look over the menu.

"You're the foodie." I said. "Why don't you order?"

"Anything you don't like?"

"Beets and lima beans."

"No worries. How about radishes? They have this great radish dish with bread and their homemade butter."

"Yum."

I perused the cocktail menu and decided on something called a *Lush Life* with pineapple bourbon and Jamaican rum, lime, and two other ingredients I didn't recognize. Greg raised his eyebrows at me. I guessed this wasn't the girly drink he'd expected me to order.

"I've had a rough several days," I said.

Greg ordered a beer from a local Georgetown brewery and several small plates: mussels and sweet potato fries, a charcuterie plate, and the radishes. "They make their own sausage too," he said, licking his lips.

"Sounds good to me."

As the waitress went off in the direction of the bar, I admitted I'd Googled him too and wondered why he had no internet persona. "Especially if you really were an animal trainer in Hollywood."

"Right. Well, that part's easy," he said. "Back then I used the name Giorgio Costello. Giorgio is a family name. I thought it sounded more Hollywood." He shrugged. "As a cop, of course, I don't want anything personal to be public. You can find my name if it's mentioned in the press. Usually, police press is not good press. I try to stay out of it, as a rule. Hope that doesn't offend you. "

"Not at all. I get it."

The waitress arrived with our drinks, and I took a sip of mine. "Ooh, that is yummy. But strong. Don't let me have more than one of these."

"I will not be policing your drinks," he said. "You can have as many as you want. You can always walk home if you need to sober up." He lifted his glass. "To neighbors!"

I touched the rim of my cocktail glass to his beer bottle. "Neighbors."

"Tell me about working with animals in Hollywood. That sounds very exotic."

"The filming part is pretty demanding and not all that much fun – a lot of waiting around and then a lot of takes until the director gets the shot right. Training is what I liked."

I nodded. "Did you work on any movies I may have seen?"

"*Must love Dogs*?" He suggested. "The movie never got great reviews, but the dogs were awesome."

"I loved that movie! Well, I love John Cusack in anything," I admitted. "But the dog, I can't remember much about the dog." I wracked my brain. Got nothing.

"Large shaggy black dog called Mother Teresa in the movie." Greg said.

I laughed. "Great name. What kind of dog?"

"Newfoundland. Actually, two Newfy puppies played Mother Teresa, two litter mates, Molly and Mabel."

"Nice." I said. "Now I remember the dog. He was huge! They were puppies?"

"Yup. Newfies are big dogs."

"How did you pick them?"

"We didn't. The director found them, then hired us to train them."

"Nice." I said. "And why was it your favorite film to work on?"

"The dogs were great, smart and eager to please. Also, it was my first solo run. Before that, I'd worked with Bud or someone else from the ranch. I liked the challenge."

"Got it." I nodded. "What's the biggest challenge in filming dogs?" I asked.

"You're pretty good at the interview," he said.

"Sorry. Occupational hazard. Also, I love dogs, and movies. This is fascinating."

He smiled. "Hmm, biggest challenge. It depends. In that film, keeping the drool out of sight with the camera rolling, that was a challenge. The drool is the Newfy's downfall—so much slobber, all the time."

I laughed.

"Getting the dogs in and out of the rowing shells without tipping them was also a challenge. Would never have worked as you see it in the movie. Those boats were totally held down with ropes. Oh, and the dogs had a lot more fun in that scene than we did. They love to swim so they were happy we had to do so many takes. The rest of the crew, not so much." He chuckled.

"Sounds like a great career to me. How'd you end up a cop?"

"Some things happened," he said. " I started to think maybe I should do something with my life that would be more useful. Make a difference maybe."

"There are lots of other career paths you could have chosen."

"Right." He said. "But, like I said, some things happened. I have an uncle who's a cop in LA. I've always admired him. He took me to the police academy to check it out. The rest is history."

The waitress brought the charcuterie plate then and, after describing the different sausage and cheese types and serving up a plate for me, Greg dug into his own helping with the same delight I'd noticed at Bakery Nouveau. We fell into a comfortable silence, enjoying the food. Greg finished off the last of the bread, took a gulp of his beer and smiled at me. I liked how his face lit up and the little lines that appeared around his dark eyes when he smiled. I also liked the softness of his face. There were no hard angles, just a permanent five o'clock shadow that I wanted to touch.

"All this time I've been talking about myself when I'd much rather know more about you. From what I read about you on the internet, I know you've been involved in some pretty intense situations."

"Yeah. But those were anomalies." I said. "You read the education blog? That's my bread and butter."

"I did, actually, read some of those blog entries. Loved the fourth-grade teacher video."

I laughed. "Me too. That thing went viral on YouTube."

"My mom was a teacher," he said. "Boy did she have the stories. You were a teacher too. Why'd you switch to journalism?"

"Oh, you know." I shrugged. "Like Woodward and Bernstein, or the Spotlight team, I thought I'd right wrongs and uncover the truth."

Greg nodded as the waitress arrived with the mussels and sweet potato fries. "I'll have another one of these," he said, lifting his empty beer bottle. "Ann? You want another?"

"No, no. I'll switch to wine. You have a Pinot Gris?" I asked the waitress.

She went off to the bar and once again we were quiet while we ate. The mussels were perfect, firm and flavorful in a white wine and herbed butter sauce. The fries were sweet and salty, just right.

"Mmmm, this is good stuff," I said.

He nodded. "So, have you?" he asked. "Been able to right wrongs and all that? Seems like you uncovered the truth of that scam church."

"Yeah, but that sleezeball is probably already preying on vulnerable women somewhere else. Neither he nor his partner in crime did any time. Far as I'm concerned, it was murder. They didn't pay for it. Not really."

"Yeah. It happens."

"What's your experience? As a homicide detective, I mean. Do the guilty usually pay? Go to jail?"

"Sometimes," he said with that serious look again. "It's frustrating. Mostly I feel like I'm doing damage control." He shrugged, then continued. "I see people at their worst. I see what poverty and desperation does to them. I see homelessness. I see how badly the system has failed the mentally ill. How they end up on the streets instead of in treatment."

"Like the guy who killed the cop in the U District," I said. It was on my mind.

He shook his head. "That's just one more example of how dangerous it is out there for the police. People think de-funding is the answer. It's so much more complicated than that."

"Yeah. Most things are complicated." Everything that happened over the past few weeks came reeling forth in my brain. "It was random though, the stabbing, right?"

"I don't know all the facts, just that the officer was trying to calm the guy down. But he got more agitated and frightened, lashed out with the knife. Who knows what demons he was fighting? The officer became the demon."

I nodded.

"Why so interested?" He asked. "You covering the crime beat now? Is that why you were at the scene of Robert Clark's death?"

"No, no. I was there because I knew his daughter. Also, I sort of know Officer Tompkins's wife. They're both in a class I'm taking."

"Wow. What kind of class?" Greg asked.

I shook my head. "It's going to sound really weird, but my editor insisted I take it. He knows the instructor."

"Okay." He waited.

"It's a *Happiness* class."

"Happiness?" I couldn't read his face. He sipped his beer. "The class teaches you how to be happy?"

"That's the idea. I'm writing a series of articles about how individuals cope with stress, and my editor wanted me to find out how a class like this could help people deal with it." Greg looked skeptical.

"Hey, Happiness is a hot topic these days. Every other self-help book is about Happiness."

"Okay." he said. "But it's ironic, don't you think?"

"What?"

"Your friends in this Happiness class are facing a world of sadness right now."

"Yeah. I've been thinking about that. And there's something else too. My friend Alex Rhodes's colleague drowned in his hot tub a couple of weeks ago."

"She's in the class?"

"Yes. It's why I asked if Officer Tompkins's stabbing was random." I said. "I mean, two suspicious drownings and then a random stabbing. I don't see how they can possibly be related, but still."

I could see him processing that while he focused on his beer. He probably thought I was crazy or a conspiracy theory lunatic.

"Hey, I'm sorry I mentioned it," I said. "Too much rum on an empty stomach. I really don't want to think or talk about it right now. Okay?"

"Okay," he said. He took another sip of beer.

In the silence between us, I focused on the background music for the first time. When had they switched to opera? I closed my eyes and listened to Pavarotti, the passion so clear in his voice. When he hit the famous high note, I felt it in my chest and tears filled my eyes. *Vincera! Vincera!*

Greg touched my arm. "Are you crying?" He asked. "I'm sorry about your friends."

"What?" I asked, having forgotten what we'd been talking about as soon as I heard that unmistakable voice coming through the ceiling speakers. "Oh, no, not crying. It's just Pavarotti does this to me every time. *Nessun Dorma* from *Turandot*."

"Oh, right. You love opera." He smiled. "Never been to one in my life."

"You *are* missing out." I said, happy to change the subject. "Still, it's not everyone's cup of tea. I haven't been able to really enjoy it since last Spring. But I don't want to think about that right now either."

"I read about that. How you were kidnapped with an opera singer. It's impressive, the way you got out of there alive."

Before I could respond, the waitress showed up, saved me from having to talk about Franco Albanese. She asked if we wanted another drink, or dessert. I declined.

"I should probably get back to the dogs." I said. "This is the first time I've left them alone."

"I'm sure they're fine," he said. "If it were nicer out, I'd insist on taking you to Molly Moon's."

"What's Molly Moon's?" I asked.

"Seriously? It's only the best ice cream in Seattle, possibly the world." He said. "It's also close by. Your new neighborhood is filled with great things." Greg said, just as a couple dripping with rain entered the bar bringing a gust of wind with them.

"Maybe in July,"

Greg chuckled. "Right."

When we pulled up in front of the house, I felt the usual first date awkwardness. *Would he walk me to the door? Would he kiss me? Did I want him to?*

"It's wet," I said. "You don't need to walk me to the door."

He turned off the car and looked at me. "Oh yes I do," he said. My father taught me that a man always walks a lady to her door after a date."

He smiled and unclipped his seatbelt. "Kissing, though, is optional." He got out of the car, and I felt myself flush. Didn't he want to kiss me? I undid my seatbelt and before I could find the door handle Greg had opened it for me.

"It's nasty out here," he said, "better move fast."

He took my hand, and we ran up the front porch steps together. Still awkward, I opened my purse to search for my keys, avoiding the moment of truth. I could hear Doozy barking from the kitchen where I'd left him.

I pulled out the keys and looked up at Greg. "The dog's barking," I said stupidly.

"I hear him," he said, meeting my eyes. He leaned in.

"I had a really nice time tonight," I said, lifting my face.

"Me too." He bent down to kiss me, his lips touching mine softly, tentative, only once, but enough to send the zing from my mouth to my other parts. He pulled back and smiled.

"Shall we do this again?"

I felt the heat in my face. Did he mean kiss? Go out again?

"Um, yes?"

"Is that a question or an answer?"

"An answer. Sorry. Yes. I'd love to see you again."

"Good," he said. Then he pulled me into his arms and gave me a real kiss, nothing tentative about it and I felt myself melt into it, then light up, all systems go. It had been a long time, but my body remembered how this worked all too well. *Too soon*, that little voice in my head told me at the same time Greg pulled back and smiled.

"Nice," He said, and I mumbled something like mmm, then, "Better take care of that barking dog."

"Good luck with him. And, hey, call me anytime if you want help with Doozy. Really, I'd be happy to work with him."

"Thanks. I may take you up on that." I unlocked the door and went in feeling buoyant and a little light-headed. That feeling lasted for about thirty seconds, the time it took me to walk through the house and into the kitchen. I opened the door and Doozy leapt at me then ran through the dining room and into the living room doing laps and ricocheting off the furniture as I stared in disbelief at the mess he'd left on the floor. Somehow, he'd managed to open the cabinet door and knock over the yard waste bin. Coffee grounds and orange peels were crushed into the rug and smeared on the hardwood floor. He'd also gotten into the recycle and shredded the paper, leaving soggy bits of it strewn around in small piles.

"Oh my God!" I said out loud. Then I saw Pooch sitting in the entryway to my bedroom, ears back and looking guilty, even though I knew she had nothing to do with this chaos.

"Hey, Pooch, come here!" The dog wagged her tail and slowly approached, nudging her head into my hand. I scratched her ears and kissed her wet nose.

"What are we going to do with this guy, Pooch?" At the sound of my voice Pooch sat and cocked her head. "Yeah, it is confusing, I know. But we'll figure it out."

CHAPTER SEVENTEEN

"Each night before going to sleep, write down at least five things that made or make you happy – things for which you are grateful." Tal Ben-Shahar, *Happier*.

Despite Doozy's bad behavior, the glow I felt after my date with Greg Costello returned and lasted through the night and into the next morning. He'd texted less than half an hour after he left me on my doorstep saying that he'd had a really nice time. I replied: *Ditto* - not wanting to sound too eager. I settled in with a Stephen King novel—the last in the Mr. Mercedes trilogy—in front of the fire, one dog at my feet and one next to me on the sofa. I didn't even try to train that behavior out of Doozy since it was neither destructive nor necessary. The Salton's would expect him to sit on the sofa when they returned from South Africa. Who was I to judge?

On Wednesday afternoon I got an email from Mary Summers cancelling Happiness Class, not just for that afternoon but for the rest of the session. Mary had cited a "family emergency" and promised to send a prorated refund. Since I hadn't paid for the class, the refund didn't matter to me. What mattered was that Mary was leaving town before I could talk to her about what was still bothering me. She'd been dismissive when there had been two deaths. Now there were three. I called her, went straight to voicemail. I listened to her chirpy message: *I'm so happy you called! Please leave me a brief message and I'll call you back just as soon as I can!* Then I hit the red button on my phone and wished I knew where she lived.

I turned to my computer and did a White Pages lookup. There were six entries for Mary Summers but only one in Seattle: age sixty-one, Green Lake neighborhood. Yes! I love the Internet. Under the *past locations* heading, the listing noted Summerville, South Carolina. That explained the hint of a Southern accent I'd heard in her voice. Sometimes it was so easy to do detective work. I copied the address into Google Maps on my phone and headed to my car. Mary's apartment was twenty minutes away.

When the voice in my phone announced *You have arrived*, I stopped in front of a modern apartment building complex called *Circa Green Lake* on Green Lake Way North. There was no place to park so I circled around to the back of the building and pulled up on the side street behind a blue Corolla with the trunk open. I stepped out of my car just as the owner of the Toyota arrived with an armful of clothing which she laid on top of the boxes already in there. She slammed the trunk closed and looked my way. It was Mary.

"Mary! What's going on? Are you moving?"

"Oh gosh, Ann. Hello!" She smiled at me. "Yes, turns out I'm heading back to California. My brother has had a heart attack. He needs me there."

Flabbergasted, I stared at her. "Wait. What about the happiness class?"

"Didn't you get my email? I'm giving everyone a pro-rated refund."

"I don't care about the refund. I care about the three suspicious deaths. You can't just up and leave."

She turned to face me, her forced smile turned into a frown. "Of course, I can." She got into the driver's seat, waved over her shoulder, and drove away while I stood there with my mouth open. I was tempted to jump into my own car and follow her. But, then what?

I stood on the street for a minute trying to decide what to do next while all the questions spun around in my brain. Did her brother really have a medical emergency? Why didn't she just visit him? Why would she completely clear out unless she was afraid to stay? Why was she afraid? I walked around to the front entrance of the building, thinking I might find a neighbor who knew Mary, someone who would be willing to tell me something about her. Any information would be helpful at this point. Finding the front door locked, I looked at the names next to the apartment numbers, each with their own button. I raised my finger to ring a random person when the front door opened and a young guy in running clothes and earbuds pushed out onto the sidewalk. I grabbed the door and let myself in. With a nod to me, the guy headed toward the path around the lake for his afternoon run.

I took the stairs to the second floor and Mary's apartment, number 235 according to the listing out front. I thought I'd simply knock on one of her neighbor's doors, see if anyone was in and willing to talk to me about Mary. When I got to Mary's door, I found it ajar. Lucky for me, Mary had been in such a hurry that she'd forgotten to close it. I pushed the door wide and took a tentative step inside.

"Mary?" I said loudly, just in case someone was in here. When I was sure that the apartment was empty, I closed the door softly behind me and looked around. The apartment was furnished in a mid-century vibe. The small galley kitchen had a granite countertop dividing it from the living room, with two white molded plastic chairs pushed up to it. The living room had two facing loveseats, a coffee table and a gas fireplace. Two large windows looked across a shared courtyard to the building opposite. I walked down the short hallway to the bedroom, bed stripped and closet door open. All empty, not even a dust bunny in the corners. The place was small, about six hundred square feet, with a tiny bath and a washer/dryer behind sliding panels in the hallway. I went back into the kitchen and opened the cabinets. Only a couple of cartons of organic butternut squash soup and a half-empty box of Rye Krisp on the shelves. The fridge held some condiments and a gallon of spring water. Wow, Mary had really cleared out of this place fast. I took another walk-through, peeking under the bed and opening drawers this time. Nothing. I opened and closed the washer and dryer doors and was about to slide the door shut on them when I noticed a small recycling bin next to the dryer. I pulled it out and dumped the contents onto the floor. I picked up an issue of Yoga Journal magazine, tossed it aside, then sifted through the rest of the contents: a few Odwalla juice bottles, rinsed clean, a *Real Change* newspaper and a catalog of classes for Winter Quarter at the Phinney Neighborhood Center. Nothing of note. As I began to replace the contents of the bin, I noticed a small card wedged into the bottom corner. I managed to extract it but not before it sliced through my index finger.

"Shit!" I sucked the drop of blood from the paper cut and read the card: Hans Bergman, PhD, Professor of Psychology, University of Washington. I tucked the card into my pocket with plans to look up Professor Bergman later.

I closed the door behind me and headed for my car trying to figure out the best route to the daycare to pick up the dogs. Given that it was rush hour, the traffic would be terrible whichever route I chose. Google maps suggested I take a circuitous route over surface streets, over the University Bridge, east on Boyer and up and over Capitol Hill. I looked at the map on my phone and found a solid red line on I-5 through the city, so I went with Siri's plan. By the time I picked up the dogs and got back to my place on Capitol Hill, an hour had passed. I was hungry, my nerves were frazzled from the drive, and I was still trying to make sense of my interaction with Mary. Something was off. I was determined to find out what.

I fed the dogs, poured myself a glass of Pinot Grigio and considered calling Greg. He was a police officer and I felt I could trust him. Could I? Instead of calling, I scrambled some eggs, added a piece of toast, and called it dinner. I took my laptop into the living room, turned on the gas fireplace and settled in to do a little more detective work. I entered Mary Summers into Google and clicked on the same White Pages site I'd checked earlier which had listed Mary's address in Seattle. A popup indicated that *A comprehensive background check on Mary Summers is available.* I clicked on that and set in motion a series of *verifying data* line entries which went from zero to one hundred percent and finished with a checkmark. I watched as the following data was verified: personal background, address history, marriage records, relatives and associates, licenses and permits, lawsuits, sex offender status, arrest and criminal records, social network profile. All this took just a few minutes. I clicked on the *view full report* box only to discover that I would need to fork over my credit card and agree to the site's terms and conditions. I clicked the box saying I understood the site was not warrantying any of the information (meaning it could all be false) and then authorized a credit card payment to the tune of fifty bucks. I took a deep breath and entered my Visa number.

After downloading the full report, I scanned it quickly for anything interesting. I learned that Mary was born Mary Ellen Stone in Summerville, South Carolina, graduated with a B.A. from a small college in Oregon, had a Master's in Psychology from the University of Washington. She was licensed as a therapist. She'd married a man named Brian Winters in Seattle twenty-five years ago, divorced him five years ago and had a restraining order against him at the time of the divorce. That was interesting. She had also changed her name from Mary Winters to Mary Summers around the same time. There were many previous addresses. She'd lived primarily in Seattle and Bellevue, Washington, Summerville, South Carolina, and San Diego, California, after her college years in Ashland, Oregon. Besides her ex-husband, Mary was related to Peter Stone of Charleston, South Carolina. I decided to look him up next, hoping he was the brother with the medical emergency even though Mary had told me he lived in California. The White Pages came through immediately with an address and phone number for Peter and listed his age as sixty-four, just the right age for Mary's older brother. I noted his number and planned to call him in the morning. It would be too late to phone Charleston now.

I went back to my search results and clicked on Mary's website. I'd seen it before. There were photos of Mary teaching yoga classes and schedules for yoga and happiness classes. I clicked on *Background*. Here she'd listed her extensive training in yoga and mindfulness meditation first, her master's degree in psychology from the UW last, like an afterthought. I hadn't noticed that before. Or hadn't focused on it. From there I clicked onto her

Happiness blog and began flipping through the archives. I found a post entitled *Dr. Bergman's Positive Psychology Class Gets National Attention*. The article described how University of Washington professor Hans Bergman had been interviewed by NPR about his extremely popular class, how Psychology 245 went from a handful of students when he first offered it, to the most popular class on campus. Since the class had a wait list of hundreds of students, Professor Bergman put his lectures online. Mary had provided a link. Curious, I clicked on the first lecture.

Dr. Bergman stood at the front of a large lecture hall. He looked to be in his mid-to-late forties, with flecks of premature gray highlighting his curly dark brown hair. He had a lean frame and his brown eyes radiated warmth. He smiled and opened his lecture by saying how happy he was to be teaching the class. He said he first got interested in positive psychology when he was studying economics at Stanford. Although it seemed like he had everything going for him – he did well in his classes, was successful in sports and had a good social network – he was not happy. He wanted to find out how he could become happier, so he began studying positive psychology. He explained that positive psychology comes out of academia rather than the self-help (or New Age) movement. He joked that the typical academic paper is read by about seven people (including the author's mother) whereas there have been millions of copies of self-help books sold. His intention was to build a bridge between academic science and self-help. He said that this course would require rigorous academic work but that he would also require students to step back and look inward, asking themselves: *How can I apply this to my life?*

I was immediately drawn in. Before I knew it, the ninety-minute lecture was over, and my head was swimming with information about the history of positive psychology. Dr. Bergman said this class would be rigorous fun based on research and I believed it. He said it was built on simple ideas but would not be simplistic. I liked what he had to say. I liked him. I knew I would watch all the lectures. Somehow, I believed, as Dr. Bergman said, that this class could be transformative for me too, that I could uncover the source of my own barriers, my fear of failure and perfectionism by asking the right questions. This was the first example of a happiness class that made sense to me.

When he suggested that we start by keeping a gratitude journal, that made sense too. The idea is to keep a notebook next to your bed and write down five things you are grateful for right before you turn off your light to sleep. I clicked off the lecture and went searching for a notebook I could use. I found one that had been a gift from Nancy, a soft coral pink cover with drawings of lemons and vines intertwined on it. The word *notebook* embossed in gold. I placed it on the nightstand next to my bed and set my favorite pen on top of it.

I thought about the things I was grateful for today while I let the dogs out for their final trip to the outdoor potty. I found myself smiling at Doozy as he took his usual victory laps around the yard. I called, and he did not come. I went in search of a dog treat and returned to the yard. I approached Doozy and showed it to him then closed my hand around it. I went back to the door and called him, showing the palm of my hand. He bounded to me and licked my closed hand. "Sit first, big boy," I said as authoritatively as possible. He sat, and I backed into the kitchen. I showed him the treat and said, "come!" He came in and I opened my palm, offering up the cookie. Success! I hurried through my bedtime routine and hopped into bed. I propped myself up on a couple of pillows, got under the down comforter and picked up my gratitude journal to write the five things I was grateful for today.

The next morning, I called Hans Bergman and left a message. I told him my name and that I was writing an article for *The Seattle Times* about happiness. I expressed my interest in positive psychology and hoped he would take some time to talk with me about his work. I didn't mention Mary Summers. Most people would rather talk about themselves. I also called Peter Stone in Charlottesville. Straight to voicemail. If Peter was Mary's ailing brother, he might not be in any condition to answer his phone. I decided against leaving a message. I would try him again later, after the funeral.

CHAPTER EIGHTEEN

".... death is the light by which the shadow of all of life's meaning is measured. Without death, everything would feel inconsequential, all experience arbitrary, all metrics and values suddenly zero." Mark Manson, *The Subtle Art of Not Giving a F*ck*.

Ryan Tompkins's funeral was set for eleven o'clock. I knew that a large contingent of officers from the Seattle Police Department would show up in solidarity for one of their own slain in the line of duty and wondered if Greg would be there. I also realized that we'd just danced around the discussion of Ryan Tomkins' murder the last time we talked. How did I feel about that? The few butterflies that showed up were smacked down by the weight of grief I felt as I pulled on my clothes: black skirt and grey sweater, black tights and boots, black raincoat. I managed to throw some color into my morning by wrapping a coral scarf around my neck and hoping it wouldn't appear too festive. I'd texted Alex and arranged to meet her at my office then take an Uber to St. James's Cathedral in downtown Seattle. We'd consider lunch afterwards if either of us had any appetite. Over five hundred police vehicles were expected to join in the procession beginning at 9:00 a.m. at the University of Washington, winding through the city and ending up at the Cathedral. It would be tricky to get to the church, and grim once we got there.

It took the Uber driver a long time to get to us and once we got into the car it took even longer to drive the few miles to First Hill. We got out at Fifth and Marion and trudged up the hill on foot, sharing Alex's umbrella. We walked under an archway between two fire trucks, past hundreds of flags at half-mast and arrived at

St. James soaked and silent. The cathedral is an imposing structure built in the early 1900's. I'd been inside once before for a Christmas concert. I remembered thinking then how this gorgeous church felt like it belonged somewhere in Europe, with its Renaissance architecture and beautiful bronze doors, rather than here in the Pacific Northwest.

We stepped inside the Cathedral's grand sanctuary and walked down the center aisle admiring the black and white marble tile under foot. The seats immediately inside the door and to either side of the main aisle were all filled. After much jostling through the crowd and scanning the available seats behind and on either side of the altar, we finally found two spots in the side back tucked behind a marble pillar. The space was breathtaking – all pillars and arches and stained glass. The walls were awash in white paint with gold accents. Large pendant light fixtures hung from the ceiling. A skylight illuminated the stunning white marble altar. I noticed Alex looking up at it too.

"The eye of God." I said.

"What?"

"The skylight is meant to symbolize the eye of God."

"Meant to be watching us? Creepy."

My eyes rested on the large pots of flowers flanking the stand meant for Ryan Tompkins' coffin. I looked at my watch, anxious for the funeral to begin, just as the first piercing notes of plaintive bagpipes rang out, echoing off the stone walls. We stood as one. The mournful music resonated in my chest bringing tears to my eyes. We watched the coffin's bleak procession to its place in front of the altar. Alex pulled out a package of tissue and handed me one, her eyes dry but on the verge. As the pallbearers placed the casket on its stand, I looked for Jennifer and her girls. The officers saluted and took their seats. Other uniformed policemen and women entered from some side door, filling the chairs in the choir loft. Jennifer and her daughters came forward then to place flowers on the casket. They looked tiny and vulnerable from this vantage point, and I couldn't help but think how vast their grief would be. I thought about Robert Clark's memorial service, noted the difference between the two and wondered whether there was any good way to honor the death of another human being. Never a good way, I decided. Just necessary. Inevitably I thought about Ben's memorial service. Time had blurred the details. I only remembered the pain.

As this would be a full-blown Catholic funeral Mass, I knew we were in for the long haul. There would be no personal stories today about Ryan Tompkins, that would have happened at the wake last night. Alex and I had talked about attending the wake when Courtney emailed the details to us, but we'd decided against it. I would write a personal note to Jennifer instead. It was the best I could do. We stood to sing a hymn – an adaptation of a Dvorak piece and quite lovely. The priest began by giving praise and thanks to God for Christ's victory over sin and death. I began to have some serious doubts about the service. Giving praise and thanks to God that a man with a wife and two children was killed at the prime of his life made no sense to me. The priest reminded us of Christ's experience of suffering, death, and new life. Death no longer has the last word, he said. Really? Death sure seems final to me.

There was a reading from John, the bit I'd heard in the Lutheran church every Easter, where Mary comes to the tomb and finds Jesus gone. I tried practicing some mindful breathing and letting the priest's words wash over me. When the priest began what he called a reflection, I was pulled back in.

A loved one is a treasure of the heart and losing a loved one is like losing a piece of yourself. But the love does not leave, for the essence of the soul lingers. Cling to your memories of love and joy and let them find their way to heal you. Let the beauty of love stay behind to embrace you. Keep your heart beating with your loving memories and trust in your faith to guide you through.

I don't think there was a dry eye in the entire Cathedral after that one. Luckily, there was one more opportunity to stand and sing. We were back to asking Jesus to take us home. Instead of singing along, I looked at the rows of police officers and tried to find Greg Costello among them. No luck.

We stood once again as the organ played another sorrowful song and the casket made its way back down the center aisle followed by Jennifer Tomkins, her two daughters, and hundreds of police officers. I thought I'd spotted Greg briefly but wasn't sure. Out on the street we saw the uniformed cops on motorcycles start up and, with lights flashing, lead the hearse north on Marion towards the cemetery. The rain had stopped, and Alex and I stood looking down the street while the rest of the mourners slowly walked off toward the rest of their day.

"That was rough," Alex said. I nodded.

"Ann!" I turned and smiled at Greg walking up the steps towards us.

"Hey." I said. "I thought you might be here."

"Yeah," he said. "Terrible thing."

"Yeah," I replied. There was nothing else to say. Alex broke the silence to introduce herself.

"I'm Alexandra Rhodes."

"Greg Costello." They shook hands and we were awkward for another minute.

"So, you're not going to the cemetery?" I asked.

"Nah, just the motorcycle guys. I gotta get back to work. You?"

"Back to work too."

"How's Doozy?" he asked, and his expression changed.

"Better maybe? At least I'm telling myself that. I've been working with him a bit." I turned to Alex. "Greg's met Doozy too. He's been giving me some advice on training."

"Ah." Alex nodded. "He's a real piece of work, that dog." she said.

Greg shrugged. "Oh, he's not so bad. I'm sure Ann can whip him into shape."

He touched my arm. "Hey, I'll give you a call?"

"Sure." I said as he turned and walked briskly down the street, my eyes on his back.

"I see what you like about him. He's hot." Alex said, watching his receding form. "Too bad he's a cop."

"He's a nice guy. Used to be an animal trainer in Hollywood."

"What?" she scoffed. "You have a bad dog and coincidentally this guy's some famous dog trainer?"

"Really, he is! Worked on the movie *Must Love Dogs*. I like him. Not all cops are bad cops you know."

She shook her head. "Trust me," she said. "It feels different when you're on the wrong side of the interrogation table."

"How's that going? Have you heard anything more from the police?"

"No. You have any luck finding the mysterious Jacqueline Forte?"

"No."

Alex and I walked down the hill and stopped for a quick bite at a sandwich shop on Fifth where we spent some time talking about the three deaths.

"It's really bothering me," I said. "It can't be coincidental."

"You think Mary Summers is trying to keep everyone in her class happy by killing off the people who made their lives miserable?"

"Of course not. When you put it that way it sounds ridiculous," I said. "And yet, it still worries me. Also, why did Mary pack up and leave so abruptly?"

My cell phone vibrated, and I pulled it out of my pocket. Unknown caller. I picked it up anyway.

"Ann Dexter."

"Oh my God! I'm so glad I got you. This is Holly Nelson. I live across the street from the Saltons. You're the house sitter, right?"

"I am."

"I'm calling because Doozy has the mailman cornered on the front porch."

"He what? How is that even possible?"

"It looks like he jumped out the front window! Anyway, I tried to get him to calm down, but he won't. He's just barking and barking." I could hear barking in the background. "I'm at home with our baby," she said. "I called my husband to come home. He works at Kaiser up on Fifteenth. But you should get here as soon as you can."

"Did he bite the mailman?" I asked, my voice louder than it needed to be.

Alex looked at me wide-eyed from across the table.

"I don't think so. He's just barking like crazy. I think the guy is too scared to move."

"I'm on my way."

I hung up the phone and punched in a request for an Uber ride. The guy was ten minutes away. "Shit!" I said. "I'll never get there in time."

"Your dog bit the mailman?" Alex asked, incredulous.

"No! Not my dog! Doozy! Oh, shit." My mind was reeling. What the hell could I do? "I'm calling Greg," I said. "The East Precinct is closer to the Saltons' than I am right now."

"Are you sure?" Alex asked.

"Of course not!" I replied, my voice shrill. "I don't know him well enough. But all bets are off when your dog is holding the mailman hostage on your front porch. He can always say no."

Instead, he answered on the first ring and didn't even miss a beat.

"I'll meet you there," he said.

I paid my bill and paced around the front of the restaurant until finally my phone pinged with a message: "Farah is arriving in a Blue Prius, License AWJ482." As the car pulled up, Alex gave me a look. "Good luck," she said. "Keep me posted."

When I got to the house, all was quiet. No mailman on the front porch, no neighbors standing around, nothing. As I walked up the front porch steps, I could hear laughter inside. The door was unlocked. Greg and a young man in hospital scrubs were sitting in opposite chairs. Doozy and Pooch were both lying at Greg's feet. When he saw me, Doozy barked. He would have lunged if Greg hadn't been holding his collar. He gave Doozy a command and the dog lay down while Pooch approached, greeting me with a wagging tail and a nose in my crotch. I scratched her head.

The man in scrubs stood up to greet me. "I'm Todd Nelson," he said, "from across the street. I got here as soon as I could. But your friend Greg already had the situation in hand." He extended his hand in greeting.

"Hi. Ann Dexter, thanks. What a crummy way to meet my new neighbors." I said.

Todd smiled. "Hey, we all know Doozy. He's quite a character."

"An understatement. He's impossible!" I said, looking over at Doozy who cocked his head at my voice and moved his ears back at my approach. "Oh Doozy! How did you do it?" I leaned down and scratched behind his ears. His tail thumped.

"Did you leave the front window open?" Greg asked. "Because Doozy jumped out through this window. It was open when I arrived, the screen popped out."

I looked at the scratches at the bottom of the frame. "Uh, I did leave the window open a crack last night for some fresh air. I guess I forgot to close it completely." I said, feeling like an idiot.

"That's all it took for Doozy to escape."

"I'd better get back," Todd said. "Hey, nice to meet you both. Next time at our house? Holly and I have been meaning to have you over for dinner."

"Don't you have a new baby?" I asked. "I think I owe you dinner over here sometime."

"Sounds great," he replied. "See you both."

That was awkward. The guy clearly thought Greg and I were something more than acquaintances. I turned to Greg. "Hey, I can't thank you enough. Really, it was above and beyond for you to head over here."

"I'm happy I could help. It's been a weird day." He looked at me and shook his head.

"No kidding."

"Look, Ann. There's something I want to talk with you about. You have a minute?"

"Sure. My workday's all shot to hell anyway. Have a seat." We sat across from each other, Doozy at Greg's feet, Pooch at mine. "What's going on?"

"I've been thinking about your friends in the Happiness class, the deaths."

"Okay. But remember I told you that under the happy hour privilege."

He smiled sadly and nodded. "I knew about Mr. Clark and Tompkins, of course. After you mentioned what happened to your friend Alex's co-worker, I contacted the Bellevue detective working on Matt Downey's case."

"And?" I asked, hoping he had found out something I had not.

"You must know that Alex is their prime suspect?"

"It's ridiculous," I said. "I know they found her fingerprint on a glass, but she was there about work. The guy was sabotaging her career. Had been for years! It's just another example of an over-reaching prosecutor looking for the great white defendant and some over-zealous cop is looking for the easy way to close a case." Greg looked as if I'd slapped him, but I kept going anyway.

"Alex was *not* the last person to see Matt Downey alive. He had someone else over there for dinner that night, after Alex left. That's who the police should be looking for." I stood and paced the length of the living room, not wanting to meet his eye.

"Hey, hey, Ann. Calm down. Come and sit. I'm not saying your friend Alex had anything to do with Matt Downey's death. They're looking for a woman named Jacqueline Forte. They know that she may have been at Downey's that night. But they've come up empty on her."

"Right." I said, not elaborating about how I knew that too.

"Did the police get a description of her? I couldn't get any information about that."

"They did. The description is generic though: white woman, in her forties maybe, medium height, medium to slim build, long black straight hair. She wore designer clothes and very high heels. Also, according to the people at the table with her and Downey, Ms. Forte got drunk and couldn't keep her hands off Downey. Table captain said she figured they would get a room."

"Well, the description doesn't fit anyone I know." I thought a moment longer.

We sat in silence for a while. Finally, Greg said, "Look. I think we both know that these murders aren't coincidental. I've started questioning the individuals in your happiness class, beginning with the instructor, Mary Summers."

"When did you interview Mary?"

"Yesterday morning. Why?"

"Because yesterday afternoon, she cancelled the rest of the happiness classes and left town."

Greg shook his head. Said nothing.

"Wait!" I said. "How did you even know Mary's name?"

"Easy. I just Googled *Happiness classes in Seattle* and her name came right up. Her website showed the dates of her ongoing classes, that she's in the middle of an eight-week class now. I figured that's the class you're in, at the Phinney Neighborhood Center?"

I nodded, my stomach in a knot.

"Why did she cancel the classes?" he asked. "And how do you know she left town?"

I told Greg about my trip to visit Mary yesterday afternoon. I didn't mention that I'd let myself into her apartment.

"What did you think of Mary?" I asked. "Any insights from your interview?"

"She has an alibi for Matt Downey's death – she was teaching a yoga class at the time. Robert Clark's is trickier. She says she was at home, alone, asleep. I didn't have any reason to doubt her."

"Right."

"She was nervous, upset about the deaths. Seemed a little frightened. But I'm used to that. It comes with the territory."

"She seemed scared to me too. I think she knows something. Maybe she's hiding something. She doesn't seem like a murderer. But then, I have less experience with that than you do."

Greg nodded.

"And I can't find anything that these three men had in common. One was a high-powered lawyer at the peak of his career, one was a sad old man with dementia and the other was, I assume, a well-regarded police officer. I mean, it doesn't fit any serial killer kind of profile, right?"

"Except that they were related to women all taking the same happiness class," he replied.

"Yes." I thought about that for a minute. "Also, I'd say that each of these women was unhappy *because* of their relationships with these men. It's a big stretch from that to Mary Summers is killing the people who are making her students miserable. Even saying that out loud sounds insane." Pooch sat up and placed her paw on my lap. The dog has amazing empathy.

"Agreed." Greg said. After a moment, he asked, "How was Ryan Tompkins making his wife unhappy?"

"He was controlling. Her friend Courtney thought the way he tried to control their daughters and his wife, Jennifer, was borderline. I don't think there was any physical abuse."

"Courtney's in the class? I'd like to talk with her. I'm sure I have her contact information on the list that Mary Summers provided."

"Wait a minute. I want to talk with Courtney first. I'm writing about the happiness class and my friend is a suspect in a related murder. I can't stay away from it now. Please don't tell me to leave it alone or to leave it to the police. That's not going to happen."

"I hear you. But I also need you to know that this is a police investigation and, as such, I'll expect you to let me in on anything you find. Agreed?"

"Sure," I said, following that up with, "I've already done a little online investigating of Mary."

Greg raised an eyebrow.

"Her maiden name was Stone. She was born in South Carolina, has a Master's in Psychology from the University of Washington and had been a licensed therapist. She was married to a Brian Winters for twenty-five years, divorced him five years ago, and got a restraining order against him at the time of the divorce. She then changed her name to Mary Summers. She's lived lots of places, mostly on the West Coast after leaving South Carolina. She's related to Peter Stone of Charleston, South Carolina, possibly her brother, though she told me her brother lives in California."

A smile was spreading across Greg's face.

"What?" I asked.

"I like your tenacity," he said. "Your investigative skills."

"Are you patronizing me?"

"No, no! Seriously, I'm impressed."

"Well, don't be." I said. "Those things are all in the online databases. Cost me fifty bucks and about five minutes to find that out."

Greg was still smiling.

"I've told you everything I know. I'll continue to do that if you agree to let me in on everything you find. Deal?"

"Deal," he said. Then his face got serious again. "There's one more thing I need to ask you."

"Okay."

"Is there anyone making your life miserable?"

His question felt like a punch. "You think someone else might get killed?"

He looked pained. "It's possible," he said. Following that up with, "Is there?"

"No. Of course not. I'm taking the class so I can write about it, remember? Not because I'm looking for happiness."

After Greg left, I tried to stay calm. I had to get back to work. If only I could focus. Instead, I kept thinking about Greg's question: is there anyone making my life miserable? No! I mean, I wasn't happy that Nancy had been dating Victor, but I was pretty sure I hadn't mentioned that in class, just at happy hour that one time.

I got back to the *Times* and went looking for Jeff. He knew Mary. He'd gotten me into this class. I needed to talk to him about what had been going on. But Jeff was out and hadn't said when he'd be back. I sent him a vague email saying I wanted to talk. Then I pulled up the happiness class roster. It was alphabetical. Bradford, Winkie, was first. I punched in her number. Cheerful as ever, Winkie said she'd be happy to talk with me about what's going on in the class and that she'd be available tomorrow afternoon.

"I'd love for you to come here, if you can," she'd said, and gave me her address.

CHAPTER NINETEEN

"Ask questions. It's a way to show interest and engagement, and most people love to talk about themselves." Gretchen Ruben, *The Happiness Project.*

On Friday afternoon, I drove the short distance from the *Times* to Winkie's houseboat on Lake Union. It reminded me of the old movie *Sleepless in Seattle.* Living on a houseboat had seemed very romantic to the inner Midwest girl in me when I'd first moved to Seattle. I'd even looked at one for sale. What if I'd bought a houseboat instead of the house in Shoreline? I would not have met Ben. Funny how random decisions could change the course of your life.

Parking nearby was reserved for houseboat owners, so I circled around twice before I found a spot. The rain had stopped but the sky was low and gray. The wind pushed me along as I walked quickly to the dock and opened the gate to the floating homes. Winkie lived in number seven, the coveted spot at the end, the one with the very best view across the lake. I continued down the central dock checking out the houseboats on either side. No two were alike. A couple of them were brand new and huge, actual floating homes, but the rest were funky and small, genuine boats, painted all sorts of colors. I passed a sunny yellow and a royal blue. The modern homes were done up in a more subdued palette, stained wood, and what looked like natural stone. Winkie's house loomed out over the water like an ocean liner, all steel-gray and concrete-colored panels. Wondering how this massive structure could even float, I stepped onto the side dock and looked for the door. At first, the place appeared impenetrable and unwelcoming. But then motion sensor lights flashed on and I spotted the front door, flanked by colorful pots of winter evergreens and red coleus. Soft recessed lights and heat lamps set into the tongue and groove entryway offered some welcome warmth. I paused to take in the view before ringing the bell, inhaling the mossy damp scent of the lake. Even on this dreary Seattle autumn afternoon, the view was stunning. Floating homes on either side and the buildings across the lake on Westlake Avenue were all lit up, their reflections shimmering on the water.

"You like it?" Winkie's voice startled me.

"I sure do. Wow! What a place to live."

"Come on in and I'll give you the tour."

I followed Winkie in the wake of her expensive perfume through a small entryway into the living room. The room had a minimalist vibe, continuing the gray tones of the exterior but punctuated here and there with splashes of color, mostly peacock green and turquoise, in pillows on the sofa and most spectacularly, the Chihuly glass chandelier in the vaulted ceiling overhead. Smaller glass pieces, these in fiery red and orange, had been set atop the large linear gas fireplace which blazed brightly. I was drawn to the fire and the glass, craving warmth in this cold space.

"Winkie, this place is incredible," I said. "Spectacular, really."

She beamed at me. "Oh, I'm so glad you think so! That means a lot to me. Come this way." She walked up a step and into the kitchen. Here, the stainless appliances and white and gray marble continued the neutral tone. Only Winkie's hot pink and gold mobile phone stood out on the countertop.

"Would you like a glass of wine? Or a cup of tea?"

"No thanks to wine," I said. "It would put me straight to sleep today. I feel a bit ragged. How about you? How are you holding up?"

Winkie shrugged, "Oh, I'm okay. Like you, I guess. A little ragged." She hesitated, opened her mouth as if to say something else, but turned instead to one of the gray-stained cabinets. She took out an ornate wooden box, set it in front of me and opened the cover. Lined up under the red satin lid were rows of teabags each in its own individual colorful wrapper: carrot orange

Darjeeling, grass green peppermint, sunny yellow chamomile, and, of course, gunmetal Earl Gray. I chose the sun while Winkie chose the gunmetal. She turned on the burner under the stainless tea kettle and suggested we finish the tour.

"It's small but it's all I need now," Winkie said, an odd edge to her voice. "I mean, there's just me and Ziggy." As if on cue, a huge gray tabby slinked into the room and jumped onto the counter. "Off!" Winkie swept the cat off the counter and out the door in one brisk movement, like a drop kick.

"Through here is the powder room and laundry, also a guest room," Winkie said, as she moved through the space. I watched Ziggy slink along on the outside deck rubbing against the floor-to-ceiling windows while he moved, as if clinging to the warmth.

"Up here is my room and access to the roof-top deck." Winkie gestured to the spiral staircase and began ascending it. I followed her up and into a small hallway. French doors to the left opened to a deck even larger and better appointed than the one downstairs. I peeked into Winkie's room before following her outside. Nothing remarkable there, just a queen bed all done up in silver and black, the numerous shimmering pillows piled onto the bed continuing the *Fifty Shades of Gray* decorating scheme. I shivered as we stepped out onto the deck, but Winkie flipped a switch and a double-sided glass fireplace flared into flames.

"That is so cool!" I said. "An indoor-outdoor fireplace!"

Winkie looked pleased. "The architect who designed this place is a genius. I spend hours out here," she said.

"When I first came to Seattle, I actually considered buying a houseboat." I said. "But I chickened out. Bought a standard issue house in Shoreline instead. It was more affordable, less risky."

Winkie gave me a tight smile. "It's not for everyone, I guess. Still, I love it out here on the water. There's the tea."

Drawn to the whistle of the kettle, we made our way back into the main living area and I looked around some more while Winkie poured the hot water over our teabags and opened a tin of shortbread cookies. I perched myself as close to the fireplace as possible for warmth and sipped my tea, thinking of the questions I wanted to ask, while Winkie brought her tea and the cookie tin into the room and placed them on the glass coffee table between us. Kicking off her high heels, Winkie sat on the edge of the sofa facing me, tucked her legs underneath her and began biting her thumbnail.

"What do you think of Mary cancelling the happiness classes?" I asked.

"Personally? I think it's a terrible idea," she said. "I mean, we all need that class now more than ever, right? I guess if Mary had a family emergency, it can't be helped." Winkie shifted in her chair.

"I'm still hoping the deaths are not connected in any way," I said.

"What do you mean?" Winkie picked up a cookie and began nibbling around the edges of it.

"Don't you think they're connected?" I asked.

"No. I mean, they're *related* because they happened to people in our class. I know your police officer friend is nosing around, but that's what he's paid to do." Winkie crossed and re-crossed her legs, then began bouncing her right foot restlessly. I watched the motion of her foot and noticed the crimson polish on her toenails.

"You've talked with Detective Costello?"

"I have. He came over earlier today. Had a bunch of questions." She shrugged.

"Like?" I raised my eyebrows. Seemed like Greg was always one step ahead of me.

"Like, how long I've known Mary, Alex, Emily, and Jennifer. Had I noticed any tension between Mary and the others? Things like that. I don't think I helped him at all." She looked down at her foot, stopped jiggling it and looked back at me.

"I think he's looking for someone to blame. Maybe Mary. But that's ridiculous. Mary could never." She shook her head. "Anyway, I'm going to miss the class and the women I've met there. I feel like you're my best friends."

Her comment struck me as odd. Surely Winkie had tons of friends at the tennis club or in the opera guild or wherever else she spends her time.

"Did you grow up here in Seattle, Winkie?" I asked.

"Oh, no. I grew up in Chicago," she said. "I came here for nursing school and, besides a job in California right out of school, I've been here ever since."

"You're a nurse?" I asked, again surprised. I didn't see Winkie as the care-giving type.

"Was." She replied. "It was a long time ago." Winkie sipped her tea and I wanted to ask her how long it had been but knew from her comments in class that she was extremely sensitive about her age.

"Your ex-husband is a doctor, right? Is that how you met?"

Winkie set her mug of tea on the coffee table and shot me a quizzical look. "You know Larry's a doctor, Ann," she said in a scolding tone. "I mentioned this in class. Or maybe at one of our happy hours?" Winkie shook her head. "He's a cosmetic surgeon, likes to make things beautiful. He liked working on me until he got bored and needed a new challenge. A younger challenge." Winkie's smile twisted into a grimace. She began rubbing her temples, a distress signal I'd noticed before.

"I'm sorry to bring up a painful topic, Winkie. I didn't remember that you were a nurse."

"Oh yes, I was a nurse. Of course, my parents wanted me to be a doctor, but I saw what that did to them, and I wanted a life, not just a career. Ironic now, isn't it? Now that I have neither of those things." Again, the temple rubbing.

"Your parents were both doctors?"

"Yes. Very important surgeons," she said with obvious contempt. "They didn't have much time for me though. I don't even know why they bothered having a child. I suppose I must have been an accident. My mother is Catholic. So, no aborting me." She forced a smile.

"You said you started out your nursing career in California." I said. "What brought you back to Seattle?"

Winkie picked up another piece of shortbread and took a bite. she shrugged. "I worked in a hospital in San Diego – so depressing. So much suffering. I did the best I could. Then I saw a job advertised in Larry's clinic here in Seattle. Cosmetic surgery sounded glamorous, so I applied. I thought it would be different. It was." She shook her head. "There was still suffering. But it was self-inflicted. I mean, when it comes to cosmetic surgery, the patients know there will be pain, but they do it anyway. It's the price they're willing to pay for beauty."

I looked at Winkie's perfectly symmetrical features, her tiny nose, cool blue eyes under long lashes and her flawless pale skin. Her hair fell to her shoulders, straight and full with blonde highlights. Again, I wondered about her age but was too chicken to ask.

"Yeah. That's kind of depressing too." I said, then worried that I'd offended her again. Winkie had chosen cosmetic surgery for herself after all. Or maybe her husband had insisted. Either way, it gave me the shivers.

"Are you still going to write about the happiness class?" she asked. Before I could answer, she plowed on. "I mean, I hope you're not going to write about the bad stuff. There's so much that's positive about the class."

"I'm not sure what I'll be writing," I said.

"Wait," she said. "I just had a great idea. Why don't we all meet anyway? Without the class? We could still meet every Wednesday afternoon. We could meet here!" Winkie looked so bright and expectant that I hated to burst her bubble.

"I don't know, Winkie. I doubt that Jennifer and Emily are up for any more happiness classes. They're still hurting from their losses."

"Oh, they'll be fine after a while," she said. "In the meantime, we can get together, support each other, help them through."

I shook my head, but Winkie kept on going.

"Alex is already fine, right? I mean, she's happy now that Matt Downey is out of her life."

"It's true that Matt's not around to torment her at work, but Alex no longer has a job to go to. She's not too happy about her forced sabbatical or about being a suspect in his murder."

"Oh, the police don't know anything. I mean, cops aren't exactly known for their brains, are they?" I immediately thought of Greg, his keen intelligence.

"Even the police know Alex didn't do it." Winkie continued. "They couldn't pin it on her. It sure looks like an accident. Guy had a ridiculous blood alcohol level, fell asleep, drowned. Oops." Winkie grinned and finished off her shortbread.

"Want another?" She picked up the tin and offered me a cookie. I declined. "So, what do you say?" She looked at me expectantly.

"About Matt Downey's death?" I asked, trying to get my head around Winkie's comments.

"No, silly, about getting the group together here on Wednesdays. I could give everyone a call and see about starting next week. We still have that time frame blocked off on our calendars."

"Like I said, I think Jennifer and Emily need time to grieve. They need professional help."

Winkie frowned. "What about you and Courtney and Alex? It would be a nice opportunity to see each other regularly, right? Girls' night kind of thing?"

"No Winkie," I said. "It would be too weird, given what's happened."

Winkie frowned again and bit her thumbnail. "I mean, I thought we were friends, but I guess I was just being stupid. As usual."

"You're not stupid, Winkie. I just think we all need some time. Maybe after the police investigation is over. You know, you can always call me if you feel like it. We could have lunch sometime." Why had I said that? Winkie was the last person I wanted to have lunch with.

"Sure." Winkie didn't sound too enthusiastic either.

"I guess I should head out," I said. "Friday night traffic and all." I stood with the intention of gathering my things and taking my teacup into the kitchen.

"How's your sister?" Winkie asked.

"Um. She's fine." I said.

"Still screwing around with your boyfriend?"

I sat back down and shot her a look. "Wow, that hurts, Winkie," I said.

"Really? Because I thought you were over it."

"I am. I mean, I don't like to think about it. Nancy and I have buried the hatchet."

"I just wondered if you were really okay." Winkie looked genuinely concerned.

"I am. Okay, that is." I stood a second time. "Thanks for the tea and cookies. And, for the tour of your amazing house."

Winkie shrugged, her face sad. "No worries," she said. "And remember what I said about meeting with the group. I think it could be good for all of us."

I nodded. "I'll be in touch."

Winkie opened the door and Ziggy zoomed back into the room and leapt onto the cat bed in front of the fireplace shining his green eyes in my direction. Time to go.

CHAPTER TWENTY

"You can survive losing a piece of your heart without losing the core of who you are. More than merely surviving the loss, you can thrive." Rachel Hollis, *Girl, Wash Your Face*.

I drove to pick up the dogs thinking about Winkie. She seemed so needy. She thought we should just go ahead and schedule our own happiness classes on her houseboat because we'd all become such great friends? Weird. And her comment about Nancy worried me. If there was a happiness killer out there, could Nancy be a target? No. I was pretty sure I hadn't mentioned Nancy and Victor in class, just at one of our happy hours, which meant that Mary didn't know anything about it. That was something.

After the chaos of getting the dogs into the car, I called Ooink, a newish restaurant on Pike which Greg told me had the best ramen in Seattle. A nice bowl of hot noodle soup sounded like just the ticket – comforting on a cold night. When I walked into the house with my takeout, it seemed particularly chilly and unfamiliar, like it belonged to someone else, which it did. I turned up the heat and turned on the gas fireplace. In the kitchen, I poured the ramen into one of the Salton's beautiful cerulean blue soup bowls and then moved to the dining room where I lit the pillar candles in their decorative arrangement on the table. Not exactly mindful eating – what with the distraction of the computer in front of me – but it was the best I could do in this moment. I looked over at Doozy curled up in the corner quietly snoring and smiled. Thank goodness for daycare. A tired dog is a good dog. Pooch sat in front of me with her big head in my lap. I scratched behind her ears with my free hand until her eyes lolled and she flopped down on the floor at my feet. I started to feel better, ready to click into gear.

First, I called Peter Stone again before it got too late in Charlottesville. This time, I left a vague message saying I was a friend of Mary Summers from Seattle and asking him to give me a call. Then, while slurping noodles, I created a document called "Happiness Interviews," and typed in my thoughts on my meeting with Winkie. It was a process I'd always used while researching a story. I added some questions that needed follow-up. Then I went over my notes one more time. It still didn't make any sense, the deaths, Mary's leaving. Discouraged, I wrote a couple of questions that I wanted to ask Courtney during our meeting tomorrow.

I checked my phone several times for a text from Greg. Nothing. Just when I was getting ready for bed, my phone rang, and my heart thumped with anticipation. The display read *Betty Petersen* and I picked up with another kind of emotion surging through me.

"Hey, Betty."

"Hi Ann. I hope I'm not disturbing you too late, but I wanted to let you know that I had a call from an agent who showed your house tonight to a young couple who are very interested. Tom – he's the agent – thinks they'll be writing up an offer tomorrow."

"Wow! That's great news, Betty," I said, my stomach clenching.

"I don't want to get your hopes up if nothing comes of it, but we haven't really talked since you moved out, so I figured it was a good idea to give you a call."

"Right. Well, thanks."

Betty yammered on for a while, giving me the details on how many agents had been through the house in the first week, what a great job the stager had done, etcetera. I sat listening while a whole other stream of thoughts raced through my mind.

"Ann?" Betty interrupted my busy brain.

"Sorry Betty. I'm here. It's just such a surprise. I guess I didn't think the place would sell so quickly. But that's great news." I feigned enthusiasm.

"Fingers crossed. I just want to make sure you'll be available tomorrow. In case we have an offer to review."

"Oh, I'll be available," I said. "And Betty?"

"Yes?"

"I think I'd like to stop by the house tomorrow. Would that be okay? Or will I run into the prospective buyers?"

"That's fine, Ann. It's still your house. You can see it anytime. I'm sure you'll be pleased with how it's showing." Betty added a few more comments about the strong real estate market, the scarcity of inventory in Seattle and ended with a perky goodbye.

I clicked off the phone and remained on the sofa. Pooch woke up at the sound of my voice and plopped her big head on my lap once again.

"I should be happy, Pooch. Why do I feel so weird?" The dog nudged under my arm, so I scratched her head. "Yeah, well, I guess we might end up truly homeless if this deal goes through. At least we have this place. And Doozy. Where *is* Doozy?"

I got up and returned to the kitchen where Doozy had the cardboard takeout bowl from Ooink wedged against the refrigerator while he licked it clean of any remains of the ramen I may have left in there. The dog had an amazingly long reach. He'd already trained me to put all food items at the back of the counter. Apparently, I'd lapsed.

I got into bed and reached for my Gratitude Journal. Then, on a whim, I opened my laptop and clicked on Dr. Bergman's second lecture from his positive psychology class.

* * *

First thing Saturday morning I drove to the University of Washington Medical Center where Courtney worked as an anesthesiology resident. The University of Washington campus is enormous, over seven hundred acres of land with more than thirty thousand students. A huge banner greeted me at the main entrance: "The Best Hospital in the State," it said. And a sign in the front lobby declared the place "An Award-Winning Magnet Hospital."

Courtney had suggested we meet at the espresso stand on the first floor, just past the Cascade elevator bank. I followed the signs—the place is a maze—and finally found the right corridor. Then, I just followed my senses, the warm dark aroma of coffee and the whoosh of milk steaming in a stainless-steel pitcher. I searched for Courtney in the crowd of bleary-eyed doctors and nurses waiting in line for their jolt of espresso. I didn't see her, so I joined the end of the line. When Courtney appeared around the corner in her blue hospital scrubs with her red hair pulled back into a messy ponytail and her face free of makeup, I thought she looked way too young to be a doctor.

"Hey, Ann. Sorry I'm late but I'm crazy busy with my new rotation here."

"No worries. I appreciate you taking the time to talk." We picked up our coffees and Courtney stopped at the door to the outdoor seating area.

"Too cold out there, let's head down this way." I followed Courtney into a waiting area for *Surgical Specialties and Transplantation.*

"Wow, that's intense," I said. "You do transplants here?"

"Sure do. About fifty lung transplants this year already. We have one of the top surgeons in the country. I worked that rotation back in September. Happiest patients in the hospital, lung transplants. They're just so thrilled and grateful to be alive and to breathe without oxygen tanks. They're my favorite patients for sure." Courtney smiled brightly, and I tried to get my head around the idea of a lung transplant. Wild.

"Nothing going on down here on a Saturday," she said. "We might as well take advantage of the quiet." We sat in a corner of the empty waiting room. Courtney took a sip of her large coffee then pulled out her phone, which must have vibrated in her pocket. I hadn't heard a sound. She briskly thumbed in a message, then put it back into the puffy vest she wore over her scrubs.

"Sorry. Occupational hazard," she said.

"No problem," I replied. "First, I want to talk about how Mary cancelled the rest of the happiness classes." I said.

"Okay. What's that about?"

"Apparently, her brother had a heart attack," I said. "But the weird thing is Mary has left town completely, moved out of her apartment and took off."

"She's left Seattle for good. That's intense," Courtney said, pulling out her phone again and thumbing around, only then did I notice the small tattoo of a bluebird on the inside of her forearm. She looked up, saw me noticing it.

"Were you looking at Chirpy?" She smiled. "Long story. Not particularly interesting but followed an all-nighter in medical school. Up until the crack of dawn, birds were chirping. Sorry. Told you it was not particularly interesting." She smiled again at the memory.

"Let's talk about what happened to our happiness class," I suggested.

"You mean all the deaths?" she asked.

I nodded.

"They could be connected." She said. "If Mary, or someone else in the class, is some kind of twisted Dr. Death, killing off the individuals who are making lives miserable."

"That seems very far-fetched." I said.

"Why? We learned about this kind of thing in medical school. There have been more than one psychopathic nurse or doctor who've done exactly that. They get so caught up with their power and they start to believe they know the best time for people to die. Angels of death. I know of one case, where the nurse pulled the plug on patients, just so she could try to resuscitate them and look heroic to the patients' families. More than one family sent the nurse flowers after the funeral."

"That is sick," I said.

"Agreed."

We sat with our own thoughts for a moment.

"Okay," I said. "Let's go with that idea. Think like the police. Let's say Mary, or someone else in our class, has this perverse motive. What about opportunity and means? We know someone was with Matt Downey the night he died, a woman he was expecting for dinner."

"Mary's a little too old for Matt, right? Isn't he around forty-five?" Courtney asked.

"Yes, he was somewhere around there." I said. "And the woman he had a date with is apparently younger. She, like Mary, is MIA."

"Okay," she said. "But what about Emily's dad? How did someone get to him in the middle of the night and lure him to Lake Union? Unless it was Emily or someone else in her family."

"That's absurd. Emily loved her dad."

"Of course, but she was at her wits end taking care of him. Maybe she just snapped. He got out, she followed him to the lake, they argued, she pushed him in. Maybe she got the idea from Matt Downey's drowning."

"No way," I said. "Someone else could have done that." I thought about it. "It's Ryan Tompkins murder that can't be connected," I said. "That was a random mentally unstable person lashing out at a cop."

"Seems like it." Courtney agreed. "Is that guy dead, by the way? The mentally ill person? Or was he killed by Ryan's partner?"

"Good question. I know he was shot by Ryan's partner. Last I heard he was at Harborview in serious condition."

I made a note to ask Greg about that. I couldn't get into Harborview to interview the suspect, but Greg could. I would need to call him now that I had something to discuss.

Courtney's phone vibrated again, and she stood up. "Sorry, Ann. This one I really need to respond to. Surgery in ten minutes, and I have to hit the bathroom first."

I thanked her for taking the time to meet with me. "One last thing," I said. "I talked to Winkie yesterday and she's all for having us *gals* meet at her house for our own private happiness class."

"Seriously?" Courtney asked. "I'd rather have a root canal."

I made my way to the correct elevator bank for the garage and rode with a distracted older woman carrying a large clear plastic bag filled with random items of clothing, a watch, a wallet and a pair of glasses. I hoped the patient was being released and that the woman was on her way to a pickup at the front door, rather than the alternative. She didn't make eye contact, her expression locked down. We both watched the elevator buttons light up as we descended to the garage. Thinking how depressing it must be to work in a hospital, I got out, found my car in the huge underground garage with a click of my door opener and sat for a minute, thinking about my options for the rest of the day. I hadn't yet heard from Betty about the offer, but it was still early, and I wanted to head over to my house to take one last look and say goodbye. I also wanted to call Greg. There was no cell reception in the bowels of the UW parking garage, so I exited, turned right onto Montlake Boulevard, and took the ramp to the I-5 north. Pleased that traffic was not too bad this early on a Saturday morning and that the fog was beginning to dissipate, I drove toward Shoreline mulling over my conversation with Courtney.

My phone pinged with a text message before I got to the exit at 145th. I ignored my strong desire to dig into my bag to retrieve it while driving. Instead, I turned on the radio and listened to the NPR station's broadcast of the quiz show, *Wait, Wait, Don't Tell Me!* A favorite. They'd just got to the part where the moderator reads three possible newspaper articles and the contestants guess which one is true, each one more outrageous than the next. I picked the only possible true option. Wrong again.

I turned off the radio and was about to pull into my driveway when I saw a white sedan parked there already. I pulled up across the street instead and retrieved my cell phone. The text I'd received while driving was from Greg suggesting we get together for dinner later. I smiled and began tapping in a response when the front door of my house opened, and a young, happy-looking couple emerged from it. The woman had an infant wrapped into one of those cloth slings around her belly and over her shoulder. Her husband placed a protective arm around her and guided them to the car while their real estate agent locked up my house, then sprinted to the car to open the back door for them. Everyone smiling.

Mesmerized, I watched the man help his wife extricate the baby from the sling while the agent went around to the driver's side and started up the car. It's just what this house needs, I thought, a family with a baby. The neighbors will be so pleased. Then why did I feel so wretched? I felt the squeeze in my gut. *This should have been us, me and Ben.* That's why. The tears welled up and spilled down my cheeks. I swiped at my face with the back of my hand and forced the emotions back into place as best I could. The car drove slowly past me, and the woman caught my eye, smiling from the backseat. I swallowed hard and tried to smile back. When they were finally out of sight, I started up the car and pulled into my driveway.

I took a deep breath and remembered Greg's text. *Sure! I'd love to see you later!* I tapped into my phone, then erased it as too eager. *Sure. I'm available later.* I wrote instead. *Where and when?* I looked up at my house and thought about the first time I'd seen it, how excited I'd been at the prospect of home ownership. I'd felt so grown up, pleased to be putting the small inheritance I had from my parents to good use. When I found the correct key on the ring, I squared my shoulders and strode to the front door. Once inside, I gasped. *Holy shit*, I said aloud. The place didn't look anything like my house anymore. *It isn't your house anymore*, that little voice in my head reminded me. The stager had transformed the space into a mid-century hip vibe that certainly was not to my taste. The modern art on the walls, though colorful, appeared huge and blurry, a different framed Rorschach test in every room. There were vases filled with silk greens, a fake orchid in the entry hall next to a glass bowl filled with cards from real estate agents who had passed through. Mirrors were placed strategically throughout to give the impression of spaciousness. The powder room had its own orchid and candles and plush white towels.

My mouth agape, I walked through to the living room. Faux fur throws and pillows were piled onto a gray sofa. A square glass coffee table held a bottle of red wine and two glasses on a tiled tray. An orange accent chair sat in the corner. It was amazing how much bigger the rooms looked decorated in this minimalist way. Very clever. I laughed when I went into the kitchen. Here a beautiful cookbook lay on the counter, *Tuscan Cooking*, the cover photo a sun-drenched shot of a stucco villa set amidst rolling hills planted with old vines and olive trees. A small wrought iron holder next to the book displayed three more bottles of wine. Several copies of the colorful sales brochure Betty had made were piled into a basket. I picked one up and looked at the photos of my house not looking like my house at all, more like a more sophisticated modern version of it.

I couldn't wait to see what she'd done upstairs. The same color scheme, gray with silver and pops of orange continued in the master bedroom and bath. Here were more displays of flowers and candles and French soaps in a bowl. No dirty laundry or dog hair or hairdryers or toothbrushes. No real life, in other words. This was good for me. I could say goodbye to a place that had already moved on without me. It wasn't until I got to the garage that I broke down. The silliest thing. The steel shelves Ben had installed for storage were mostly empty, just a hammer on the shelf next to the door. Ben's hammer. Where the hell had that been? I thought I'd packed up all the tools and boxed them up safely for storage, for use in my new life somewhere else. I picked up the hammer and felt the heft of it in my hand. I carried it upstairs, flopped down on the cold gray sofa, cradled the hammer in my lap and began to cry, quietly at first and then huge gasping sobs. I felt sorry for myself, for the loss of Ben, the love of my life, for my childlessness, for the sorry state of my relationships, for the loss of this house, our house. I let the memories flow until I cried myself dry.

Eventually, I stood up, slipped the hammer into my handbag, and went into the powder room for a tissue. My phone began ringing from somewhere in the front hall. I ignored it. I blew my nose and splashed water on my face, wiping it dry with the bright white hand towel that had nothing to do with me, except the black smears of mascara I'd left behind. I ran the faucet and cupped my hands to drink from it. I wiped down the sink and replaced the towel on the rack turning the stains inside the fold. I went into the front hall and pulled out my phone.

We have an offer! read the text from Betty. I also had two missed calls and a voicemail, one from Betty and one from a number I didn't recognize, an 843 area code. I pressed the phone icon and listened to the Betty's excited voice telling me that the offer was full price, it came with a twenty-thousand-dollar earnest money deposit and the standard inspection clause contingency. *Call me back as soon as you get this!*

I stood there for a while listening to the silence of the empty house, hesitant to return Betty's call, even though I felt as ready as I'd ever be to move forward with my life, even though I knew I would be happier somewhere else, away from the memories of the different life I'd once shared here with Ben. Something Dr. Bergman said in his lecture popped into my brain: *What matters in terms of long-term happiness is how individuals face challenges.* I'd been feeling sorry for myself, for the loss of the life I'd had in this house with Ben. The reality is that I have many things to be grateful for. Those things I wrote in my gratitude journal just last night, for example: the renewed relationship with my sister; the great place I'm living with Pooch rent-free; my new friendship with Greg. Now I could add: the fast sale of my house for a solid price. I pressed the button to call Betty.

My brief meeting with Betty at the Shoreline Windermere Real Estate office proved how simple it could be to sign all the necessary paperwork transferring my house to Alison and Josh Gordon. I didn't want to read the personal letter they'd written to me saying how much they loved my house, how they were looking forward to raising their family in it. There were no competing offers, so they needn't have gone through this step that has become common in the competitive Seattle real estate world. I glanced at it and handed it back to Betty.

"Nice." I said.

Betty arched her eyebrows at me but let it go. Then she began talking business. "The buyers have been pre-approved for financing, so everything should move quickly. They'd like to be in the house by December 15, in time for the holidays. Does that work for you?" Betty asked. I nodded.

"Why not?" I replied. The sooner the better.

Betty smiled, pleased with the deal she'd put together. We shook hands on it, and I drove back to my non-home in Capitol Hill, planning to take the dogs for a run around Volunteer Park and hoping it would be therapeutic for all of us. It was not. Doozy was his usual naughty dog self, barking and lunging at squirrels. At least he didn't pull me down this time. I spent the rest of the afternoon watching another lecture on positive psychology, finishing my weekend chores, and looking forward to my date with Greg. At five o'clock my phone rang, again that 843 area code.

"Ann Dexter."

"Well, hello Ann Dexter, this is Peter Stone. You're a persistent gal. I must have five recent calls from you, but only one voicemail. Should have left one sooner mentioning my little sis. I would have called you back first thing. Is Mary okay?"

I listened to Peter Stone's charming Southern accent and scrambled to think how to answer his question.

"I don't know," I said. "I haven't been able to get a hold of her and I wondered if she might be in Charleston visiting you?"

After a large belly laugh, Mary's brother said, "You can't be a very close friend of Mary's or you'd know that she left Summerville when she was eighteen swearing she'd never set foot in the South again. So, no. She's not visiting me now and hasn't in over forty years."

"Maybe I have the wrong brother, then. Mary said she was going to visit her brother who'd had a heart attack?"

I heard Peter take a deep breath. "I'm right as rain and I'm also Mary's only brother so I guess my sis has told you one of her stretchers, Ma'am."

"Stretchers?"

"Mary always has been a good storyteller. She's good at stretching the truth so long as it suits her. Does she owe you money or something?"

"No, no, nothing like that. I was taking a happiness class with her and, like I said, she left saying her brother needed her."

He chuckled. "A *happiness* class? Now that sounds just like Mary Ellen. I know she's been into yoga and all kinds of woo woo things."

I waited.

"Doesn't sound like she's too happy then, if she's run off." He scoffed. "She got a man she's running from? Never did know how to pick a good one."

I thought about the public records I'd seen, the no-contact order she had against her ex-husband.

"She never mentioned anyone," I replied.

"Well, that's just like Mary Ellen too. Quiet. Secretive even."

I took that in. "You said your sister hasn't visited you in forty years. Do you keep in touch at all?"

"You know, we exchange Christmas cards, the occasional phone call but we've not been close for a long time. When I heard your voicemail, I thought maybe you were calling to tell me she'd passed. I figure someone will call me when that happens."

"Has Mary been sick?" I asked.

"Not that I know of Ma'am. It's just, neither of us is getting any younger, if you know what I mean."

I asked Peter Stone to call me if Mary got in touch and he promised he would but, he said, "There's a snowball's chance in hell that'll happen."

We said our goodbyes and I wrote down some notes about our conversation, something I could share with Greg later.

CHAPTER TWENTY-ONE

"Happiness comes from solving problems." Mark Manson, *The Subtle Art of Not Giving a F*ck.*

Greg picked me up at seven and we drove to an Italian restaurant on Fifteenth called Rione XIII. The restaurant, warm and intimate with white linen napkins, flowers, and flickering candles, felt romantic. I wondered whether Greg had selected this place because of the ambiance or the food. I hoped it was both. He had been chatty and easy-going on the drive, making no mention of Mary Summers or the murders surrounding the happiness class. I hadn't brought it up either. I guess I wished we could just have a normal date, or at least start out that way. Greg asked me about Doozy and about selling my house. I didn't want to risk getting emotional again about the house, so I told him about running the dogs, how Doozy nearly pulled my arm out of its socket every time he spotted a squirrel. We laughed, and Greg assured me that Doozy was trainable, indeed making progress, and I agreed.

Only after we ordered wine did we broach the subject of the happiness class.

"I interviewed Winkie Bradford yesterday." he said.

"Right. I talked with her too. What did you think?"

Greg took a sip of his Chianti before responding. "Lonely? Tries too hard. Probably spent a fortune on cosmetic surgery." He said. "But her houseboat is really something."

I laughed. "I think your investigative skills are right on, detective. Except that all that cosmetic surgery was free, thanks to her ex-husband, Dr. Lawrence Bradford. Apparently, he has moved on to another human guinea pig." Greg looked puzzled, so I elaborated.

"He has a new, *younger*, wife. Poor Winkie. I never really paid much attention to her in class because all her comments seemed so first world, so white, so top one percent. Maybe that's not fair. She seems so eager to please. Also, I discovered that she's a nurse. That really surprised me."

Greg listened without saying anything. I was about to tell him about my phone call with Peter Stone, Mary's brother, when our waiter arrived to take our order. Greg suggested we split the *ensalata mista* along with the Carciofi *alla Giuda* which was a fried artichoke with aioli, and something called *pangrattato*.

I nodded. "Sounds good."

"You like some spice?" he asked.

"Spice is good."

"Then try the bucatini al'Amatriciana. Simple but fresh and fabulous."

"What's bucatini?" I asked the waiter.

"From the Italian, *buco* means hole. It's like a thick spaghetti noodle with a hole through it. Holds up to a spicy sauce quite well."

"Sounds great. This guy hasn't steered me wrong, *yet*." I handed the menu to the waiter and gave Greg a look.

"So, tell me about your day." Greg said. "Anything happening on your house?"

"Yes! I got an offer today."

"That's amazing,"

"Right? I now have twenty thousand dollars of earnest money in my bank account. Looks like it's a done deal."

"Nice," he said. "What now? You going to look for another house right away?"

"No idea. I'm still processing the whole thing. Might just take the money and run." I said, surprised that I'd said that out loud. Greg looked concerned. "Don't worry. That's not my usual M.O. I've never really been much of a risk taker."

"Ha!" He scoffed. "Aren't you the same person who risked your life to free some opera star?"

I laughed. "No, I'm the reporter who stupidly thought she could outsmart the kidnapper. Plus, that had to do with my job.

Risks at work are so different from risks in my personal life. I usually don't go there."

Greg studied me for a while, long enough to make me uncomfortable. He shook his head. "That's too bad," he said.

The waiter arrived with our salads, simple fresh spring greens, shaved parmesan and drizzled with a raspberry vinaigrette. The savory and sweet tastes combined with the cold, crunchy lettuces for a perfect blend of flavors and textures. I smacked my lips and Greg smiled. "Delicious, right? Have a bite of this." He cut the artichoke heart in half and dragged it through the aioli before presenting it to me.

'Mmmm. Very nice." I said.

We finished our first courses in an appreciative silence. With impeccable timing, our waiter picked up our empty plates and returned with a steaming plate of ravioli for Greg and the spicy pasta for me. Greg watched me wind the pasta around my fork and put it into my mouth. He smiled at my wide-eyed reaction.

"Told you so," he said, reaching over to touch his napkin to my chin, dabbing off the drop of red sauce. Embarrassed, I wiped my chin again for good measure.

When Greg picked up his cell phone, silent but vibrating between us, I frowned. He frowned back and stood up. "Sorry. Gotta get this."

He went outside. I watched him through the plate glass window talking into the phone while I continued to shove pasta into my mouth. I couldn't tell from his body language whether the call was upsetting or not. When he returned the phone to his pocket and walked back into the restaurant, I wiped my mouth again and took a sip of wine.

"Sorry," he said. "But you'll be interested. That was the duty officer at Harborview. Ryan Tompkins' killer has regained consciousness."

"He's lucid?" I asked.

Greg shrugged. "Well, he's awake, ranting about things. I want to get over there and talk to him before the doctors give him another sedative. He might have something to say."

"Now?" I asked. "You're going there now?"

"I'm sorry, Ann. I have to go."

Greg looked over my left ear, apparently finding something fascinating in that direction. I turned and saw only rows of liquor bottles lined up and gleaming from the lighted shelves behind the bar. I reached over and touched his hand.

"What's the connection?" I asked. "There's something you don't want to tell me. Something that connects this guy with the other murders."

Greg pulled back his hand and took a sip of wine. "I just need to talk with the guy first. Then I'll know more."

"I want to come with you."

He looked at me like I was a crazy person. "Can't happen," he said. "It's a police matter." Greg shoveled the last two raviolis into his mouth, polished off his wine and got up to catch the waiter standing at the bar's computer screen. He handed over his credit card while I silently fumed. I'd fully intended to pay for my share of this dinner, but I'd changed my mind. Greg could go for it now that he'd cut things short and cut me out.

"Ready?" He stood looking down at me.

"No thanks. I'll finish my wine and walk home in a bit. You go ahead."

"Don't be pissed, Ann. Come on, it's cold out there."

"It's not raining. I'll be fine. It's only a few blocks. Let me know if you find out anything you can share."

After Greg left, I flagged down the waiter, ordered a cup of decaf and considered the dessert menu. I pulled out my phone and checked my email. It made me feel less alone, more in control. I considered calling Alex, or maybe Nancy, to tell them about my house sale. But all the emotion around that had combined with my feelings about Greg, and our date that wasn't a date, Ryan Tompkins's killer, the other deaths, and Mary's disappearance. I needed to sort it out somehow but needed more information. I needed Greg. I sent him a text: *Let me know what happens at Harborview,* tucked away my phone just as the waitress arrived with the profiteroles I'd ordered.

By the time I left Rione, the rain had started up again, a constant sideways drizzle, tiny needle pricks hitting my face. I hurried along, cursing myself for not letting Greg drive me home. My trench coat could not keep out the rain or the cold and my shoes were cute, yes, but good for walking, no. By the time I heard Doozy barking behind the front door and put my key into the lock, I was drenched and shivering, with a blister on the back of my left heel. I pushed open the door and Doozy jumped up on me. I didn't even care.

"Okay, okay. That's enough." I hung my coat to dry on the rack in the front hall, kicked off my wet shoes and set them on the radiator. I peeled off the rest of my clothes on my way upstairs to the master bathroom. I didn't usually go in there, but a hot soaking tub was just what I needed. With the water running, I wrapped a thick towel around me and went back to the kitchen to warm a cup of milk for cocoa and grabbed my favorite pajamas from the chest of drawers in my bedroom. Once I'd lowered myself into the steamy fragrant water, I considered what movie to watch afterwards – escapist or gripping drama? I'd thought about *Sleepless in Seattle,* while visiting Winkie's houseboat, but couldn't do the romantic comedy tonight, not when my real life resembled a romantic disaster story. Lately I'd been more interested in movies that took me to exotic places. I decided on *The Constant Gardener.* I could travel to the middle east and remind myself of the kind of journalism that makes a difference in the world. I could dream about a future when I might do the same.

When the skin on my fingers began to shrivel and the water turned from hot to tepid, I got out and toweled off, knocking the cocoa cup into the draining water and cursing myself for it. Descending the stairs, I saw a shadow moving across the front porch. I stopped and squinted toward the small leaded-glass window in the door. From that distance, I couldn't see anything but the pool of yellow light from the porch fixture and the rain falling harder now. Doozy continued to snooze at the top of the stairs and apparently hadn't heard anything. I continued down and chalked it up to exhaustion and a too-vivid imagination. I hung the towel over the back of a chair in my bedroom and got into my pajamas when my cell phone pinged from somewhere with a text message. I couldn't find it. Funny how the sound could travel but not identify its source. I went from room to room until I found the phone back where I'd started, in a pile of damp clothes on my bed. I'd missed three texts, all from Greg. Smiling, despite myself, I began reading the first one when the doorbell rang and both Doozy and Pooch started barking.

I jumped, then read the last text, *I'm at your front door. Can we talk?* Shit. Here I was looking like a drowned rat in my most tattered and least presentable pajamas.

"Coming!" I commanded both dogs to sit and opened the door to Greg.

"Sorry to barge in, Ann. But I'm pretty sure you'll be interested in what I heard at Harborview." His face softened as he looked closer at me. "You look great in those retro pajamas with your hair up," he said. "Very Audrey Hepburn."

I felt the heat in my face. No one had ever compared me to Audrey Hepburn.

"Can I come in?" he asked.

"Yes. I wasn't expecting. . ."

"I know. I'm sorry. But you need to know this. Can we talk?" I realized I'd been standing there dumbly holding my empty cocoa cup with one hand and giving the dogs the sit command with the other one. Amazingly, Doozy was sitting beside Pooch, wiggly but successfully suppressing the urge to jump up on our visitor. I released them and closed the door, while Greg crouched down to scratch Doozy's big dopey head, then gave some attention to Pooch.

We moved over to the seating area surrounding the fireplace, Greg on one of the oversized leather chairs while I settled into the corner of the sofa, cross-legged, a decorative pillow on my lap.

"So, what did the guy have to say?"

"First, I should tell you the connection I discovered." He leaned forward in his chair and drilled into me with those intense brown eyes. "Mary Summers didn't always teach yoga and happiness classes. When her name was Mary Winters, she worked at Seattle Public Health as a therapist for over ten years, mostly at the downtown clinic on Second, just a few blocks from one of the homeless shelters."

"Okay."

"It's the shelter where the man who murdered Ryan Tompkins spent most of his nights."

I took that in. "There's lots of homelessness in Seattle. It's a huge issue."

"Yes, but this guy, Luke Mitchell is his name, Mary saw him on a regular basis. The department got access to his mental health records. Turns out Mary saw him off and on for two years."

"How long ago was this?" I asked.

"Five years ago."

"Just about the time she got divorced and quit doing therapy."

"Exactly," he said.

"There's something else I discovered about Mary that will interest you," I said. Greg's face got serious. "Mary does have a brother, Peter Stone. He lives in Charleston, South Carolina, not far from where he and Mary grew up in Summerville."

"Is Mary there tending to him? He have a heart attack?"

"No. Mary hasn't been back to the South since she was eighteen and left for college. They're not particularly close. He's in fine health."

Greg frowned. "Looks like we'd better find Mary. We need to talk with her about her relationship with Luke Mitchell."

"You never told me what he said when you saw him just now."

"Nurse on duty told me that when the guy woke up, he started ranting that he wanted to talk to the angel, that he'd done what the angel had told him to do."

"Delusional behavior." I said. But Greg had planted the seed, making me worry even more about Mary.

"Right." He agreed. "When I got there, I asked him about the angel, and he lit up. *I did it! He said. He can't hurt anyone again. I stopped him from hurting them.* When I asked him who he was talking about, he said, *The policeman. He can't hurt anyone anymore.* He just kept repeating that. Then he asked to see the doctor. He wanted to tell her how he'd done just what she'd told him to do."

I shook my head. "I don't know, Greg. It's so far removed. Even if someone wanted to kill Tompkins, convincing a delusional man to kill seems unlikely."

"I'm just saying that it's possible. Was Ryan Tompkins hurting his wife? His daughters?"

"No. Like I said before, it sounds like he was overbearing and controlling, but not physically abusive."

"Remember that Mary had an abusive husband herself, that she'd gotten a no-contact order against him," he said. "She had no tolerance for abusive men."

"Right. Mary ran from her ex-husband, changed her name and moved to San Diego." I thought for a moment. "Is he still around?" I asked. "Her ex? Maybe we should talk to him about Mary."

"He died in a boating accident on Lake Washington just a few months after the divorce."

"What kind of accident?" I asked with a very bad feeling in my gut.

"Brian Winters was an avid sailor. He took his sailboat out on a sunny July day, alone with a bottle of scotch. Just as the sun went down, along comes a seventeen-year-old kid, also drunk, going like a bat out of hell. Struck the side of the sailboat, Winters went into the water and drowned."

"Did the kid get charged?"

"Not with murder. Judge ruled the death accidental. Kid got a hand-slap. He's an upstanding college student now."

I stared at Greg in disbelief. "Shit," I said.

"Shit, indeed." Greg replied.

"So, you're thinking that if Mary had something to do with her ex-husband's death maybe she's moved on to killing others?" I asked. "But why?"

"I don't know. I've seen a lot of murder. It's usually personal. It happens when something, some emotion, love maybe, morphs into something else, something twisted, causing a once rational human being to consider murder as the right thing to do."

"Hard to imagine," I said. "When I talked to Courtney today, she told me about some case she'd read about in medical school where a nurse was pulling the plug on terminally ill patients, then trying to resuscitate them, so their families would think she was a hero."

"Yeah. Remember the case in L.A. about eight years ago? Nurse was giving terminally ill patients overdoses of morphine when he decided it was time for them to die. All through the trial, he kept saying that he just wanted to ease their suffering. They were going to die anyway. He believed he was an angel of mercy."

"Mary does look pretty angelic," I said. "that halo of gray curly hair. She's beautiful."

Greg nodded. "Beautiful or not, I need to talk to her. I'll start by putting out a bulletin in the National police database. We might get lucky and find her that way."

"I don't know, Greg. I have a hard time imagining Mary as a killer. Really, she seems very grounded and, well, happy."

Once we'd exhausted the topic, we were awkward with each other, any romantic vibes between us had faded to the point of extinction. Greg left, and I went to bed confused and frustrated. I considered watching another of Professor Bergman's positive psychology lectures, but it was late, and I knew it would probably amp me up. Instead, I turned on the Waves app on my phone, hoping the sound of the surf would lull me to sleep.

CHAPTER TWENTY-TWO

"You don't see things as they are; you see things through the lens of what you think and feel and believe. Perception is reality . . ." Rachel Hollis, *Girl, Wash Your Face.*

Jolted awake by my cellphone's annoying ringtone, I rummaged around under the covers as it blared on, eluding my grasp. Clutching it at last, I squinted at the display, groaned, and hit the green "accept" button.

"Jesus, Nancy, it's seven-thirty on Sunday. Just because you can't sleep."

"Sorry, Sorry, but I need to talk to you."

"What's wrong?"

"I think someone's following me."

I sat up and the dogs stirred from their beds, scratching and stretching and then bounded to the back door to be let out. I followed them with the phone pressed to my ear.

"Wait, what?" I said to Nancy. "You think someone's following you? Have you seen someone? Explain."

"Okay," she said. "Last week I noticed a woman outside the studio. You know, just standing in the doorway at the little shop next door, talking into her phone, but watching through the window. I didn't think much of it. I mean, that's why I put up blinds. I like the natural light, but no one likes to be watched during yoga. Well, not everyone does."

"Go on," I said.

"Then I saw her, or someone, the other night when I was at the studio late, going through some new poses after class. I heard the outer door open, and I figured someone had forgotten something and came back to get it. No one answered when I called out, and when I poked my head out the door, I saw someone dashing around the corner, almost running."

"Weird." I agreed.

"Yesterday I had coffee at the Fuel just a few blocks from my place, like I often do, and as I walked home, I had the distinct feeling that I was being followed."

"Did you see anyone or are you just being paranoid?"

"Yeah, that's what I thought. Just paranoid. Later, when I walked over to get some takeout Thai from that place on Fremont, I had the same creepy feeling again, but I didn't see anyone."

"Okay," I said, getting a bad feeling in my own gut.

"Here's the really creepy thing." She said. "Last night, I went to bed early and I was half asleep when I distinctly heard the back gate open and close. I jumped up to look out my window and saw a car driving off down the alley."

"Shit," I said. But I didn't know what to think. I needed some coffee. I put the phone on speaker while I turned on the Salton's espresso machine.

"Did you see anyone in your yard?" I asked.

"No." Nancy said. "But just now, when I was heading out for my morning walk to Fuel, I found a package at my back door, a gift package with coffee and a cup wrapped in cellophane. No note, nothing. Weird, right?"

"Yeah. Weird. You should throw it away. The coffee, I mean."

"It's that blend I like from Common Grounds, oh, and a bottle of my favorite vanilla syrup." I could hear Nancy unwrapping the cellophane. "This is weird," she said. "You sure you didn't send it?"

"Of course not, why?"

"The cup says *Life is better with Sisters*."

The knot in my stomach twisted with the kind of intuitive bad feeling that needs to be recognized and trusted.

"It was probably Heather," Nancy said. "You know how Heather and I always pretended to be sisters growing up? I'll give her a call."

"Seems like a stretch." I said. "Are you even in touch with each other these days?"

"A little. We send Christmas cards, occasionally a birthday gift if we find something perfect."

"Your birthday isn't until February."

"Yeah."

"Nancy? Maybe you should come and stay with me and Pooch. There's plenty of room."

After a long pause, she replied, "Thanks Ann, that's tempting, but not necessary. I feel better just talking about it. I'm probably overreacting. I'll let you know if it happens again. And I'll let you know what Heather says."

"Okay," I said, thinking this is so not okay, trying not to overreact.

"Ann?"

"Sorry. What?"

"I asked about your house," she said. "Any bites?"

"Oh geez, I can't believe I didn't tell you. There's been so much going on. I have an offer! Pretty close to a done deal. Full price, contingent on inspection."

"Wow, that's great. Now what? You looking for another house?" she asked.

"No. Not yet. The whole thing has been emotional. I actually started crying when I walked through the house yesterday."

"Of course, it's emotional," she agreed. "I'd be surprised if you didn't cry. I mean, even you – the quintessential ice maiden – has some feelings."

"Hey! Who are you calling an ice maiden? Just because I don't cry over every little thing doesn't mean I'm emotionally broken. I'm just tough. I've always had to be tough."

"Yes, you have," Nancy agreed.

I changed the subject to avoid the emotions aroused by Nancy's empathy.

"How are you doing, Nance? I mean, otherwise."

"Pretty good. The yoga classes are going well, and I've started taking a training for teaching mindfulness."

"Ah yes, mindfulness," I said. "Everyone is into that now. I imagine it could be quite lucrative."

"Yeah, well, that's not my motivation," she replied. "That reminds me, how's the happiness class going?"

"It's over. The last few classes were cancelled," I said. "The teacher had a family medical emergency."

"That's too bad."

"Yeah. And, Nance, promise to call me if anything else happens, okay?"

"I promise," she replied.

"And let me know if Heather sent that gift."

"Will do."

I took the dogs for a long walk in the Arboretum for a change of scene while I worried about Nancy. Was she in danger? If Mary had had something to do with the happiness murders, as I'd come to think of them, she couldn't be here stalking Nancy. Of course, I knew Mary had lied about where she'd gone and could be anywhere. I thought about calling Greg. We were connected by the investigation into these deaths but also at the beginning of a dating relationship. It felt tricky. I didn't want him to think I was needy, the kind of person who couldn't handle things on my own. Instead, I decided to watch another positive psychology lecture when I got back to the Salton's. Pleased that Dr. Bergman had agreed to meet with me next week, I'd planned to be as familiar as possible with his work. After watching the lecture, I felt better, like lots of things were possible – maybe I could find a new house or maybe I could find a new job, or travel, or somehow combine the two. I believed I could move forward in any way I chose. These lectures seemed to help me think in a new way. I'd even convinced myself that I didn't need to worry about Nancy.

* * *

On Monday afternoon, in the middle of an education lab meeting, my phone vibrated with a series of texts, a call, and a voicemail. We had a strict policy against cell phones during meetings, so I ignored them as best I could. As soon as Neil finished his report on disparities in access to IB and AP classes in high schools around the state, I dashed out of the meeting and into my cubicle to see who'd been sending me all those communiqués. What the hell? Victor! The texts were just some variation of please call me as soon as possible. It's important. I steeled myself to push the button on the voicemail. I didn't want to hear his voice. Deep breath. Go!

Ann, It's Victor. I know I'm the last person you want to hear from, but it's extremely important that we talk. I think your sister is in danger. There's a persistent spirit trying to get through, I'm seeing water, drowning.

Oh my God. The stalker! Nancy needs my help. I stared at the phone for a while then decided to call Nancy. I couldn't do it from my cubicle where my voice would carry and everyone within earshot would be listening. I took the stairs down, left the building and found an empty bench outside of Starbucks. When my call went straight to voicemail, I looked at my watch. Damn. Nancy must be in the middle of her four o'clock yoga class. I took a few deep breaths, pressed the *recent calls* icon, then held my breath, waiting for Victor to answer. He picked up almost immediately.

"Ann. Thanks for calling me back," he said, his voice stirring something in me I didn't want disturbed. He continued, "You know I wouldn't call if it wasn't important."

"I know."

"I'm getting very strong signals from a persistent spirit. I've been shown water, drowning, a woman. Also, the name Nancy is appearing, there's fear around it. Can you tell me if something is going on? Nancy won't return my calls."

"Really?" I asked.

"Yes, really. This is serious. Life and death. You know how these things work."

"I do," I said, wishing wholeheartedly that I did not. "What should I do?"

Victor suggested that we meet as soon as possible at his office, try to find the connection between this persistent spirit and Nancy.

I went back to the office and finished up for the day. There were no deadlines that couldn't wait. On the drive to Victor's office, I tried thinking about this in a new way, using the skills

I'd learned from the positive psychology lectures. What questions could I ask about this encounter to frame it in a new way? First: Could Victor help me protect Nancy? Yes. Also, if this spirit was connected to the happiness murders somehow, could Victor help solve them? That also seemed likely. He'd done it before.

I drove to Capitol Hill thinking about the proximity of Victor's office to the Salton's house. I'd thought of that when I'd first moved into this neighborhood but had been successful in pushing it to the back of my brain since then. More compartmentalizing. I was a master at it! A moving truck blocked access to the parking spaces in front of the old Victorian which now housed several offices, including Victor's. Frustrated, I drove around until I found a spot around the corner and down three blocks. I walked past the movers carrying out what looked like dental chairs, sinks and equipment. Looked like the teeth whitening business had gone belly up. The front porch seemed less welcoming than I remembered—no pots overflowing with flowers, the paint a little worn in places. Still, the inside hallway was bright and well-lit. There at the top of the stairs, the end of the hallway, the sign, Victor Lloyd, Psychic Medium, made me smile, the absurdity of hanging out your shingle as someone who talks to dead people. Yet, here I am.

I pushed open the heavy door and entered. As I stood in the entry alcove and looked at the familiar artifacts – three marble horses set on the wooden table, the vase of red flowers – I felt a shudder of the past rushing back. Just breathe, I told myself. Return to the breath. I heard faint voices from behind the closed shoji screen, Victor's voice and a woman's. I couldn't make out their words, so I sat down in the small wooden chair to wait. More time to breathe or consider my questions. I couldn't sit still, so I stepped out into the hall to leave Nancy another voicemail without disturbing Victor. When Victor's door opened and a woman brushed past me and headed down the stairs, I watched her go, all flowing gray hair, loose flaring black slacks and heavy ankle boots. A purple wool jacket, more like a blanket/wrap kind of outer garment with one big wooden button and a multi-colored scarf finished off her ensemble. I smiled. She looked familiar. I didn't know her personally, but I'd seen this type of late middle-aged woman frequently in my new neighborhood. The liberal earth mother I called them. *Your time will come*, that little voice reminded me.

Back in Victor's entry hall, with the screen now open, I could see Victor at his huge antique oak desk framed by the bay window facing the street. He clicked away at his computer, deep in thought. Only when I slid the screen all the way open and said, *knock, knock*, did he look up. He did not smile. He just fixed me with those gray eyes that always pulled me in. I met his gaze but looked away first. I didn't want to play this game, or any game, with Victor.

"Hi Victor."

"Ann."

"I'm here and I want to hear everything you have to tell me about this persistent spirit, but I don't have any interest in getting involved in the conjuring of said spirit. Okay?"

He smiled, shrugged. "I've missed you, Ann."

"Don't," I said.

"I just mean that I've missed your cynicism, your bullheadedness. Here you are."

"Here we are back to where we began. You getting messages about my sister and all. Tell me what you've got."

"Like I said over the phone, something about this spirit feels like a warning for Nancy. I need more information from you to make sense of it."

"Tell me what you're getting."

"I've been shown water, a lake or a pool. I've felt intense pain at the back of my head, like being hit with a hard object, falling into the water, going under, feeling heavy, unable to get back up."

"I suppose you read about my friend Alex, how her boss, partner at Turnbull, Proctor and Samson, drowned in his hot tub?"

Victor took a moment to respond. "The lawyer," he said. "Yeah, I read about that. Had no idea you were friends."

That struck me. I guess I never mentioned Alex to Victor. Of course, it had been less than a year since we'd reconnected, and just over six months since I'd last seen Victor. So many things had happened in that time. He'd started and then finished dating my sister. I'd sold my house. We'd both moved on. Hadn't we?

"Ann?"

"Sorry. Distracted. Where were we?"

"You were telling me that your friend Alex's boss drowned in his hot tub under suspicious circumstances. Like being hit on the head after having had too much to drink and going under."

"There's never been any suggestion that Matt Downey was hit on the head. But Mr. Clark, he had blunt force trauma to the back of his head, possibly from hitting the dock as he fell in."

"Mr. Clark?"

"Mr. Clark is the father of another woman in a class I'm taking."

"What class?" he asked.

"It's a happiness class," I said, straight-faced.

Victor raised his eyebrows. "You're taking a *happiness* class?" He suppressed a smile.

"Look, Victor, the only reason I'm here is because I'm afraid for Nancy. I'm afraid that your warning might be connected to the shit that's happening to people in my happiness class."

"What's the shit?"

"Two people have died under suspicious circumstances and one was definitely murdered."

"These are people in your class? No these are people connected to people in your class."

"Right. These are the people who were making these women unhappy. Matt Downey was making Alex's work life miserable, and Robert Clark had dementia. His daughter, Emily, in my class, was his caregiver. Life with him was very difficult for her, as you can imagine. He wandered away in the middle of the night and drowned in Lake Union. Again, suspicious."

"And the murder?" he asked.

"The husband of woman in my class, Jennifer Tompkins, was a cop killed by a crazy man."

"The police officer who was stabbed in the University District?" I nodded.

"I read about that too." Victor sat quietly for a moment with his thoughts and his own ghosts, or whatever happened when he got that slightly scary look on his face.

After a while, he said, "Nancy could be in danger because she's making your life miserable. Is Nancy making your life miserable somehow?"

"No, she's not." I said, squirming a little under his gaze. "Not now, anyway." I could see the understanding dawning in his eyes. "Okay, I'll admit that I was pretty miserable when you two were dating. I believe I mentioned that in one of the happiness classes, too." I felt the anger and then the fear. Shook my head. "Oh, shit!"

Victor sat back in his chair, studied my face for a moment, then shook his head. "I see. You were miserable when she and I were dating. That's why she ended it, right? I should have known. It felt like things were going great and then boom, Nancy says she doesn't want to see me anymore. That was you, right? You told Nancy you didn't want her to see me." Victor stood up and turned his back to me, looking out the bay window facing the front garden. When he turned around to look at me again, I could see the sadness in his eyes.

"Let's get back to the reason I'm here," I said. "Some persistent spirit is using you to warn Nancy. Is that how you see it?"

"Yes, but it would be a whole lot clearer if Nancy would work with me. I'm more likely to get something directly through Nancy, or her spirit guides."

Ugh. Spirit guides. Here was Victor using this whole psychic medium vocabulary that I'd been happy to erase from my personal lexicon.

"Okay, so you want me to call Nancy? Get her to come in here and work with you to channel this spirit?"

Victor again fixed me with those eyes. "I think that would be best, yes."

"Let's call her now," I suggested, looking at my watch. "She should be finished with her afternoon yoga class. We'll put her on speaker."

Victor nodded, and I hit Nancy's number on my phone and set it on the table between Victor and me. We listened as it rang. On ring five, the voicemail clicked on and I left a message: "Nancy, it's Ann. I'm here at Victor's office and there's something we need to talk with you about. Can you give me a call back as soon as you get this?"

Victor and I sat staring at my cell phone for a while. I avoided his eyes and willed the phone to ring, for Nancy to call back. After several uncomfortable minutes, I picked up the phone, put it back in my bag and stood up to leave.

"I'll have Nancy call you as soon as I talk with her."

"Fine." Neither of us said goodbye.

Back out in the street, I called Nancy again. Direct to voicemail. I looked up at Victor's second floor window and saw his backlit silhouette large and looming. Something about it gave me the shivers, a premonition of something I didn't want to see.

CHAPTER TWENTY-THREE

"Happiness is other people: studies show that good social relationships are the strongest predictor of a happy life." – Ruth Whippman, author of *America the Anxious: How Our Pursuit of Happiness is Creating a Nation of Nervous Wrecks*.

I needed a plan. I also needed to see Nancy and make sure she was okay. Since she wasn't answering her phone, I figured she might be teaching the six o'clock yoga class. I'd get the dogs from daycare, get them fed and head over there. Traffic going west was jammed, as usual at rush hour. I made it over the University Bridge okay, but it took me fifteen minutes just to make the left turn onto fortieth and past the Google offices on Lake Union. The techies were all filing out of their cubicles and a traffic cop was stopping every westbound car to let two cars out of the parking garage. By the time I made the turn off Fremont Avenue onto the side street and into the alley behind Nancy's apartment, my nerves were shattered. I pulled my car behind Nancy's little blue Honda, hoping she was at home. When she didn't answer the doorbell, I let myself in with the key she'd given me just in case.

"Nancy? Anybody home?" The pendant light above the kitchen sink was on and I looked around briefly—registering nothing amiss—before moving through to the dining/living room. I flipped on the wall switch and jumped when I heard a thump behind the sofa. "Hello?" I moved toward the sound and exhaled when I saw the huge orange tabby stretching there having hopped off his make-shift bed – a fluffy yellow towel placed on top of the radiator under the window. The cat rubbed up against my legs before slinking off into the kitchen, in hopes that I would prove to be a new food source. Surprised that Nancy had adopted a cat without mentioning it, I glanced around the neat room, smiled at the familiar minimalist decor, and called up the stairs.

"Nance? You up there?"

I ascended the stairs, getting that empty house vibe and figuring Nancy was either out for dinner or at the yoga studio. I peeked into the bedroom, bed made, no clothes on the floor. In her office everything was in order, only her closed laptop and a lime green vase of flowers on the desk. The subtle fragrance of creamy freesia sweetened the air. The bathroom too was sparkling and empty. I pulled the shower curtain aside just to check for Tony Perkins before heading back down the stairs. The tabby jumped onto the kitchen counter and began purring when I stroked his silky fur.

"What's your name? I asked, checking his collar for a tag. *Harvey* was etched into the round metal disc hanging from his black collar decorated with a row of cherry red hearts. It included a phone number that was not Nancy's. She must be cat-sitting, I deduced.

"Well Harvey, where's Nancy?" The cat bumped his big head under my hand then shined his emerald eyes at me before hopping off the counter and rubbing up against my legs again. "What a whore you are, Harvey. I am not here to feed you." I looked down and saw a small ceramic bowl half-full of kibble and another filled with water. I picked it up and refilled it with fresh water before picking up the pad of paper on the counter and writing a note. *Nancy—been trying to get a hold of you. Checking the yoga studio now. Call me if you see this before you see me, okay? — Ann*

I locked up and got into my car, trying to remember the exact location of the yoga studio. I knew it was close, within walking distance for sure. Rather than wandering aimlessly I pulled out my phone and typed *yoga* into Google Maps. *Fremont Power Yoga* came up immediately with an address on Fremont Avenue, just a few blocks north. I should have walked but the rain and dark put me off. I drove to the studio instead and then drove around for five minutes trying to find a parking place on the street with no luck. Out of desperation I pulled into the small parking lot at the market across the street, hoping that the *Fremont Market Parking Only—Violators will be Towed!* sign didn't mean me. The homeless guy selling *Real Change* newspapers made eye contact and I handed him two dollars, hoping that some good karma would come of it.

I crossed the street and entered the yoga studio where a young woman sat at the front desk behind a sign that read, *Silence please, Class is in session!* and below that, *Please silence your cell phones!*

"Is Nancy Dexter teaching the six o'clock class?" I whispered. "I'm her sister."

The woman looked me up and down and nodded, "Class is over in ten minutes," she said quietly. "You're welcome to wait here until then."

"Sure." I sat down on a narrow wooden bench against one wall and looked around. Long butterscotch velvet draperies separated the class from the entryway and pooled at the floor. I heard Nancy's muffled voice but couldn't discern her words. I took out my phone to silence it and to check emails. Then I scrolled through my text message history with Greg. When the draperies opened, I watched the class participants, mostly women, roll up their mats and pile them into a large wooden bin at the back of the room. I stood, hovering around the entrance until most of the women had filed past me and out the door. Nancy was at the front of the room talking to a woman. I did a double take.

"Winkie! What are you doing here?"

She turned and smiled at me. "Hi Ann! I'm here trying out this class, hoping to get back into a regular yoga practice now that Mary is gone and no longer teaching. I've been taking classes all over the Seattle for the past few days. This class has over twenty great Yelp reviews and I can see why. Nancy is an amazing instructor."

"Nancy is my sister." I said, and Winkie looked from Nancy to me. "Really? I had no idea. I do see a bit of a family resemblance, now that you mention it."

"So, six degrees of separation, right?" Winkie said.

Nancy smiled at Winkie and gave me a look.

"I was just asking Nancy about the details, you know, whether I need to sign up monthly, or if there's a drop-in policy. I don't want to take up too much of her time."

Nancy turned to me. "What a nice surprise to see you, Ann. I'll be with you in a moment." She turned her attention back to Winkie and I stepped away, thinking about coincidence. When I heard Winkie thank Nancy, I followed her across the room where she placed her yoga mat into the bin.

"Your sister is lovely, Ann. Such a good teacher." Winkie looked more serene than I'd ever seen her. Maybe the yoga had helped. "Any news about Mary?" she asked.

"Still MIA," I said. I didn't want to talk about the rest of it. Not now.

"See you later," Winkie said, heading out the door.

I looked back to Nancy as she gathered her things at the front of the class and walked my way.

"You know Winkie, I guess?" Nancy asked. "Nice lady, interesting name." She pulled a goofy face and I laughed.

"Right?"

"Winkie is in my happiness class."

"Oh, right. Anyway, what's up? You never show up at my classes. In fact, you've only been to my apartment one other time. Something wrong?"

"I've been trying to get a hold of you. Oh, Nancy!" I wrapped my arms around her and held on tight.

"Hey, hey, what *is* wrong?" She pulled back to look at my face, her hands on my shoulders. "Let's go back to my place where we can talk. I must feed Harvey. Is that okay with you?"

"Sure." I said, relieved that she wanted to talk to me. "I met Harvey earlier, by the way. I stopped by your place to see if you were home before coming over here." Just changing the subject calmed my emotions. Compartmentalizing. Again. It's a pretty good coping strategy.

"Really?" Nancy raised her eyebrows at me and took her jacket from the peg in the closet next to the bin for yoga mats. After she said goodbye to the woman at the front desk, we walked out of the studio and across the street to my car.

"You can't park in the Fremont Market parking lot! People get towed from there all the time. I tell the people in my classes to never park there, to move their cars anywhere else." she said.

I pulled out my keys and bleeped the doors open. "Luckily, I wasn't here very long."

We got into the car and Nancy asked, "How'd you like Harvey? Isn't he a sweetie?

"Yes, he is. But, Nancy, I've been trying to call you. Why aren't you answering my calls or my emails or my texts?"

"Oh, sorry. I've imposed a twenty-four-hour ban on technology. No looking at devices. I think it's healthy to do that regularly, don't you?"

"No! I mean, yes to social media, but your phone? I needed to talk with you and got plenty worried when you didn't answer. You called me *yesterday* when you were afraid you were being followed, remember? Then you just dropped off the radar. No, not a good idea. You could have called to tell me."

"But then I would have had to use my phone." I heard the amusement in her voice, and it made me angry.

"It's not funny! There's a lot of bad stuff happening and I'm worried about you." I pulled into the driveway and walked with Nancy to her back door.

"You left all the lights on!" She said, ignoring my comment while fumbling for her keys.

"Yeah," I said. "More importantly, I saw Victor this afternoon. We left you a message earlier today."

"Victor! What has Victor got to do with anything?"

Nancy stood with her hand on the doorknob looking at me wide-eyed. As soon as we walked through the door Harvey made a beeline to Nancy, the same routine he gave me earlier, rubbing against her legs, jumping up onto the counter. Nancy opened a can of Fancy Feast and placed it on the floor. She remained quiet until she opened her fridge.

"If we're going to talk about Victor, we're going to need some wine." She said, pulling out a bottle of Albariño and rummaging around a drawer for a corkscrew.

"We are." I agreed, taking two wine glasses off the open shelves next to her sink.

"I have some lentil soup I made earlier and some bread. You hungry?"

"I'll start with the wine."

Nancy poured the wine into the glasses, handed me one and sat at the kitchen table. I sat across from her. "Okay, Victor," she said, taking a sip. "Shoot."

"Right." I told her about how Victor had called me, told me about the persistent spirit, the way that Matt Downey and Robert Clark had died. Then I told her about Ryan Tompkins's murder, the homeless guy, the angel doctor. I ended by telling her about Mary, how she'd been a therapist who'd seen Tompkins' murderer, how her brother didn't have a medical emergency, how her ex-husband had died.

"Mary, the happiness teacher?" Nancy asked. "You think she's been killing these people? That I might be her next victim? That's why Victor has been getting warnings?

"Well, I . . . "

"But why me?" she asked, wide-eyed.

"Maybe she thinks you've been making my life miserable," I said. "I may have mentioned something about you and Victor in that class."

Nancy took a big gulp of her wine. We sat in silence for a while.

"This is a lot to take in, Ann."

"I know, and I am so sorry. I know the police officer working this case, Greg Costello. I'm going to call him, tell him about Victor's concern. He's the best. I know we can protect you."

"You think this police officer is going to believe in Victor's spirit warnings?" she asked.

"I think he'll take the threat to you seriously," I replied. "I'll tell him how you've been followed, see if he can get someone to watch out for you."

"Really? You think the police department has the resources to send bodyguards out whenever someone thinks they're being followed."

"Greg will find a way."

"Greg?"

"Detective Costello. I've gotten to know him over the past couple of weeks. From the murder investigations but also on a more, uh, personal basis," I said, feeling the heat in my face. "He lives in my neighborhood."

"Okay. You're on a first-name basis with this homicide detective. Good. You'll call him." I nodded.

"Let's get back to Victor," she said, refilling our wine glasses. "Do I have to see him in person? Can't he call up this spirit without me?"

"No." I said. "So, yes. You should see him in person. I know it won't be easy. I had a rough time myself, seeing him today." I lifted my glass for emphasis. "Even though I'm so over him."

Nancy touched her glass to mine and kept her eyes on mine. "Here's to Victor being wrong this time." We sipped our wine.

"Will you come with me?" She asked.

"No. I can't. You'll be fine on your own," I said. "You should call him to set it up."

"Now?" Nancy asked.

"Yes. You go ahead and call. I'll heat up the soup. We need to eat something. No more wine on an empty stomach."

"Okay." Nancy picked up her cell and walked through to the living room. I tried not to eavesdrop. After a few minutes, she appeared in the doorway. "Done," she said. "Four o'clock tomorrow."

"Thanks," I said.

Nancy nodded, took a loaf of Macrina Cassera bread from the counter, slipped it from its brown paper sleeve, sliced a few pieces and handed me one, along with the butter bell she always kept filled with a special French butter. I slathered it onto the bread and took a healthy bite.

"Mmmm."

"Good, right?" she asked. "Do you know that Leslie Mackey, the owner of Macrina, first tasted this bread in Italy? She tracked down the recipe from a bakery there and has been baking it here in Seattle ever since. She's named it *cassera* which means *house bread* because it's her favorite."

I smiled. "How do you know that little tidbit?" I asked.

"I saw her on a cooking show," Nancy replied.

"Of course," I said. Unlike me, Nancy had always loved cooking, and cooking shows. She ladled up the soup and we ate quietly, each with our own thoughts. Although the bread, wine and the warm fragrance of homemade lentil soup had a calming effect, the worry persisted.

"Why don't you come and stay with me tonight?" I suggested. "You know there's plenty of room, and I have these two great guard dogs. No intruder would get past Doozy." I forced a laugh.

She thought about it. "No, I don't think so. Harvey's been alone all day, and I have an early morning yoga class. I don't want to have to drive from Capitol Hill at five-thirty a.m."

"I'd stay here except I know I can't leave Doozy overnight."

"Don't worry. I'll come straight to your house to de-brief after I meet Victor tomorrow. I'll be extra careful," she said. "But hey, didn't you say that Mary Summers packed up and left town? She can't hurt me if she's no longer in Seattle."

"True," I said, without much conviction. "Promise to keep your phone on and call me immediately if anything strange happens."

"I will," she promised.

We said our goodbyes and I left feeling just as worried as I had been earlier. Now I had to call Greg and find a way to protect Nancy.

CHAPTER TWENTY-FOUR

"Lasting happiness requires building upon your strengths, persevering, and being gracious with yourself and others—it's really not about personal achievements or experiencing fleeting, positive thoughts and feelings." Zelana Montminy, Mindbodygreen: *Why Resilience Is The Key to Lasting Happiness + How to Cultivate It,*

Greg called me back while I was in bed and watching another positive psychology lecture on my laptop. The lectures calmed me. Also, I wanted to get myself into the right frame of mind for my appointment with Dr. Bergman tomorrow morning. I paused the lecture with a power point slide frozen on the screen defining resilience: *resilient individuals take initiative and responsibility, have confidence, can forgive, and forget. Resilience leads to optimism and hope.*

"What's up?" Greg asked. "You sounded worried on your voicemail."

I gave Greg the most concise version of what was going on with my sister and he seemed concerned. When I told him about Victor, however, the silence on the other end of the line was deafening.

"Greg?"

"I heard what you said, Ann, I'm just trying to get a grip on it. You're telling me that a psychic medium you know has been visited by spirits who say your sister is in danger. Did I get that right?"

"I know it sounds crazy, but I know Victor very well. It's a long story I'll share with you another time. For now, can you just suspend disbelief for a while and consider that Victor knows what he's talking about? If Victor is getting messages, I've got to take them seriously. We have a history."

"Okay," he said. "There's no way I can get anyone over to watch your sister's house tonight. I'll see what I can do as soon as I can."

"Thanks," I said, glancing at my computer screen. "Greg, do you have any leads on Mary yet? Has she been spotted anywhere outside of Seattle?"

"Nothing yet," he replied. "I'll let you know as soon as I do."

We hung up and I clicked off the positive psychology lecture with thoughts of resilience swirling around my brain. I picked up my gratitude journal and jotted down the five things I am grateful for today: my sister Nancy, my developing relationship with Greg, the sale of my house, the great place I'm living in right now, and my job. Before turning out the light, I called Nancy just to hear her voice, to reassure myself that she was safe.

"I'm fine, Ann. Go to sleep," she'd said. "I have to get up really early tomorrow, remember?"

First thing in the morning, I called Nancy again. When the phone rang and rang, I remembered that she was, once again, teaching a yoga class when I wanted to talk with her. Just to be sure she was okay, I called the studio. Yes, whoever answered the phone told me, Nancy had taught the 6:00 a.m. yoga class and had left with someone to get coffee. She wasn't due back until around 11:30.

"She left with someone?" I'd asked. "Was it someone from the class?"

"No. Someone came in to meet her after class," the woman said, and my heart thumped.

"Was it a woman with beautiful gray hair?" I asked, thinking that would be the way to describe Mary.

"No, it was a man. Seemed nice," she said. "I have to go. The next class is starting." She hung up and left me speechless. A man? Nancy hadn't mentioned anyone new. I called Victor to see if they'd changed their meeting time but went straight to voicemail. I'd call again after my meeting with Dr. Bergman.

Hans Bergman had an office at the University of Washington in the Psychology Department in Guthrie Hall, Annex 2. I had to look up a map of the enormous campus to find his office, hoping it was in one of the old brick buildings in the quad. No such luck. Guthrie Hall was on the perimeter of the campus, just off Fifteenth Avenue. I loved to visit the campus at any time of year, but especially in the early spring when the cherry trees were blooming, and gusts of wind sent showers of pink and white perfumed blossoms swirling to the ground. The campus was still beautiful now, just different. I parked in the underground garage and walked through the quad anyway. On this late November day, the cherry trees stood cold and bleak, their branches as gray as the wet cement beneath my feet, their buds held tightly shut against the sleet collecting there.

Dr. Bergman's office was on the second floor of the old building. When I arrived, the door was closed, and a sign read *Advising in Session,* so I sat down on the old wooden chair in the hallway to wait. The smells of dusty books and damp wool combined with the steady flow of students rushing past on their way to class sent me right back to my own days in college. I felt my anxiety ratchet up a notch and wondered randomly if any of these psychologists studied the effect of academic buildings on stress and anxiety. The specific odors here had transported me back to Northwestern and my days as a journalism student. To relieve my anxiety, I thought about the positive psychology lectures I'd seen, how I'd come to admire Dr. Bergman's work, how he advocated for more research on positive psychology, like the qualities of resilience I'd learned about last night.

Dr. Bergman's door opened at exactly ten o'clock, the time of our appointment. A young woman emerged looking upset. She nearly tripped over my chair in her hurry to get away. I watched her dash down the hall, her boots clicking on the hardwood floor, the sound receding as she descended the stairs. Wondering why his student didn't look particularly happy, I gathered my courage and knocked on the half-open door while peeking in at Dr. Bergman. The man smiled and rose from his chair – nothing scary about him at all. His brown eyes radiated warmth behind his dark-rimmed glasses, and he looked delighted to see me. I'd figured his age at around forty-five, but he looked older somehow, flecks of premature gray highlighted his thick, dark brown curly hair. He had a lean frame, long loose limbs, and large feet which I noticed when he stepped from behind his desk. He wore red Chucks and a forest green V-neck sweater. What a lovely Christmas gift he'd make for someone I thought, then tucked that idea away as I noticed his wedding band and the photo of him with his family – beautiful wife and two adorable children.

"Ann Dexter, yes?"

"Yes."

He shook my hand. His was large and dry and warm.

"Your student didn't look very happy," I said.

"Oh, Nora is terribly upset that she got a B on her latest paper. These days Bs feel like failure to overachieving students. Grade inflation is alive and well," he shrugged.

"I guess she didn't convince you to change it."

"Of course not. Please, sit down." He nodded to the only other chair in the room, the one recently vacated by the worried young woman. I sat while he wheeled his executive chair out from behind the desk and sat facing me, clasping his hands in his lap, and leaning toward me, relaxed.

"How can I help you? You're writing an article for the Seattle Times about positive psychology? Is that right?"

"I am." I said, with an enthusiastic smile I could not suppress. "I came across your lectures online and have been watching them over the past few days. I love what you have to say about focusing on positive factors, healthy psychological traits, rather than the old disease model where psychologists look at what's wrong with the person and treat that."

He nodded at me, looking pleased.

"I watched your lecture on resilience last night and thought it was brilliant!" I said. "I've actually started keeping a gratitude journal."

"That's a great start." He said. "You're writing about the lectures in *The Seattle Times*? Or writing about positive psychology generally?" he asked.

"I'm not sure. I have a few questions."

"Sure," he said. "Where would you like to begin? If you're watching my lectures, you know the basics of my focus. Is there something specific you'd like to ask me about?"

"Yes," I said, pulling out the pad in which I'd been taking notes on his lectures. "I'd like to begin with some background about you, how you decided to focus on positive psychology when you were a grad student at Stanford."

"Okay," he said, launching into the story I'd already heard online about how he found himself at Stanford, successful in school, in sports, in his social life. Yet he was unhappy. He decided to focus on positive psychology to find out how he could become happier.

I asked him about the teacher he described as his mentor. "Yes, yes, she is quite an inspiration for me. I highly recommend that you read her book," he said.

I was flipping through my notes when he added, "It seems like you've done quite a lot of research on me. Why don't you write up your article and email it to me and I'll look it over?"

"Okay," I replied, thinking I was about to be dismissed and wondering how to broach the subject of Mary. "Actually, there's something else I'd like to ask you about."

"Sure. Go ahead."

"I've been taking a class on happiness with Mary Summers. I think you know her?"

Without missing a beat, he said, "Yes, I know Mary. How are you enjoying her class?"

"Honestly, there are aspects of the class that I've liked, but some of it seems a little shallow, kind of silly. Are you familiar with laughter yoga?"

Dr. Bergman let out a large belly laugh, and I smiled. When he continued laughing, it was contagious, and I laughed too.

"It works though, right?" he asked, still grinning.

"Yes, but only temporarily. Your approach makes more sense to me: re-framing questions, focusing on positive characteristics, understanding that happiness is a process, not something one can accomplish in a couple of days," I said.

"Yes, that's true. That's why I like the way Mary planned to present several happiness methods and theories in her class. Of course, many of those, like laughter yoga, come from the self-help arena, but I believe Mary also planned on sharing some of my material in her class, presenting the science-based research as well. That is, she asked me for permission to do so when she came to see me."

"I think she was planning to use one of your lectures in her last class. The problem is, Mary left Seattle last week and cancelled the remaining classes."

Dr. Bergman frowned. "Why did she cancel the classes?" he asked.

"She said her brother had a medical emergency."

"That's unfortunate," he replied. "Is there some way you think I can help?"

"I don't know. You see, terrible things have happened to three people in Mary's class, the police are involved, and it looks like Mary chose to run off rather than cooperate."

"What terrible things?"

"Two people connected to individuals in Mary's happiness class have died under suspicious circumstances and one was murdered."

Dr. Bergman's eyes widened with a flash of shock, then narrowed as he shook his head and rubbed his jaw. "I am so sorry to hear this. You said Mary's brother had a medical emergency. It would be natural for her to go to him. That's not running off."

"Apparently her brother is in perfect health and hasn't seen Mary in forty years."

He shook his head, looking sad. "Again, how do you think I can help? I have not seen or spoken with Mary since early in the Fall. We are not close friends, though I've known her professionally for several years. I knew her when she was Mary Winters, when she practiced here in Seattle."

"Did you know her husband?"

Dr. Bergman ran his index finger around the collar of his shirt, like it had suddenly become too tight. "I'm sorry, Ms. Dexter, I don't feel comfortable with the way this conversation has shifted." He said. "Are you writing an article on positive psychology or about Mary Summer's disappearance?"

"I'm not writing about Mary's disappearance." I said. "But I'd like to help find her. I believe the police need to question her."

"Do the police believe Mary had something to do with these deaths?"

I paused, weighing my words before responding.

"Do you?" He asked.

When I didn't reply, he continued, "No. I cannot believe this. I know Mary well enough to know that when she's faced with unpleasantness, when she is frightened, her tendency is to run away."

"Like she ran from her husband after her divorce," I suggested.

"Yes."

"Did you know her husband died in a boating accident shortly after that?"

"I did. No wonder Mary is frightened. These deaths, the police involvement – it must have brought back that painful time for her."

"Do you think Mary is capable of murder?"

"I think this is the wrong question, Ms. Dexter. Perhaps any human being is capable of murder. Another question to ask would be: Why would Mary kill? She is a happiness practitioner. Her goal is to become happier and to help her students, the people around her, to become happier as well."

"Maybe Mary believed that killing these individuals would ultimately make her students happier by eliminating the individuals who were making their lives miserable," I suggested.

"I see. You believe that you understand why these three individuals died. It is a known pathology, *angels of death*." He shook his head. "I'm sure you and the police suspect the wrong person. Mary is kind, loving, and psychologically healthy. I am certain of this. Now, if you'll excuse me. I need to prepare for my next class." He stood, and I collected my things but stayed seated.

"There's one more thing that worries me," I said. "It was a former patient of Mary's who murdered Officer Ryan Tompkins."

"The police officer who was stabbed in the University District?" he asked, sitting down again to face me.

"Yes. He was the husband of someone in the class. Mary had treated him off and on for a couple of years when she worked for Seattle Public Health."

"I'm sure she treated hundreds of individuals suffering from mental illnesses during her tenure there. It's the reason she turned to happiness. She'd had enough of treating psychological diseases. Like me, Mary decided to change her focus to psychological wellness. To happiness."

"Okay. Except that the guy says an angel, the angel *doctor* told him to kill Ryan Tompkins, so he couldn't hurt anyone again."

He shook his head. "The poor soul is delusional."

"Yes," I agreed. We sat with that for a while.

"I'm sorry I can't help you, Ms. Dexter. You might consider asking yourself why you've become involved in this investigation." He looked closely at me, and I almost told him about my sister.

"Perhaps a better question would be, how you can help Mary? Let the police continue their investigation. If there is a psychopath behind these deaths, let's hope the police will soon find whoever it is." He stood, picked up his laptop case and collected some papers from his desk. "I must get to class."

"Thanks for seeing me."

"I know you're here with the best intentions, Ms. Dexter. If you think of anything I can do to help Mary, please let me know."

"I will."

"Also, if you decide to write an article on my work, please email it to me and we can talk again."

I left Guthrie Hall feeling different about Mary. If Dr. Bergman was correct, and Mary was not behind the murders, then who was? I drove back to my office mulling over the things that Dr. Bergman had said. As soon as I pulled into to the *Seattle Times* parking lot, I called Greg.

"Hey," he said, sounding sleepy.

I told him about my conversation with Hans Bergman, emphasizing the man's belief in Mary's innocence and her psychological health.

"If it isn't Mary, then who is it?" I asked. "Have you interviewed everyone in the happiness class yet? Is there anyone you have a hunch or a bad vibe about?"

"We have interviewed all the class members, he said. "No one stands out."

"Can I take a look at the interview notes?" I asked, listening to Greg exhale on the other end of the line.

"No, Ann. You'll just have to trust that we're doing our job here." More silence. "Hey, your sister is fine by the way. I had coffee with her this morning."

"You saw Nancy?"

"You were so worried about her last night that I decided to spend my night parked in front of her house. Just to make sure. I took a nap in my car while she taught that early morning yoga class, then I introduced myself and we had coffee."

Stunned, I didn't know what to say. "That is one of the kindest things anyone has ever done for me," I said. "Thank you."

"Part of the job," he said. "I liked her, by the way. There's a slight physical resemblance between you two. But there's a big difference in your personalities."

"What? She's serene like a Golden Retriever and I'm a Pit Bull?" I suggested.

He chuckled. "I wouldn't have made that exact comparison. I guess you know yourself better than I do."

We agreed to check in with each other with any news about Mary, or if we came up with any other leads.

"Good luck with the psychic." Greg said, following that up with, "Call me if you need me."

I hung up feeling better, reassured that Greg would not let anything happen to Nancy and that, in keeping with my new positive psychology mindset, I might even weather this terrible time and come out stronger and healthier. As I walked into the *Times* building, trudged up the stairs and into my cubicle, I tried to re-focus my mind on my work. Our Education Lab group was planning an event at Town Hall early next year called *Ignite Education*. The idea was that we would invite a few educators to give a five-minute talk about a positive experience they had with schools and learning. I was slogging through the sixty applications we'd received so far and instead of inspiring me, my eyes were glazing over. Most of their stories focused on the value of relationships — between teachers and students, parents, and children, and among everyone involved with schools. Many of the stories were great, they just needed a fresh open mind, which I couldn't offer right now.

All I could think about was the meeting that Nancy had set up with Victor for this afternoon at 4:00. I wondered what would come of it, and how they would handle being in the same room together. Not that I was too worried about that. Mostly I was relieved that I would not be there and hopeful that any spirits Victor might conjure up would have something useful to say. Nancy had promised to stop over to debrief afterwards, and I didn't want to be late. At 4:30, I packed up and headed home, hoping Jeff didn't notice that I'd come in late and left early once again.

CHAPTER TWENTY-FIVE

"Our deepest fear is not that we are inadequate. Our deepest fear is that we are powerful beyond measure." Marianne Williamson, *A Return to Love*, quoted in *Happier*, Tal Ben Shahar.

Nancy was waiting on the front porch when I got home with the dogs.

"That was quick," I said. "You were supposed to text me."

"I did."

Doozy barked and lunged at Nancy. "No Doozy, it's my sister! Sit!" The dog lowered his big head and his tail, gave Nancy one more sniff, then obeyed. After Nancy greeted the dogs in turn, we followed them into the kitchen where they sniffed around for dinner. I poured kibble into two bowls and Nancy filled their large water bowl. Once the dogs were fed, Nancy opened the fridge.

"In the door," I said. Nancy nodded, pulled out the bottle of Pinot Grigio and opened a cabinet looking for two glasses.

"Where are the everyday ones?" She asked, holding up the Waterford crystal.

"Yeah, I know. That's all they've got. I'm trying to be very careful."

I brought out a container of Marcona almonds and poured some into a small wooden bowl. We went into the living room and sat facing each other.

"Okay, spill," I said, just as I would when we were kids, and I knew Nancy had something to tell me about a date or something that had happened at school.

She shook her head and took a sip of the wine. "The whole thing with Victor was very weird," she said. "Just like you said it would be."

"Tell me what happened."

"At first, nothing. That's what was weird. I mean, just being there was strange enough and then Victor couldn't make anything happen. I mean, no spirits showed up."

"You mean, he went through his whole schtick and nothing?"

"At first. It rattled him, like performance anxiety or something." She looked over at me.

I giggled. "Sorry, my bad. Keep going."

"Just as I got up to leave, Victor cried out in pain. He clutched the back of his head and collapsed onto the couch. His breathing was raspy and labored. I totally freaked out. I sat next to him and searched his face. He looked at me but didn't see me – like he was in a trance or something."

"Yeah. I've seen that before."

He said that one of my spirit guides was with us and he asked about the things he'd been shown and how they were connected to me, the head pain, the gasping for breath.

"*Was someone connected to Nancy killed with a blow to the head*? He asked but wasn't getting anything. Then he asked if I was in danger." Nancy shook her head. "This part was scary," she said.

"Tell me."

"He said, *I'm getting the sense that it's someone to the side of you. That usually means a sibling. Is Ann in danger?* And then his face went pale, and he said he was being shown a circle, that usually means a circle of friends."

"Oh geez," I said. "He's just parroting what I've already told him. The circle of friends are the women in my happiness class, and he knows there have been three deaths. Did he tell you anything at all useful?"

"Before he lost the connection, he put his hand over his eye, like he'd had a sudden pain there. He kept opening and closing it, like it hurt, or he had a speck of dust in it. When I asked him about that, he said he'd gotten the image of an eye, felt some clue there, but didn't understand it."

I thought about the eye of God shining down on Ryan Tompkins' casket at St. James Cathedral. "Well, shit," I said. "I'm sorry you had to go through all that hocus pocus with Victor, and for nothing."

"Yeah." Nancy took a sip of wine and shook her head. "It was an interesting experience though. You know Victor is not faking this stuff. It's pretty disconcerting."

"Yes. Victor has a connection with spirits or a different dimension or something. I haven't forgotten how his special power—whatever the hell it is—helped me find you, maybe saved both of our lives if you think about it. It's just that the messages are so vague that it's frustrating."

"And, frightening, don't forget that," she reminded me.

"So how did you leave it with Victor?" I asked.

"He told me to be careful, and that you need to take this warning seriously too. Of course, if he gets anything else, he'll be in touch."

"Great."

"Oh, I almost forgot to tell you," Nancy said. "I met Officer Friendly this morning – Greg?"

I laughed. "I know, he told me."

"I liked him," she said.

"He liked you too," I replied. "Don't get any ideas!" She laughed. "Did Greg tell you that he's got a police officer watching you now?"

"He did. It made me feel a little foolish. I mean, maybe I imagined someone following me. I haven't had that feeling since."

"Better to be cautious," I said, finishing my wine. "Want to get something for dinner?"

"No thanks. I need to get home to Harvey. I'll just heat up some leftovers," she said. "Speaking of leftovers," she said. "Thanksgiving is Thursday. That's just two days from now in case you've forgotten. Have any plans?"

"Nope. You?"

"Well, I've been invited to dinner with some women in my yoga class. None of them has family here and so they rotate hosting Thanksgiving and invite all the other strays they know for a potluck. I'm sure they'd love to have you too."

"Thanks. I'll keep that in mind," I said, thinking that I'd rather have my fingernails pulled out one by one than spend a holiday with a bunch of Nancy's yoga ladies.

"No plans with Greg?"

"No. He has plans with his family in California."

"Well, why don't the two of us go out for Chinese then? I don't particularly like turkey anyway. I'd rather spend the day with you than with several near strangers. We could watch some old Christmas movie. *It's a Wonderful Life* maybe?"

"Maybe." I said. It sure sounded better than any other option I had at this point. "Let's talk about it tomorrow."

After Nancy left, I checked my fridge for anything edible and came up with a couple of eggs and some cheese, so I whipped up an omelet, added a piece of toast and called it dinner. I considered watching another one of Dr. Bergman's lectures but knew that was just my brain's way of avoiding what it really needed to work on. If not Mary, then who? I thought about Dr. Bergman's suggestion as I left his office, that I leave the investigation to the police. I know Greg is competent, but so am I. I know the individuals in the happiness class better than he does. We'd spent five weeks together. All of them had opened in class and talked about their struggles to find happiness. It was Mary's way of creating a cohesive group. I wracked my brain trying to remember if anyone had said something off. Did any of them seem like a psychopath? No.

I had some time, so I dug into the process which had always worked for me. I turned on my laptop and opened the file I'd started on Matt Downey's death, back when the police suspected Alex. I re-read all the notes I'd written on each person I'd interviewed. My methodical process of taking notes and poring over them again and again afterwards often sparked some idea, a bit of a lead to follow. Not tonight. The only real lead was missing, along with Mary Summers. I thought about the physical description Greg had given me for Jacqueline Forte: medium height, long, straight, dark hair, expensively dressed. The description, though generic, didn't match anyone in my happiness class. I had an idea scratching at the back of my mind, but I couldn't see it clearly. Not yet. I needed to speak with Mary Summers. Even though I wanted to believe Dr. Bergman's assertion that Mary was not a killer, I also believed she knew something, something that had made her run.

I opened my browser and went to Mary's website. I clicked on the *Contact Me!* button at the bottom of the page, thinking hard about what to say, and how to say it. I knew it was a long shot, but I remembered Dr. Bergman's question: *How can I help Mary?* So, I composed what I hoped was a persuasive email asking for her help, suggesting we could help each other.

I woke up on Wednesday morning with that sketchy idea still whirling around my head. It clicked into place as I drove to the office. I'd been mulling over what the spirits were trying to tell Victor yesterday, and the one clue I'd almost missed. Now I understood, but I needed proof. I wanted to collect the damning information on my own.

As soon as I got to the office, I called Courtney and told her my suspicions. Once the initial shock sunk in, I told her about Winkie's career as a nurse in Southern California and how I wanted to check into that. Courtney agreed to help. She said that hospitals were highly unlikely to give out any information about employees, but that she would help once I knew which hospitals to check. It was a long shot, but I needed to follow it. I also needed to talk with Mary. She held the key. I felt sure of it.

I started my research by putting a name into Google and hoping something would pop up. Nothing, except that someone with a similar name had been a Democratic member of the South Carolina General Assembly. Then I began a more pointed search for suspicious deaths in California hospitals. A frightening amount of hits on this one including the nurse who was convicted for killing over twenty-five of his patients by injecting them with a lethal dose of pain medication. Then I found an article on a nursing home which was closed by authorities after several patients died because of understaffing. The patients were simply not monitored closely enough. Getting nowhere and feeling extremely distressed now, I went at my research in a different way, more systematically. I made a list of all hospitals in the San Diego area and began calling their Human Resources departments pretending to be checking references for a job applicant at a hospital in Portland. It was mind-numbing work. There were sixteen hospitals in the city of San Diego alone. If you added the greater San Diego area, that included another eighteen. Again, I considered calling Greg. Surely the Seattle Police Department had rookie cops with desk jobs who could help with this task. But then, I didn't want to get him involved until I had something to go on.

"Ann?"

I looked up at my editor, Jeff Skinner, standing in my cubicle and quickly clicked off the hospital website knowing he'd seen my computer screen.

"Everything okay?" He asked.

"Sure, sure." I replied. He probably thought the hospital had something to do with Nancy's breast cancer. I wasn't going to disavow him of that idea, though it made me feel a little guilty since he'd caught me doing this during normal working hours. "What's up?" I asked.

He sat in the only other chair in my cubicle wearing his concerned face. "That's what I wanted to ask you, Ann. You're distracted. I'm wondering if everything is okay. Is your sister doing okay?"

"Nancy's fine, thanks. Sorry, I guess I have been preoccupied with selling my house, moving and, of course, the happiness murder investigation."

"What's going on with that? Mary still missing? I still can't believe she's involved in any way."

Jeff and I had had a conversation about Mary right after she left town. He'd talked to their mutual friends. No one could imagine Mary as a murderer.

"Are the police still investigating her?"

I looked at Jeff. He's a nice guy and a great boss and he knows me well. I could see it dawning in his face.

"Oh, no. Ann, you're not." He shook his head. "Of course, you are. You're investigating, aren't you? Listen to me. You need to leave this up to the police."

"It will be a great story."

"No, no." He shook his head. "The story I want you to be working on involves positive experiences in education. Have you been through all the applications for the event?"

"I'm on it boss." I gestured to the pile of applications in my inbox. "I'll have my recommendations to you this afternoon." I said, affecting a smile and a light tone I didn't feel.

"I'll leave you to it then." Jeff stood, and I watched him head back to his office.

Around four, with the applications finished and Jeff in a meeting in the fishbowl, I resumed the task of calling hospitals. After the first eight calls, I got lucky. A hospital connected with the University of San Diego and one in La Jolla confirmed my hunch. I called Courtney immediately, and she agreed to make some follow-up phone calls to a doc she knew in La Jolla. Half an hour later, Courtney called back to tell me that I was right. Winkie had not only worked at these two hospitals, she'd been fired from both.

"What are you going to do now?" Courtney asked. "You should call the police."

"I will. I'll call Greg," I said. "Thanks Courtney." I hung up and was about to call Greg when Jeff appeared in my cubicle for the second time this afternoon.

"Hey boss. Here you go—my top ten recommendations for the positive education talks. I handed him the applications and the memo I'd written. "It's a very solid group. They all have great stories – lots of variety too."

"Thanks. I'll compare them with Craig's and Lindy's and come up with a decision. Then you can contact the top five and we'll be good to go."

"Right. See you tomorrow then."

He gave me a look. "Tomorrow's Thanksgiving, Ann. Home and hearth. I'll see you on Friday."

"Right, right. Nancy and I are going out. I guess it snuck up on me."

"Have a nice holiday, Ann."

"Thanks boss. You too."

"Please remember what I said earlier. Leave the murder investigation to the police. Just do it. I have to know that you're working your real job one hundred percent, okay?"

"Duly noted, Jeff. Happy Thanksgiving."

"Happy Thanksgiving." He shook his head before heading out the door. We both knew I wouldn't leave the investigation to the police, but I would try hard not to let it interfere with my real job. I needed a real job after all.

I did one final check of my email and took a deep breath when I saw Mary had replied. I clicked on it: *You have reminded me of the right question to ask: How can I help? It's true that I ran because I was frightened. Now I see that I can help by asking some more questions. Once I have done that, I will call Detective Costello and tell him what I know for certain.*

I forwarded the vague message to Greg and called him. Straight to his voicemail box, which, the robotic voice informed me, was full.

"Shit!" I sent him a cryptic text about my discoveries then got into my car to drive home and consider my next steps. I was heading East on Denny when my cell phone rang. Generally, I had a no cell phone calls in the car rule but when I saw the caller's name, I picked up anyway.

"Mary!" I said. "I'm so glad you called."

"Ann, I believe there's been a huge misunderstanding and I think we should talk in person."

Mary's voice sounded wobbly. Nerves or fear, I couldn't tell.

"Okay, Mary, where are you?" I asked. "Are you back in Seattle?"

"I am," she said. "Actually, I'm here with Winkie – at her houseboat."

My stomach clenched. "Sorry, Mary, you're breaking up a bit." I said, trying to quiet my brain. I took a deep breath. "Did you say you're at Winkie's?" I asked. "Is everything okay?"

Mary replied so softly that I could barely hear her. "Of course," she said. "Can you come? Winkie and I both think we should all have a conversation."

"I'll be there in fifteen minutes."

At the next light, I called Greg again. Straight to his full voicemail box. Where was he? I made a U-turn and drove as fast as possible to Winkie's dock off Eastlake, where I illegally parked my Camry in the nearest spot reserved for owners. I'd been imagining the scenario in my head on the way over. Either I was about to face down a psychopathic killer, or I'd made a big mistake. With my heart pumping faster than my heels clicking on the dock, I hoped for the mistake.

When the door opened, I saw Winkie wearing hospital scrubs and a black wig. I had no doubt now that she was the murderer. I remembered the description of Jacqueline Forte – remarkable only because of the long, straight black hair. The wig was a clever disguise. When I spotted the name tag, Winnifred Bradford, R.N. pinned to her shirt, I could hear the blood pulsing in my ears. My knees felt shaky. I'd read about serial killers who sometimes wore a costume, a disguise, when they committed murder. It was something about role performance, the killer emotionally and physically getting into a *uniform*. It's an integral part of the elaborate fantasy they're playing out.

"Ann, come in," Winkie said. "Mary and I were expecting you." I tried to turn and run but Winkie grabbed hold of my coat sleeve and pulled me into the front hall.

"Oh dear, if only you'd have left well enough alone. But no, you had to do your little investigative reporter thing, didn't you? Now two more people are going to have to die."

I couldn't move, and I couldn't find any words.

"I know you were hoping that Mary could help out. Maybe you were planning on taking me straight to Harborview for a commitment? No, no, not this time. Ha! You should see your face right now." Winkie laughed, a high-pitched and slightly hysterical trill. I felt cold. Paralyzed.

"I said, come in!" Winkie pulled me though the doorway and into the living room, her grip surprisingly strong and the fear making me weak. I stopped and looked around, unprepared for the scene around us.

"Mary!" I rushed over to the sofa where Mary appeared unconscious or asleep or worse. I thought I might faint. I knelt, placed my hand on her chest to check for breathing. I couldn't tell so I touched her wrist to feel for a pulse.

"Stop that!" Winkie yelled, then slapped me with such force that I fell against the coffee table, hitting my head against the glass top. Dazed but not bleeding, I scrambled to my feet and faced Winkie, my back pressed against the wall, as far from her as I could get in that small space. I looked to the door, planning my escape. She caught me, shook her head, and reached into what looked like a black medical bag open on the coffee table. When she pulled out a revolver, small and shiny, I thought it might be a toy.

"Come over here and sit down." Winkie waved the gun to indicate the gray sofa. I sat.

"What did you do to Mary? What did you give her?"

"Oh, she's fine, just a little sedative for now to take the edge off. You know, I don't really want to hurt either one of you. You see how you've messed things up. I just wanted to help. I would never hurt anyone who didn't deserve it."

"Did Matt Downey and Robert Clark and Ryan Tompkins all deserve to die, Winkie?"

She looked at me wide-eyed, disbelief shining back at me. "You know as well as I do that those individuals were ruining our friends' lives. Life is a gift, Ann. When you ignore that gift and use it to inflict misery on others, well then, no, you don't deserve it. It's quite simple."

"What about Mary? She doesn't deserve to die. Mary has helped so many people in her lifetime. She helped you too, didn't she? You can't mean to hurt her."

"Mary and I have been through a lot together, it's true. I don't want to hurt her!" Winkie stomped her foot like a spoiled child. "But she knows what I've done now. Unless I help her slip away, she'll tell that policeman friend of yours and I'll go to jail. I can't let that happen."

"You won't be helping her *slip away*, Winkie, you'll be *murdering* her. Just like you murdered the others. You won't get away with it. The police will figure it out."

"They won't!" Winkie brandished the gun in my direction again. "The police are idiots! They have no idea how I've helped the others out of this world."

"You didn't help anyone Winkie, you killed them!"

"Shut up! Shut up or I'll shoot you right now."

"You're not going to shoot me Winkie. A gun is not your MO. You may shoot me, but it will be with a needle, not a gun. I don't believe that gun is even real. It looks like the gun my cousin Johnny and I used to play cowboys."

"You don't think this gun is real? Let's just see." Winkie pointed the gun over my head at the far wall. She pulled the trigger and the sound exploded in my head and glass shattered to the floor. Taking my only chance, I lunged, catching Winkie off guard and knocking her to the floor. I kicked her hand hard, and the gun skittered across the room. We both went for it, but I got hold of it and gave Winkie a knee to her solar plexus. She doubled over clutching her stomach and I backed away, pointing the gun at her face.

"It's your turn to listen to me Winkie. Have a seat."

Winkie smiled. "I don't think you have the least idea how to shoot a gun."

"Well, you can take that chance. There's also a chance that I might mess up your face while trying not to kill you. I may not be the best shot, but I know how to shoot it. It's one of the things I've learned while dating a police officer."

"From psychics to cops! What a gal!"

Winkie took a step towards me. I aimed the gun at her left foot, fired and missed. The shot surprised her. She jumped back.

"That was a warning. Next time I'll aim for your face." I lifted the gun and pointed it at her head, my hand trembling so hard from the shock of the first shot that I knew I had no chance of hitting her.

The door burst open, and I pointed the gun at it. Greg, along with two uniformed officers rushed into the room.

"Put the gun down, Ann!" Greg commanded, and I dropped it immediately. One of the cops grabbed Winkie and cuffed her. The other guy ran over to Mary and felt for a pulse.

"She's alive. I'll call an ambulance."

CHAPTER TWENTY-SIX

"Spending meaningful time with friends, family, or romantic partners [is] necessary (though not by itself sufficient) for happiness." Tal Ben-Shahar, *Happier*.

Greg and I sat in Winkie's living room after the uniforms had taken her into custody and the Fire Department paramedics arrived to take Mary to the hospital. I felt shaky.

"I'm really glad to see you, Greg," I said. "But why are you here? I mean, what made you show up here? Now?"

"I got your text." He said. "I called you several times, but you didn't answer. I had a hunch you'd be crazy enough to head right into a dangerous situation. You'd done it before." He took my hand and squeezed.

"And I'll never do it again," I said. "But I had no choice this time. Mary called me from here, said there'd been a misunderstanding and wanted to talk about it. I called you right away, again, but you weren't answering your phone and your voicemail box was full. Mary sounded scared. I think some part of me hoped that it really was a misunderstanding, that I had it wrong. I had to find out."

"How did you figure out it was Winkie? You never mentioned her. I never suspected her. I'll admit that."

"I just kept going over my notes, everything I'd learned from my interviews. I didn't see it until Victor had a sign."

"The psychic? You told me he didn't have any new knowledge beyond what you'd already told him."

"Yeah," I said. "But he had one feeling he couldn't make sense of something about eyes. Nancy said he kept blinking his eye, like he had a speck of dust in it. He said he felt something there but didn't understand what the spirit was trying to say."

"You made the jump from blink to wink, then to Winkie?" He laughed. Shook his head.

"Yes, but only after I remembered something Dr. Bergman said about the known pathology of *angels of death*. Most of them believed they were helping. They crossed some line convincing themselves that killing was the right thing to do, and many of them were nurses. I knew Winkie had been a nurse and I wanted to check into that. The more I thought about it, the more obvious it became. Winkie was so needy. When Mary cancelled the class, Winkie suggested we all meet anyway at her house. I knew Jacqueline Forte had dark hair and Winkie is blonde. So stupid of me not to consider that Winkie simply wore a wig. I also remembered that Forte had worn designer shoes to the fundraiser. Winkie wore Manolo Blahnik's at Ryan Tompkins funeral." I stopped to take a breath.

"Also, Winkie showed up at Nancy's yoga class several days ago," I said. "I think Nancy was her next victim. I'm pretty sure she invited Nancy and some other women from the yoga class over here for Thanksgiving dinner tomorrow." The thought sent a cold shiver through me.

"Nancy's not making your life miserable, is she?"

"No, but I think Winkie believed that she had."

"Why?" Greg asked.

"I don't want to talk about it," I said, coward that I am. I didn't want to own up to my relationship with Victor. Not yet.

"Fair enough," he replied.

"What's the connection between Mary and Winkie? I haven't figured that out."

"I can help you out there," Greg said. "For a time, Winkie worked as a nurse at Seattle Public Health – after she moved up from California and before she met her husband. She must have met Mary at that time. I expect that's where they both met Luke Mitchell."

"Why didn't you tell me this before?" I asked.

"I only discovered it today," he replied.

I looked at the twinkling lights on the shore of Lake Union, struck by the serenity of the view when I felt anything but serene. I felt angry.

"Can you believe that not one, but *two* hospitals simply let Winkie go after so many patients died on her watch?" I asked Greg. "What is *wrong* with the medical system?"

"Hospitals don't like bad press," he replied. "The medical establishment will do anything to keep a lid on a story like that."

"People died!" I stood up and paced around the room. "She was cut loose." My voice rose with my indignation. "Given license to kill. Again!"

"Whoa, whoa, Ann, calm down. She's in custody now."

"I'm going to blow the lid right off that story."

"I know you are." Greg said. "But for now, why don't you sit down? Take some deep breaths or something."

I sat. "The thing that bothers me most is that these deaths could have been prevented."

"Maybe, but you could not have prevented them. Look Ann, you and I both know that bad things happen all the time. It's how you respond to them that matters most."

I looked at him. "Wow," I said. "You sound like you've been taking a positive psychology class." He smiled, and I thought about what he'd said.

"I guess I usually respond with anger. I'm working on that. And Greg, thanks for showing up."

"It looked to me like you had control of the situation." He said. "I didn't know you had a gun, or that you knew how to use one."

"That's a funny joke. I don't own a gun. That's Winkie's gun. Luckily, I was able to get it away from her. I was far from having the situation under control. I sure as hell don't know how to *aim* a gun. I might have shot off my own foot if you hadn't shown up." I shook my head at the thought, then looked up at Greg. "Thank you," I said.

"You are very welcome." Greg opened his arms in what looked to me like an invitation. I leaned in and let him hold me.

Greg pulled back and looked into my face. "You're something, Ann Dexter," he said with a slow smile just before he kissed me. I kissed him back with an enthusiasm that surprised me. It felt so good.

"Is this even legal?" I asked.

"You're a consenting adult, right?"

"I am."

"Then it is." He kissed me again. "After we take care of your statement, we might see if this leads us anywhere else."

* * *

I knew the drill by now. We'd go to the East Precinct, and I'd write down everything I could remember about tonight's incident. Then I'd call Jeff with just enough information about Winkie's arrest to get a brief story online right away. The police process would be drawn out and exhausting. I figured Greg and I would miss the moment by having it interrupted. I was wrong. As the song goes, after my statement had been signed, sealed, and delivered, I was his. Fear and adrenaline made the comfort of another human being's touch undeniably essential.

When I woke up the next morning to the sound of the espresso machine steaming milk, my heart began pounding. Disoriented and sleepy, it took me a minute to remember that Greg had spent the night and that would be him in the kitchen making lattes. I smiled at the thought and grabbed my robe to join him. I stood in the doorway enjoying the domestic scene – Greg in a t-shirt and boxers making coffee with two dogs at his feet. I liked it. He turned at my approach and opened his arms.

"Hey sleepyhead. How are you feeling this morning?" He asked.

"Mmmm. Very good, considering," I said into his chest. Then, "Wait! What time is it?"

"No worries lady. It's a holiday."

"Oh yeah. I keep forgetting that. Aren't you supposed to be on a plane on your way to see your brother?"

"I have an hour before I need to leave. What about you? When are you getting together with Nancy?"

"We're having dinner later. So, my day is wide open. I'll probably start writing the article about Winkie."

He frowned. "Can't you let it go for one day?"

"Doubtful. Besides, if I get it all out, then I can begin to leave it behind."

"Okay. I guess I get that."

We put together a quick breakfast of eggs and toast to go with our lattes. I was surprised at how sad I felt when I walked him to the front door. We kissed, then kissed again.

"I'll be back on Sunday," he said.

"Have a great trip."

Greg opened the door and Doozy bounded out with him. I laughed. "You can have him if you want."

"Ha! Here Doozy. Back inside." The dog ran a lap around the front yard then back into the house. I closed him inside and gave Greg one more kiss before waving goodbye.

I took a shower, turned on the Macy's Thanksgiving Day Parade and called Nancy. When she answered, I could hear the broadcaster in the background announcing the arrival of the Radio City Rockettes.

"They're on!" I said.

"I know! I'm watching too," she replied. Our mom loved the parade and especially the Rockettes. She'd always wanted to go to New York and see them in person, but that never happened.

"Why does watching the Rockettes always give me a giant lump in my throat?" I asked.

"You know why. The same thing happens to me," she said. "Want to get together this afternoon and watch a movie before dinner?"

"Let's have dinner early and the movie afterwards. I've got an article to write."

"On Thanksgiving! Really, Ann?"

I told her what happened yesterday, which seemed like so long ago, ending with Greg spending the night. Nancy was quiet on the other end of the line.

"Nance?" I asked.

"Oh, I'm here. I'm just stunned. How on earth do you get yourself into these situations?"

"Yeah. I don't know."

"The ending sounds good though. Greg's a keeper, don't you think?"

"Whoa, whoa. Let's not get too excited about that. It's too soon," I said. "But he is pretty great."

Once we settled on a time for Nancy to come over – five o'clock – we hung up and I leashed up both dogs for a romp around the park. I couldn't wait to get out into the bright November sunshine. What a beautiful day! Cold and clear. It seemed like I hadn't seen the sun in ages. It lifted my mood until I began to think about writing the story, the terrifying story of how a nurse could go from caring to killing. It sickened me to think about how many murders Winkie had committed, but it was time to write the truth. I knew I could do it. I'd write a first draft today and then tomorrow I'd make some follow-up calls. Then I'd talk to Winkie. I really wanted the first-hand account of how she'd gone wrong.

By late afternoon I'd written as much as I could. I knew I'd want to add some interviews and do a little more research before I filed the story. For now, I called it finished. I stood up and stretched my neck, trying to release the tension there, while recognizing the deep feelings of sadness that overwhelmed me. There was some hope too. Winkie was in custody, and I had a wonderful man in my life. It's funny how life throws things at us willy-nilly, the good with the bad. Just when things seem impossible, new possibilities become clear.

The doorbell rang and the dogs barked, bringing me out of my wool-gathering.

"Happy Thanksgiving!" Nancy handed me a bunch of yellow mums and gave me a hug. I smiled, happy to see her.

We decided to eat at a new upscale Sichuan place on Broadway that Greg had told me about – Lionhead. I had a pang about going there without him, but he was in California with his brother and his family doing the traditional turkey thing. I hoped he was having a good time.

Right away I liked the restaurant's vibe – simple wood tables, each with a vase holding one large red mum, no tablecloths, just silverware wrapped in large ivory linen napkins and placed next to snowy white dinner plates. I studied the beautiful piece of art taking up most of one wall—several panels depicting a Chinese city. I probably should have recognized which city. I didn't. I ordered the boneless crisped duck as an homage to Thanksgiving poultry, knowing that this duck – with red pepper and sweet hot and sour sauce – would be nothing like those dry old birds of Thanksgivings past. Nancy skipped poultry altogether and ordered Ma Po Doufu, a dish combining tofu, pork, and something I didn't recognize called douban jiang. It promised to be spicy with chili oil and Sichuan pepper. We each ordered a Tsing Tao beer to wash it down and cut the spice.

"To once and future Dexter Thanksgivings!" Nancy raised her beer to toast.

"At least Granny won't show up at this one." Our maternal grandmother always showed up at holiday gatherings wearing cherry red lipstick surrounded by an overwhelming aura of dime store perfume, her hair crinkled into a curly gray cap with indentations from bobby pins here and there.

"My favorite granddaughters," Nancy leaned over the table, mimicking the words our granny always said just before she planted sloppy kisses on our cheeks. Nancy puckered up and smacked her lips, making kissing noises.

I laughed. "That lipstick!" I said. "Remember how we would rub off the greasy red smears as fast as we could?"

Nancy snorted. "Oh man, she was something!"

"Yeah." We sat quietly with our own thoughts of childhood holidays in Minneapolis – mostly good thoughts.

"Did you write the article about Winkie today?" She asked.

"As much as I could. I'll need to do a little more research and talk to some people."

She shook her head. "Really, Ann, I don't know how you do what you do."

"Yeah, I've been thinking about that too. Maybe, once my

house closes, I should just take the money and run, quit my job, light out for the territory, do something completely different."

"That's more my M.O."

"Yeah, but I can see the temptation – taking off with a windfall to chase windmills."

"What would you do? Is there something you've been wanting to do?"

"I definitely want to travel. Maybe I could sell some travel pieces to *The Seattle Times* or even to *The New York Times*. Of course, I couldn't do it for a while. I still have a commitment to the Saltons, to Doozy, and I have Pooch."

"I'd take Pooch in a heartbeat," she said. "Maybe I'd even consider taking over that sweet gig you've got going on Capitol Hill. If you were serious."

"Be careful what you wish for." I laughed.

"But what about Greg?" she asked. "He seems like an awesome guy. Maybe there's potential for something lasting with him?"

"I barely know him. But, yeah, he seems pretty great."

"Maybe you're just thinking about running away because it would be a way to run away from that. You know you have commitment issues."

"Don't analyze me, yet." I smiled. "I'm not going anywhere any time soon."

Our food arrived and we dug into the delicious combination of flavors – much better than turkey any day.

Back at my place – the Salton's place really – we discussed Christmas movies.

"I'm not sure I'm up for *It's a Wonderful Life*," Nancy said. "We watched it so often growing up that I think I have the dialog memorized."

"Yeah. Well, I don't want to watch *Love, Actually*." I replied. "I know you like that one. Have you ever really thought about the relationships in that movie? Seriously weird."

"How about the total fantasy?" Nancy suggested. "You know that one where Cameron Diaz and Kate Winslet swap their fabulous lives, Los Angeles for the Cotswolds. What's it called?"

"*The Holiday.* Yeah, let's do it."

We snuggled up under a fleecy throw, Doozy on the sofa with his head on Nancy while Pooch snored at my feet, and we watched a movie about how two women ditch their lives for something completely different. It was a fantasy for sure, but one that was growing on me. I liked the movie, and I loved my sister's company and the feeling of safety it brought me. This is the happiness that would last.

CHAPTER TWENTY-SEVEN

"Freedom grants the opportunity for greater meaning, but by itself there is nothing necessarily meaningful about it."
Mark Manson, *The Subtle Art of Not Giving a F*ck*.

I got into the *Times* early on Friday, while it was still relatively quiet, and began making phone calls. I talked with the Dean of the Nursing School at UCLA, which Winkie had attended. I also spoke with two of Winkie's co-workers at the California hospitals where she had worked. I put on my noise-cancelling headphones and began writing. After a couple of hours, I had a solid draft, which I emailed to Jeff.

> Nurse Winifred Bradford began her career with high hopes and an impressive resume. The daughter of doctors, she'd gone to the best prep schools (Lakeside School in Seattle), Occidental College and nursing school at UCLA. Medical school had been in her original plan, but she didn't quite have the grades at Occidental to go to a top medical school. Being the best was always important to her. If she couldn't be the best doctor, then she'd be the best nurse.
>
> Ms. Bradford got excellent grades at UCLA and graduated at the top of her class. I interviewed Reggie Walrath, Dean of the Nursing school at UCLA about Ms. Bradford. She said: *Winifred Bradford was a top student; she was hard-working and diligent. We all expected Ms. Bradford to distinguish herself in her nursing career.* That comment seemed prophetic. Ms. Bradford certainly distinguished herself, just not in the way that anyone might have expected.

I found that while Winifred Bradford's behavior was extraordinary, she also shared some common themes with other health care criminals. Some killers think of themselves as "angels of death." By ending their patients' lives they believe that they have eased their patients' suffering. Others apparently enjoy the attention that comes with the death of patients they tend. One such nurse studied received flowers from the families of her victims because she seemed so distraught at their deaths, while another injected drugs that sent his patients into cardiac arrest because he liked being treated as a hero when he tried, often unsuccessfully, to revive them.

A British criminologist's 2014 study of sixteen nurses who committed murders in hospitals identified other red flags that these nurses had in common. Most common was a history of depression or other psychological troubles, having drugs in their lockers or homes, and making colleagues feel uneasy around them. In some cases, problems would have been picked up if employers had checked references for nurses who switched jobs quite often.

I also learned that employer hospitals often simply fired workers with troubling patient death records rather than warning other institutions about them. Ms. Bradford had been let go from two hospitals in California. According to the employees I spoke with at those hospitals, neither had investigated the high number of deaths on her shifts or reported them to Ms. Bradford's future employers.

Here is some good news: according to one British criminologist, the health-care killer phenomenon appears to have abated in the United States. She attributes this change to the use of computerized systems that bring attention to any unusual drug use by staff in health care facilities.

Unfortunately, Ms. Bradford found a way to continue her murder spree outside of the healthcare system.

I'd hoped to write a follow-up, including an interview with Winkie. But her lawyers were pushing back, not allowing her to talk to the press, claiming it would adversely impact Winkie's right to a fair trial. But Winkie wanted to talk to me. She'd already called me from Harborview, inviting me to visit. Despite my assurances that I did not understand her killing spree, she said she knew I would understand her motives, and would write her story with empathy. She wanted me to explain her concern for our friends in the happiness class. I could not do that. No one could.

I checked my email and scrolled through the education blog, considering the next piece I might write for it. Nothing grabbed my attention. I began clearing off my desk, a habit of mine after finishing a project. Under a stack of papers, I found the book Dr. Bergman had sent me, his new book about the science of happiness. I was reading the part about the importance of meaningful work when my phone rang with an internal call.

"Ann, it's Jeff. Can you come see me?"

"On my way, boss." I smiled and stood up. I couldn't wait to debrief with Jeff about the article. I felt good about it and it was just the beginning. I'd planned to write an in-depth exposé about the problems in the health care system which allowed nurses like Winkie to practice their dark arts.

When I walked into Jeff's office, I could immediately feel his unease. He avoided my eyes and began rubbing the tops of his thighs like he did when he was agitated or thinking hard.

"You didn't like the article." I said.

"The draft is fine. I've got a few suggestions, but it's fine." He gave me a look that worried me. "Please, sit down Ann."

"Because I can re-write it." I said. "Do you want me to put in more specifics about Winkie's record at those hospitals in California? Maybe a statement from Dr. Bergman or Mary Summers?" I was grasping at straws here, even as the real reason for this meeting began to dawn on me. I felt my face get hot, my eyes begin to sting.

"Ann, I know you are aware of our dire economic situation here at the *Times*."

Oh my God, I thought. *He's firing me.* I fought the tears.

"Are you going to fire me?" Even as I said the words, I hoped he would laugh, tell me I had it wrong. Instead, he shook his head and began rubbing the tops of his thighs again.

"You know I think you're a damn good reporter, Ann. But your head's not where I need it to be, especially now. Hasn't been for some time. You were hired as an education reporter, remember?"

"Yes, but."

"I know, I know, I take the blame for letting you go off and write other stories that interested you, situations that pulled you in. You're good at it. You're not afraid to get out there, do what it takes to get to the heart of an issue. I like that. I like you. You know that." He stopped talking and pressed his fingers on his forehead, like he had a headache. Like *I* was his headache.

I knew what was coming. My busy brain whirred with the stats. When I started here there were more than 375 journalists in the newsroom. Today there are only 145. I knew my days were numbered. I also knew that Jeff was right. My head was not where he needed it to be, certainly not on the education blog. I thought about the conversation I'd had with Nancy yesterday, about lighting out for the territory. When Jeff looked up at me, I met his eyes.

"Look, Jeff, you don't need to fire me. How about I quit instead?"

"What?"

"I've been thinking a lot lately about the importance of meaningful work. You're right that my head is no longer where you need it to be, it's certainly not on education in Seattle schools, hasn't been for a while. It's time for a change. And I'm in a good position right now. I made some money on the sale of my house. I can draw on that while I figure out my next step."

"This is not how I expected this conversation to go." Jeff shook his head, smiled. "I'm sure we can figure out a reasonable severance deal."

"Thanks Jeff." I took a deep breath. "You know I've loved working with you. You're the best boss I've ever had. I just wanted to tell you that before I go."

"I've enjoyed working with you too. Wherever you go from here, I know you'll come out all right." He said. We looked at each other, a little awkward.

"What do you think you'll do?" He asked.

"No idea," I replied. I felt lighter. Sure, I felt the butterflies flapping in my chest, but in a good way, the way you feel when you're about to embark on something new and exciting. That's just what I was going to do.

"When do you need me to empty my desk?" I asked.

"You can stay until the end of the year. Or you can leave as soon as you'd like with pay through December 31."

"Okay," I said. "I have some things I'd like to finish up before I go. Let's talk nitty gritty later. For now, I think I need to celebrate."

Jeff came around the desk to shake my hand, but I hugged him instead, surprised at the tears welling up. He saw my face and looked concerned.

"No worries, Jeff. These are happy tears!" I walked out of his office and continued walking straight out of the building. I didn't want to talk with my co-workers just yet. That would be too emotional and would maybe even dampen this high I felt. No, now I wanted to celebrate. I thought about calling Greg, but he was still in California. I could talk to him after I figured out what I was doing. I pulled out my phone to call Nancy but noticed the time. She would be teaching a class right now. So, I called Alex, my original happy hour buddy.

We agreed to meet at the Sorrento Hotel. The bar had an old clubby feel that I liked—all dark wood, box-beamed ceiling, soft carpet, leather chairs and a huge fireplace. At four-thirty in the afternoon the bar was quiet. Not quite happy hour. An obviously stressed-out graying guy in a fine wool suit sat alone at a corner table texting furiously and grimacing at his phone while sipping scotch. I chose a table nearest to the fireplace to keep warm. The lights were low, and I could barely read the cocktail menu. Damned if I would get out my phone and use the flashlight feature. Only old people did that.

"Do you have champagne?" I asked the waiter when he appeared.

"We don't have authentic French champagne," he said with a furrowed brow. "But I would recommend our Prosecco. Dry and delicious."

"That sounds perfect," I said.

"A glass or bottle Madame?"

"Oh, we'd better have a bottle." I looked up to see that Alex had appeared at the table dressed for work – soft gray skirt and blazer, deep maroon silk blouse and her signature high heels. Unlike me, she'd checked her raincoat at the door instead of hanging it over an empty chair and letting it drip onto the floor. The waiter picked it up and offered to hang it for me.

"Holy shit Ann! I can't believe it! Winkie!"

"Hello to you too," I said. "Have a seat."

Alex dropped her Kate Spade bag onto the still damp chair, pulled over a dry one and sat facing me. She leaned in. "What the hell, Ann. I mean, I saw the news on TV about Winkie's arrest and I'm reeling." As an afterthought, she said, "Sorry if you wrote a piece too, I don't get *The Seattle Times*."

I laughed. "Nobody does. Get *The Seattle Times* that is. That's no longer my problem." I giggled.

Our waiter appeared and popped the cork of the Prosecco with an expert flair, poured two glasses and placed the linen-draped bottle into an ice bucket.

I raised my glass and Alex did the same. As I touched her glass with mine, I said, "Here's to endless possibilities!"

"Seriously, Ann. Are you drunk already? I want to hear all the details about Winkie and you're talking about endless possibilities. What's going on? You were so vague on the phone. Sounded happy though."

"I quit my job." I said, looking directly at Alex and taking another sip of bubbly.

"You quit?" Her eyes were wide. "That's a good thing?"

"It is. I mean, I'm pretty sure my boss called me into his office to fire me, but I quit first." Saying the words out loud made them true. Their truth and the Prosecco had me giggling again. "I'm sure I've told you how many reporters have been fired recently, right?"

She nodded. "You have."

"The newspaper world is changing fast. Like you, most people don't read the print newspaper anymore. And there are so many other online news sources. When there aren't enough subscribers, papers lose money. Newspapers are going bankrupt all over the place. You know this. I knew my days were numbered, so I decided to cut my losses and view it as a new opportunity."

"Now you can do what you've always wanted to do," she said.

I looked up at her. "What have I always wanted to do?"

"Travel the world. Write about exotic places or maybe fucked up, war-torn places. Write about female oppression in emerging economies. You know. You've told me this many times. You were so tired of the education lab blog you could choke. You did choke. You were asking to be fired and now, you've quit. I'm happy for you." She raised her glass. "To Ann Dexter journalist extraordinaire!"

I smiled, clinked her glass with mine, basking in the warm glow of the fireplace and Alex's kind words.

"I bet you made a bundle on the sale of your house. You'll have enough money to get started, right?"

"Actually, yes." I replied.

"I have something to celebrate too." Alex raised her glass. "You're looking at the newest partner at Turnbull, Proctor and Samson!"

"Congrats!" I touched her glass, but the thought of Matt Downey's death crossed my mind.

"You're thinking about everything else that's happened, right? Tell me about Winkie."

"It's bad, Alex." I said. "Unbelievable." We settled in and I told her the whole gruesome story.

"Jesus." Alex said when I had finished. "It's so twisted. I never would have pegged Winkie as a killer. She always struck me as kind of a ditz."

"Me too." I said. "And to think I suspected Mary. Poor Mary Winters who'd tried so hard to become Mary Summers instead."

"Why did Mary run away?" Alex asked.

"She was scared. She'd begun to suspect Winkie, and she just couldn't face it. She couldn't stay around and watch it happen. And she couldn't tell the police. She thought they wouldn't believe her, that they wouldn't be able to protect her."

Alex shook her head. "It reminds me of those stories you read about where someone goes ballistic, and no one saw it coming. You know, when interviewed afterwards the family and friends always say things like: *He was such a nice, polite and quiet young man.*"

"Right." I said. "I guess we can never know what goes on inside another person's head. We all have our own private thoughts. Luckily, most of us don't act on our murderous fantasies."

"True," Alex replied. We sat with that for a minute.

"It's been quite the year, hasn't it?"

"Sure has," I said. "I guess those happiness classes did us some good."

She smiled. "You know, that's true. We're both on the right career path. I think Mary would say the right work makes us happy."

"And I'm saying that good friends are the key to happiness."

"I'll drink to that!"

About the Author

Rachel Bukey lives in Seattle with her husband Dave and their Labrador Retriever, Daisy. When she's not writing or reading, she enjoys gardening, running, and hiking in the beautiful Pacific Northwest. Visit her at www.rachelbukey.com

CPSIA information can be obtained
at www.ICGtesting.com
Printed in the USA
BVHW072153200322
631576BV00005B/23

9 781603 816984